"It's obvious you've never been in love."

Is that what he thought? Chelsea's pulse accelerated as she became aware of Roberto not as an adversary but as the man she wanted so hopelessly. She ached to run her hands over his broad shoulders, to rake her nails through the dark hair on his chest.

She bit her lip and turned away. "My emotions aren't the consideration here."

"Tell me, just to satisfy my curiosity. Have you ever needed somebody so much that it was like a physical pain?" He turned her to face him.

"No, I—" She couldn't look at him, afraid he might see the lie.

"You're very fortunate." His hands were caressing her now. "I want to touch you, to excite you so much that you'll beg for completion. I want to watch your face and hear you call out my name...."

Chelsea gasped. "*I'm* the one?"

Dear Reader,

Happy February! Happy St. Valentine's Day! May this year bring you love and joy. And to put you in the mood for hearts and roses, Silhouette **Special Edition** is proud to bring you six wonderful, warm novels—stories written with you in mind—tales of love and life that you can identify with—romance with that little "something special" added in.

This month, don't miss stories from Patricia Coughlin, Tracy Sinclair, Barbara Catlin and Elizabeth Krueger. February marks the publication of *Ride the Tiger,* by Lindsay McKenna—the exciting first book in the wonderful series MOMENTS OF GLORY. Next month brings you *One Man's War,* and *Off Limits* follows in April. February is also the month for *A Good Man Walks In* by Ginna Gray—a tender tale featuring characters you've met before in earlier books by Ginna.

In each Silhouette **Special Edition** novel, we're dedicated to bringing you the romances that you dream about—stories that delight as well as bring a tear to the eye. And that's what Silhouette **Special Edition** is all about—special books by special authors for special readers!

I hope you enjoy this book and all of the stories to come.

Sincerely,

Tara Gavin
Senior Editor

TRACY SINCLAIR
If the Truth Be Told

Silhouette Special Edition

Published by Silhouette Books New York

America's Publisher of Contemporary Romance

SILHOUETTE BOOKS
300 East 42nd St., New York, N.Y. 10017

IF THE TRUTH BE TOLD

ISBN: 0-373-09725-5

First Silhouette Books printing February 1992

Books by Tracy Sinclair

Silhouette Special Edition

Never Give Your Heart #12
Mixed Blessing #34
Designed for Love #52
Castles in the Air #68
Fair Exchange #105
Winter of Love #140
The Tangled Web #153
The Harvest is Love #183
Pride's Folly #208
Intrigue in Venice #232
A Love So Tender #249
Dream Girl #287
Preview of Paradise #309
Forgive and Forget #355
Mandrego #386
No Room for Doubt #421
More Precious Than Jewels #453
Champagne for Breakfast #481
Proof Positive #493
Sky High #512

King of Hearts #531
Miss Robinson Crusoe #565
Willing Partners #584
Golden Adventure #605
The Girl Most Likely To #619
A Change of Place #672
The Man She Married #701
If the Truth Be Told #725

Silhouette Romance

Paradise Island #39
Holiday in Jamaica #123
Flight to Romance #174
Stars in Her Eyes #244
Catch a Rising Star #345
Love Is Forever #459

Silhouette Books

Silhouette Christmas Stories 1986
"Under the Mistletoe"

TRACY SINCLAIR,

author of more than thirty Silhouette novels, also contributes to various magazines and newspapers. An extensive traveler and a dedicated volunteer worker, this California resident has accumulated countless fascinating experiences, settings and acquaintances to draw on in plotting her romances.

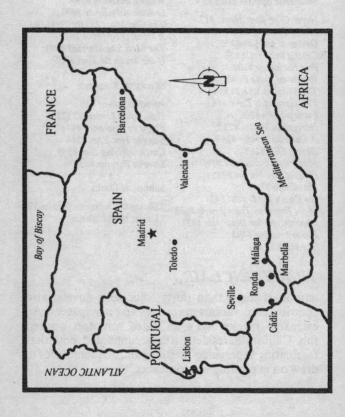

Chapter One

Chelsea Claiborne was talking on the telephone when her secretary stuck her head in the door and motioned for attention.

Chelsea frowned and shook her head. She was speaking with Oliver Worthington, her largest client. His portfolio of stocks and bonds was an important account at the investment brokerage firm of Ogilvie, Spencer and Green.

Marge ignored the warning. Approaching the desk, she hastily scribbled a note. *Your mother is on the phone. She sounds upset.*

Swift fear clutched at Chelsea. Her father was recovering from a recent heart attack. He'd been recuperating nicely, but perhaps he'd had a relapse.

After making a hasty apology to her client and promising to get back to him, Chelsea took her mother's call.

"What's wrong?" she asked anxiously.

"I need you, Chelsea," Doris Claiborne wailed. "I'm half out of my mind with worry."

"Did Dad have another attack?"

"It was more like a stroke. He was speechless. I can't believe this is happening!"

"Calm down, Mother." Chelsea's nails bit into her damp palms as she tried not to let her panic show. "Have you called the paramedics? Dial 911 and then call the doctor."

"What good will that do?"

"An ambulance can get there faster than the doctor. It will save time if he meets you at the hospital."

Chelsea could feel impatience mingling with her anxiety. Her mother had always been the helpless type, relying on other people to take care of everything. She was a throwback to an earlier era when women were treated like pampered pets. That was fine under normal circumstances, since Chelsea's father enjoyed his role as male protector, but now her mother had to assume some responsibility.

"We're wasting time," Chelsea said urgently. "I'm leaving now. Tell Dad I'll see him at the hospital."

"There's nothing wrong with your father. That's not why I called."

"You said you were worried . . ." Chelsea began uncertainly.

"I *am* worried! About your sister."

Chelsea leaned her head on her hand. So what else was new? Mindy was adorable but difficult. She'd been a headstrong child, and at nineteen she still acted like one on occasion.

"What's she done now?" Chelsea sighed.

"She's getting married!"

"When did she get back from Europe?" Chelsea asked blankly.

"She's still over there. That's what I'm trying to tell you. She's marrying some foreigner she met in Marbella."

"That's in Spain. I thought Mindy was touring England and Scotland with her girlfriend, Dawn Renzler."

"She's *supposed* to be. I don't know what I'm going to say to the Smythes and the Lockleys, after they so generously offered to show the girls around."

"Did Mindy say why she changed her plans?"

"I'm sure it was Dawn's idea. That girl is a bad influence on your sister. She probably convinced Mindy it would be a lark to run off to Spain, with never a thought to the inconvenience she was causing our friends. Not to mention the embarrassment to your father and me. I honestly don't know what—"

"Can we get back to Mindy, Mother? How did she meet the boy?"

"He isn't a boy. He's a man in his thirties! That's much too old for your sister—even if she was ready for marriage, which she isn't. A girl her age should go out with a lot of young men before she settles down."

"I wouldn't get too excited. Mindy has been in and out of love a dozen times. She'll forget about this man a week after she gets home."

"That's what I've been trying to tell you! She isn't coming home. She's getting married in some godforsaken place called Ronda—in two weeks."

Chelsea sat up straight in her chair. "That's insane."

"Exactly what I told her, but she refused to listen. You have to reason with her, Chelsea."

"What makes you think *I* can talk her out of it?" Chelsea asked helplessly.

"Mindy respects your opinion."

Only when it agreed with her own. If not, she ignored it. In all fairness, though, Mindy could hardly be blamed for being spoiled. She'd been treated like a gift from heaven all of her young life. Chelsea was already eight years old when Mindy was conceived, after their parents had given up hope of ever having another child.

"I'll see if I can talk some sense into her," Chelsea said tepidly.

"I knew I could count on you, dear. I feel better already. I've booked you a flight to Málaga. That's the closest big city. You'll have to rent a car and drive to Ronda, wherever that is."

"Wait a minute," Chelsea exclaimed. "Who said anything about going to Spain?"

"You said you'd talk to your sister."

"On the *telephone*."

"That's not good enough. We couldn't be sure that man wouldn't change her mind again. I want you to go over there and bring Mindy home immediately."

"She's an adult, Mother. I can't drag her out if she doesn't want to come," Chelsea protested. "Even if I could get away from work at such short notice, which I can't."

"You'd let your baby sister ruin her entire life because of a *job?*"

"It's more than just a job. I'm an investment counselor for a number of extremely important clients. I can't walk out on them because Mindy is pulling another of her scatterbrained stunts."

"Marrying a virtual stranger isn't what I consider a prank," Doris Claiborne said stiffly.

"She won't go through with it if we don't overreact. That's probably what she's counting on."

"I'm not willing to take the chance."

"Then you go over there," Chelsea said. "You're her mother."

"I can't believe you're suggesting I leave your sick father. This has been a terrible shock to him. You know how he worries about Mindy. It wouldn't surprise me if he had a relapse at any moment."

Chelsea knew she was being manipulated, but the possibility of a relapse did exist. Her father doted on Mindy. "Let me call her first and see what I can find out. What hotel is she at?"

"She's staying with that man. I simply can't believe it. Where did we go wrong?" Doris wailed.

Chelsea frowned. This was beginning to sound serious. "Give me his telephone number—and his name," she added.

"His name is Roberto del Machado, and this is where you can reach her." After giving a phone number, Doris ordered, "Call me right back after you talk to her."

In spite of her annoyance, Chelsea was happy to hear her sister's voice. They had different interests because of the big gap in their ages, but a warm bond had always existed between them.

Chelsea started out cautiously. "How do you like Europe?"

"It's fantastic," Mindy answered. "You can't believe how beautiful the Costa del Sol is."

"I didn't know that was on your itinerary. I thought you were only doing England and Scotland this trip."

Mindy laughed. "Have you ever met the Ian Smythes? Their idea of stimulating entertainment is a horse auction, followed by tea at the vicar's. Dawn and I came to Europe for excitement."

"It sounds as if you found it," Chelsea answered casually. "Mother tells me you're thinking of getting married."

Mindy's vivacity changed to wariness. "I *am* getting married."

"Isn't this rather sudden? You haven't known the fellow very long."

"Don't *you* start on me. Mother just finished having hysterics on the phone."

"She's concerned about you. I am, too. Marriage is a serious step."

"I didn't expect Mom to understand, but I thought you'd be on my side."

"How can I be when I don't know anything about the man?" Chelsea asked helplessly. "How did you meet him? What does he do for a living? Where do you plan to live?"

Mindy's voice hardened. "None of those things concern anyone but Roberto and me."

"We're your family. We care about you."

"Then you should be happy for me."

Chelsea felt a familiar sense of frustration. Mindy was like a little child being denied a lollipop. "We might be if we had a chance to meet him. How's this for an idea? Bring him to New York. We'll pay his fare."

Mindy laughed unexpectedly. "Roberto could buy and sell all of us. He's loaded."

"Then the trip won't be any problem for him. I would think he'd want to meet your family."

"It's not high on his list of priorities. If you want to meet Roberto, you'll have to come to Ronda." Mindy's voice softened. "Will you do it, Chelsea? I don't want to get married all alone."

Chelsea melted at the wistfulness in her sister's voice. "You wouldn't be alone if we had the wedding at home," she coaxed. In her own environment Mindy might have second thoughts.

"Roberto wants it here," Mindy said.

Chelsea's jaw set. "Let me speak to him."

"It won't do any good. Roberto makes the rules and everybody follows them."

Chelsea couldn't believe her independent little sister would let herself be bullied like this. There was more to the story than she was telling.

"Answer me one thing," Chelsea demanded. "Do you love him?"

"Yes."

Chelsea caught the almost imperceptible hesitation. "I still want to talk to him," she said ominously.

As she waited for Roberto del Machado to come on the line, Chelsea tried to picture the man. He was probably one of those flashy Latin types with longish hair and tacky clothes—pants too tight and a shirt unbuttoned to his navel.

The man who answered Mindy's summons was light-years away from that description. His dark hair was expensively cut, and his features were patrician. High cheekbones gave his face an autocratic look that was partially softened by a generous mouth that hinted at hidden sensuality. He was dressed casually yet elegantly, in gray slacks and a white silk shirt with an ascot knotted at the open neck. Unfortunately, Chelsea couldn't see any of this over the phone.

"My sister wants to talk to you," Mindy said, holding out the receiver.

"*Buenas tardes, señorita,*" Roberto said. "You wished to speak to me?"

"I certainly do." Chelsea wasn't swayed by the deep, mellow voice. She already disliked this man intensely. "I understand you want to marry my sister."

"We are going to be married, yes."

"Are you aware that she's only nineteen years old?"

"She looks older."

It was true that Mindy could look older or younger than her age, depending on the occasion. In jeans and a sweatshirt, with her glorious copper-colored hair in a braid, she looked like a fresh-faced teenager. But with elaborate makeup and sophisticated clothes, she could pass for much older. Chelsea was willing to bet that Mindy had chosen the latter during her stay on the glamorous Spanish Riviera. Not that it absolved her Latin lover. Mindy might look like a femme fatale, but anyone who spent fifteen minutes with her would find out differently. He'd callously seduced a young girl who was too inexperienced to have any defense against him.

Chelsea's blue eyes sparkled angrily. "The fact remains that she's only nineteen, much too young for marriage."

"Your sister is a woman, *señorita*. You must agree, since you considered her old enough to travel in a foreign country alone."

"We expected her to bring home souvenirs, not a husband!"

"Life is full of surprises," he answered with heavy irony.

Chelsea's temper threatened to erupt, but she reined it in. Nothing would be gained by antagonizing the man. Much as she detested him, he held all the cards at the moment.

"Surely you must understand our concern," she said in her most reasonable voice. "Mindy just sprang this marriage thing on us out of the blue. We don't know anything about you.''

"It all happened very suddenly," he conceded. His cold disinterest warmed slightly.

"I'm not questioning your love for each other, all I'm asking you to do is postpone the wedding for... oh, say six months. To get to know each other better."

Roberto's brief softening fled. "The marriage will take place in two weeks."

"Three months, then," she wheeled. "That's not being unreasonable."

"This discussion is pointless, *señorita.* "

Chelsea was aghast. He sounded like a Spanish grandee of old, laying down the law to the peons. What would Mindy's life be like? He'd crush her spirit! Somehow the marriage had to be prevented.

"All right, I see I can't convince you, but at least let us have the ceremony in New York. It's traditional for the bride's family to give the wedding."

"All the arrangements have already been made. You and your family are welcome to attend, naturally."

"Our father had a heart attack recently. He can't travel."

"I'm sorry to hear that." Roberto's reply was conventionally courteous, nothing more.

The man was inhuman! "Mindy is his favorite child. He's worried about her," Chelsea said desperately. "At least come to New York and meet our parents."

"Unfortunately I can't get away right now."

"What do you do for a living?" she asked bluntly.

"I manage the family interests."

His cool tone didn't invite further discussion, but she was neither intimidated nor impressed. Roberto del Machado was nothing more than a rich man's lazy son!

"That doesn't sound like an arduous job," she said in a clipped voice. "Surely you can take a week off for something this important."

"We have different priorities, *señorita*," he answered icily. "I will let you finish your conversation with your sister."

Chelsea was breathing hard when Mindy returned, but she struggled for composure. It would be fatal to antagonize her sister, too.

Mindy had obviously been listening to Roberto's side of the conversation and knew things hadn't gone smoothly. "I told you it would be a waste of time," she said.

"He's quite set in his ways," Chelsea answered cautiously. "Doesn't that bother you?"

"There's nothing I can do about it."

"You can think twice about marrying him!"

"Don't start that again, Chelsea. Tell me about Mom and Dad. Is he feeling okay?"

"He was," Chelsea replied succinctly. "He's worried about you."

"Don't try to lay a guilt trip on me," Mindy flashed. "I wasn't responsible for his heart attack."

"I didn't mean to imply that you were," Chelsea said soothingly. "He misses you, though. Won't you consider coming home, even if it's only for a few days? I'll send you the money for a ticket."

"I wish I could."

Mindy's voice held such longing that Chelsea was shocked. "Is there any reason why you can't? That man isn't holding you against your will, is he?" Lurid thoughts of white slavery raced through Chelsea's mind.

"Of course not." Mindy's calm answer was somewhat reassuring.

"Then why can't you come home?"

"I just can't. Take my word for it. But you could come here. We'd have such fun, Chelsea." Mindy's normal enthusiasm returned. "Ronda is an adorable little town, centuries old. We could poke around antique shops and go sightseeing. They get lots of tourists here, because there's so much to see."

"Is that where you're going to live?"

"I guess so." Mindy's animation died.

That was what convinced Chelsea that she was needed. Every time Roberto was referred to, even obliquely, Mindy became subdued. Chelsea had to find out what hold he had over her sister—and rescue her from it.

"So, will you come?" Mindy asked.

"I'll be there tomorrow," Chelsea answered.

"That's fantastic! I can hardly wait."

Chelsea was slightly cheered by her sister's high spirits. That creep hadn't hammered her into a submissive bride yet, and he was going to have a fight on his hands before he ever did.

The plane from New York landed at the Málaga airport in the late afternoon. Chelsea retrieved her luggage and went through customs, chafing at the long lines and official delay. Mindy had said she'd meet her at the airport, and Chelsea couldn't wait to see how she looked.

It wasn't difficult to locate Mindy among the crowds of Spaniards waiting to greet the arriving passengers. Her bright coppery hair was like a spotlight in the sea of brunettes around her.

The sisters greeted each other joyously, both talking at once. Chelsea wasn't immediately aware of the tall, elegant man at Mindy's side. He stood there in a detached manner while they laughed and chattered together, oblivious to the jostling crowds. It wasn't until he summoned a skycap with an imperious gesture and pointed to her luggage, that Chelsea realized this must be Roberto del Machado.

Their eyes met in mutual appraisal. Chelsea wasn't prepared for the intelligence in his dark eyes, or the finely chiseled features of an aristocrat. She'd expected him to be sexy—what else would make Mindy flip out? But this man was incredible. He had the faultless body of an Apollo, broad shoulders, slim hips and long muscular legs.

It was clear Roberto felt the same grudging approval. His eyes moved from her delicate features framed by shining auburn hair to her slender figure, expressing male appreciation along the way.

"Chelsea, meet Roberto," Mindy said.

Chelsea was jolted back to reality. "This is very nice of you," she told him coolly. "I didn't expect you to come with Mindy to meet me." Earlier doubts returned to devil her. Was he afraid she'd spirit Mindy away on the next plane out?

"I wanted you to reach Ronda safely," he answered smoothly. "Your sister's driving on our mountain roads is somewhat erratic."

Chelsea decided not to challenge him this early. "I hope I haven't inconvenienced you," she remarked politely. "Is Ronda far from here?"

"Quite a distance, but I don't think you will be bored," he answered. "There is much to see along the way."

"You're going to love it," Mindy said.

Chelsea was reassured by her sister's behavior. Mindy didn't seem frightened or stressed. Her appearance in designer jeans and white cotton shirt with the ends knotted at her slim waist was normal, and she was in high spirits.

The only false note was the lack of warmth between Roberto and Mindy. They acted more like casual acquaintances than lovers.

Chelsea was troubled as she got into Roberto's luxurious car. All three sat in front, but they weren't crowded on the Bentley's spacious front seat. Roberto was apparently as wealthy as Mindy had said.

At first she and Mindy caught up on hometown gossip, but when they reached a resort town facing the ocean Chelsea began to take an interest in her surroundings.

"This is Torremolinos," Roberto said in response to her question.

A curving line of modern high-rise apartment houses and hotels faced the Mediterranean from across a broad highway. Rows of thatched beach umbrellas stretched along the sand for shade, and lounges were positioned nearer the water for sun lovers. Sailboats and motor launches left a white wake in the blue water offshore.

"I feel right at home," Chelsea commented. "It looks like a beach resort in the United States."

"The modern part does. The old town is behind the high-rises," Roberto said.

"We'll drive back here one day this week," Mindy promised. "To get to the square you climb up worn cobblestone stairs that wind around. They're called the San Miguel Steps, and along the way are cute little shops in old buildings that used to be private homes. People still live on the upper floors."

"That's the sort of thing I'm looking forward to seeing," Chelsea said.

"Here's something else that's kind of interesting." Mindy pointed out the window. "Look over there."

They had left Torremolinos and were driving along the highway. Following Mindy's direction, Chelsea glanced to her right and saw something that made her jaw drop. Sitting on top of a low hill was a perfect replica of the White House in Washington, D.C.

As Roberto slowed the car she exclaimed, "Am I imagining things?"

He chuckled. "No, it's an exact duplication of your American White House. It was built by the king of Saudi Arabia, who was a great admirer of your president. He also built the hill for the house to sit on."

"I wonder why, if he was such a stickler for authenticity," Mindy mused. "Ours is on flat ground."

"Presumably so the house could be seen from the road," Roberto replied.

Chelsea wanted to ask a dozen questions, but they were approaching Marbella. She'd heard of this watering hole of the rich and famous, but at first glimpse it was disappointing. On either side of the broad boulevard were rows of shops that probably carried elegant merchandise but didn't look too prepossessing.

"I expected Marbella to be more glamourous," she remarked.

"It is, if you know where to go," Mindy assured her.

"Or where to stay away from."

Roberto's murmured remark was so faint that Chelsea wasn't sure she'd heard correctly. A quick glance at his grim face told her she had. Marbella was where Mindy had met Roberto. If he regretted that fact, why wouldn't he give her up?

They left the main highway and started to climb. In the surrounding hills, Chelsea caught glimpses of opulent homes with swimming pools and tennis courts. This was undoubtedly where the jet set hung out.

The road became steeper and more winding. Chelsea began to see why Roberto didn't want Mindy to drive it alone. Some of the hairpin turns were frightening. There was barely room for two cars, and the outside lane verged on a sheer drop into the valley.

Roberto sensed her tension. "We're almost there." His voice was unexpectedly gentle.

Nothing could have prepared Chelsea for Ronda. At the very top of the mountain was a medieval fortress town, its approach guarded by a towering vaulted bridge. Far down at the bottom of the sheer cliff, a river rushed over mossy boulders.

"It's like a mythical city," Chelsea breathed. "Do people really live here?"

"Some very distinguished ones have," Roberto answered. "After you've had a chance to get settled I'll tell you the history of Ronda, if you're interested."

That reminded Chelsea of more immediate matters. "Did you get me a room in a hotel?" she asked Mindy.

"You're staying with us," Roberto answered for her.

"Oh, no, I couldn't!"

Didn't he realize she'd find that arrangement embarrassing? It was bad enough that Mindy was living with him. Chelsea wasn't going to give her seal of approval.

"I thought you'd be more comfortable at my house. Ronda doesn't have a luxury hotel." His voice was dry.

"I'm not that fussy about accommodations," she answered stiffly.

"You'll love the house," Mindy said. "It's fabulous."

"I'd really prefer to stay at a hotel," Chelsea insisted.

"We'll see more of each other this way." Mindy was equally insistent.

Roberto had the final word. "I don't know if I can get you a room at such short notice. Stay with us tonight, and then if you still wish to leave I'll see what I can do tomorrow."

I'd like to leave right now, Chelsea thought mutinously. How could she trust herself not to object when her little sister went into the bedroom with that man? Chelsea was so upset that she couldn't appreciate the quaint streets they drove through or the ancient buildings that crowded the narrow sidewalks.

Roberto stopped the car in front of a stately house with an intricately paneled front door. White walls provided a sparkling contrast to the red tile roof and the graceful wrought-iron railings that bordered balconies on the upper stories.

Chelsea hadn't expected anything so opulent. A house this size would take a lot of maintaining, even with servants. Did Mindy realize what would be expected of her? She considered it a hardship to hang up her own clothes. Maybe that was the angle to take—warn her about what she was getting into.

Chelsea shelved the problem for the moment as the front door was opened by a short man in black trousers and vest over a white shirt. He was introduced as Luis, the husband of Consuela, the cook.

"*Buenas tardes, señorita,*" the man greeted her.

"*Buenas tardes,* Luis," she answered. "*¿Como estas?*" She was pleased to discover that the Spanish she had learned at college seemed adequate for simple conversation.

They entered a tiled hall that was cool and dim after the August heat outside. Beyond the hall was a courtyard with a large fountain. In the center was a sculpted figure of a laughing child. The refreshing sound of splashing water added to the coolness.

"What a lovely patio," Chelsea said admiringly.

Pots of brightly colored flowers and tubs of lemon and lime trees were scattered around the slate floor, creating the effect of a garden. Around the fountain were wrought-iron chairs with small glass tables beside them.

"Give Chelsea the grand tour," Mindy suggested.

"I'm sure she'd prefer to get settled first. Where is my mother?" Roberto asked Luis.

"She is resting, *señor.*" The man said something in Spanish that was too fast for Chelsea to catch.

Roberto turned to Chelsea. "My mother sends her apologies. She says to tell you she looks forward to seeing you at dinner."

"You invited your mother here to meet me?" Chelsea asked uncertainly. That was going to make matters even more awkward.

Roberto was equally confused. "I didn't invite her. This is her home."

"You mean she *lives* here?"

"Of course. This has been our family home for generations." After a look at her dumbfounded face he lifted one eyebrow. "I realize that in your country a man does not live with his mother, but here we have no such insecurities about our manhood."

"It isn't that! I thought you and Mindy—" Chelsea stopped in a flood of embarrassment.

"I see." Amusement replaced austerity as he gazed at her pink cheeks. "Your thoughts are quite clear. That accounts for your hostility, but I assure you, Miss Claiborne, our living arrangement is quite chaste."

Mindy was doubled over with laughter. "You're priceless, Chelsea! If that's what you were worried about, why didn't you come right out and ask me?"

When Chelsea couldn't answer, Roberto said, "Well, at least that settles the problem of a hotel room. I'll have your luggage sent up."

Mindy took Chelsea to her room, a large, airy bedroom overlooking the side yard. It was pleasantly cool, due to the thick walls and the shutters at the windows. A large bed with a carved headboard, and an equally massive armoire dominated the room. All the furnishings were Spanish in design. Even the adjoining bathroom had a Spanish motif, a beautiful mosaic floor and scrolled grillwork framing the windows. The fixtures, however, were modern.

"I'm so glad you're here!" Mindy threw her arms around her sister. "This is going to be so great. We never get to spend much time together, just the two of us."

"Aren't you forgetting something?" Chelsea asked quietly.

"What?"

"Your fiancé. Won't he expect to be included?"

"Roberto's very busy." Mindy didn't meet her sister's eye. "He's always off doing something or other."

"Doesn't that bother you?"

"No, why should it?"

"Most engaged couples want to be together as much as possible."

"We'll be together plenty after we're married," Mindy answered tersely.

"You don't love him, do you?" Chelsea asked slowly.

"What kind of dumb question is that? We're getting married in two weeks."

"Why?"

Mindy took a deep breath. "Roberto is a tremendous catch. He's rich, he's handsome, his family is top-drawer. You can't believe the amount of women who'd take him away from me in a minute if they had the chance."

"All I hear is that you're marrying him for his money, but I can't believe that."

"At least you're giving me *some* credit."

"It doesn't solve the mystery. You've never once said you love him."

"Okay, I love him. Does that satisfy you? What woman wouldn't? Have you ever seen a man that sexy?"

Chelsea was beginning to get a glimmering, and she didn't like what she was hearing. Roberto undoubtedly had vast experience with women. That taut body must have brought great joy to many partners. Mindy would be overwhelmed by his expertise.

"Satisfying sex isn't everything," Chelsea said soberly.

"You poor, underprivileged kid." Mindy grinned.

"All right, sex is great and Roberto is fantastic, but why rush into marriage? At least wait a few months."

"There's nothing to wait for." Mindy's smile was replaced by inexpressible sadness. She got up off the bed. "We have cocktails in the courtyard at eight. I'm going to get ready."

After unpacking, Chelsea took a bath to relax her tension. The warm water was so soothing that she didn't realize how late it was getting. By the time she dressed and hurried down to the courtyard, a babble of voices told her everyone else was already there.

"I'm sorry," she apologized to Roberto. "I lost track of the time. Am I terribly late?"

"Not at all. This is a family evening, nothing elaborate. I thought you might be tired after your trip."

"Not really, it's six hours earlier in New York. But you mustn't feel you have to entertain me. I more or less invited myself."

"On the contrary. You fought against it." White teeth gleamed in his tanned face as he gave her a mischievous smile.

Chelsea caught a glimpse of the great charm this man possessed when he cared to use it. Coupled with his blatant sensuality, she began to understand Mindy's fixation.

Roberto had turned to an older woman whom he introduced as his mother. Dolores del Machado must have been a great beauty in her youth and was still quite lovely. Roberto had inherited his dark, liquid eyes and patrician features from her. They also shared the same air of complete assurance.

While they were being introduced, Dolores inspected Chelsea with interest. Her eyes skimmed over the younger woman's face and figure, missing very little. Her conclusions were a secret, however. Nothing in Señora del Machado's manner told whether she approved or disapproved of her son's coming marriage.

"Welcome to our home." Whatever her feelings, she greeted Chelsea graciously.

"It's very kind of you to have me, especially at such short notice," Chelsea replied.

"We are practically family. You will be Roberto's sister-in-law."

Chelsea gave him a startled glance. That hadn't occurred to her. The idea was disturbing, somehow.

His smile this time was sardonic. "In Spain we also use that old expression, 'you can choose your friends but not your relatives.'"

Chelsea lifted her chin. "We have another expression in America that you might not have heard. 'It isn't over till it's over.'"

Dolores's face was thoughtful as she felt the electricity crackling between the two. "You're forgetting your manners, Roberto. Please introduce Señorita Claiborne to our other guests."

There were five more people in the group. Ramón and Rosa were Roberto's brother and his wife. Ramón was younger than Roberto, and deferred to his older brother on every subject that came up, Chelsea discovered later. Rosa didn't seem to mind. She was pretty and placid.

Miguel Espinosa was more interesting. He wasn't as classically handsome as Roberto, but he was pleasant-looking and very outgoing. Before they could exchange more than a few words, though, Roberto introduced her to his two aunts, elderly women who were dressed all in black, in spite of the summer season. Roberto and his brother deferred to them courteously, but they barely spoke all evening.

After the introductions had been completed, Chelsea said to Miguel, "Roberto said this was a family party. Are you a relation?"

"A cousin, many times removed." He smiled. "But to the Spanish, family is everything."

"That's nice," she said. "I approve of close families."

"You may change your opinion if you are seated between the aunties at dinner," he answered impishly. "Their only topic of conversation is who died and how long they lingered."

"I hope you're joking."

Miguel gazed into her eyes. "I would never lead such a beautiful lady astray."

Roberto joined them in time to hear his statement. "You're taking unfair advantage, Miguel. The Claiborne sisters are very gullible."

Chelsea's nails bit into her palms. He was *bragging* about having seduced Mindy! Her blue eyes sparkled with anger. "That description hardly fits *me*. Someone my sister's age might be an easy target, but any man who would take take advantage of her should be ashamed of himself."

They all turned to look at Mindy, who was pouring herself a drink from the bar cart. With an annoyed exclamation, Roberto strode over to her.

His comment was inaudible, but her answer wasn't. "For Pete's sake, lighten up, Roberto."

"I do not want you to drink," he answered firmly.

"Don't be an old party pooper. You need to loosen up a little."

A muscle bunched in his jaw as he took the glass out of her hand. "You're making a scene."

"So what?" she challenged. "Maybe it will jazz things up around here."

Dolores rose gracefully, her face serene. "Dinner is served. Shall we all go into the dining room?"

Chelsea followed the others, more troubled than she'd ever been. How could this marriage ever succeed?

Chapter Two

Dinner was an uncomfortable affair for Chelsea, although she wasn't stuck between the aunties. Dolores had given her the place of honor on her right, and Miguel was on her left. Ordinarily she would have enjoyed herself. Both of her dinner partners were charming and good conversationalists. But Mindy was seated at the other end of the table, too far away for Chelsea to try to control her.

Roberto was certainly having problems. Whenever he looked away, Mindy would pour herself a glass of wine, which he would immediately take away from her. Why was Mindy going out of her way to be difficult?

"Is this your first visit to Spain?" Dolores asked Chelsea.

"This part of it," she answered. "I've been to Madrid and Barcelona."

"I've never been anywhere before," Mindy announced.

"And now you're going to live here." Miguel smiled. "You got more than you bargained for on your first trip to Europe."

"You better believe it!" Mindy laughed, but Roberto's face was austere.

"Will you like living here?" Rosa asked.

Mindy shrugged. "I don't have any choice, do I?"

"You can call off the wedding and come home with me." Chelsea kept her voice light, as though she was joking, but her eyes held Mindy's. "We love you, no matter what you do."

"Are you trying to break up the happy couple?" Ramón asked facetiously.

"I think whirlwind courtships are terribly romantic," Rosa remarked. "We're all so excited about the wedding."

"Not to mention, surprised," Miguel said. "How long have women been trying to drag you to the altar, Roberto?"

"You tell me," Roberto drawled. "You're the one who's keeping track."

Both men were smiling, but Chelsea began to wonder if they really liked each other.

Miguel backed away gracefully. "We're indebted to you for bringing the lovely Claiborne sisters to Spain. How long will you be staying?" he asked Chelsea.

"I'm not certain yet," she replied.

"Surely you'll stay until the wedding," Dolores said.

"Of course she will," Mindy declared.

"I don't know if I can be away from the office that long."

"What do you do?" Dolores asked.

"I'm an investment counselor. It's a rather demanding job."

"Don't I have a higher priority than some rich old goats who play real-life Monopoly games?" Mindy pouted.

"Obviously, since I'm here," Chelsea answered crisply.

"Then don't go home. Make her stay, Roberto," Mindy appealed to him.

"Something tells me I'd have even less success controlling *her* than I've had with you," he answered dryly.

"The Claiborne women are formidable," Mindy agreed. She raised her glass. "Where's Luis? I want some wine."

Chelsea was really annoyed at her sister. There was nothing she could do about it at the moment, but she intended to have a serious talk with Mindy after dinner. It was time her sister started acting like an adult.

Miguel eased the tension by tactfully changing the subject. "Do you enjoy sailing?" he asked Chelsea. "It would give me great pleasure to take you out on my boat."

"That sounds like fun," she replied politely.

"How about tomorrow?"

"Not tomorrow. I haven't seen Mindy all summer. We have a lot of catching up to do." Chelsea's grim tone didn't promise the happy reunion she implied.

Dolores pretended not to notice her inflection. "It's so nice that you two have such a warm relationship. I admire that. Here in Spain, the family is all-important."

"Half the time Chelsea acts like a mother to me." Mindy laughed. "I guess that's the price of being the baby in the family."

"Or acting like one," Chelsea muttered under her breath.

Not low enough, however. Ramón heard her and chuckled. "We have our problem child, too. You have yet to meet Jorge."

"Who is Jorge?" Chelsea asked.

"Our youngest brother."

"Are there any more of you? Do you have sisters, also?"

"No, only the three of us. After Jorge, Madre Dolores decided she had enough." Ramón smiled.

"Ramón is making a joke," Dolores said reprovingly. "Jorge is a delightful young man."

"Does he live here in Ronda?" Chelsea asked, wondering why he wasn't present.

"He comes and goes in the summer," Dolores answered. "The rest of the year he is at the university."

"Ronda is too tame for Jorge," Ramón said indulgently. He looked questioningly at Roberto, "Where is he now? Living the good life in Puerto Banús on someone's yacht?"

"Who knows?" Roberto shrugged.

"He'll show up when he needs money," Miguel remarked. "Ah, to be young again, without any responsibilities."

Roberto eyed his cousin dispassionately. "Do you consider yourself overworked?"

"Not compared to you, certainly. But few of us possess your noble character, Roberto." Miguel's voice held a mocking note.

"What exactly do you do?" Chelsea asked Roberto.

"I look after our family interests." It was the same evasive answer he'd given over the phone.

"Roberto took over when his father died. We depend on him greatly." Dolores gazed at her oldest son fondly. "Of course Ramón is a great help, too," she added hastily. "All of my sons are fine young men."

"You are too lenient with Jorge," one of the aunts said unexpectedly. "That boy is a wild one." It was the first word either of the old ladies had uttered, and every one looked startled.

"He is young, *tia*. Jorge will grow up in due time." Dolores repressed a sigh.

"I know every man wishes for a son, but I can't help being happy that we have daughters," Rosa remarked. "They are so much more docile."

"Not necessarily." Mindy grinned as she maneuvered her wineglass out of Roberto's reach once more.

"How many children do you have?" Chelsea asked, trying to ignore her sister's antics.

Rosa was only too happy to give the ages, description and accomplishments of her two daughters. They were the center of her universe, along with her husband and home. Chelsea tried to appear interested, but she was grateful when Dolores suggested they move to the living room for coffee.

Mindy declined, saying she was tired and wanted to go to bed. Chelsea made the same excuse and followed her sister upstairs.

At the door to her room, Mindy yawned elaborately. "Boy, am I beat. I can't wait to hit the sack."

"We need to have a little talk first," Chelsea said ominously.

"Catch me tomorrow. I'm really wiped out."

"You'll survive. I'm not leaving until I find out what happened to you."

Mindy gave her a wary look. "What do you mean?"

"When did you start to drink?"

"When did you turn into such a prude?" Mindy countered. "So I felt like having a glass of wine. Big deal! Roberto doesn't own me, even though he acts like he does," she added in a low mutter.

"If this is the way you feel now, think how much worse it will be after you're married."

"Why do you think I wanted a drink?" Mindy asked sardonically.

Chelsea was speechless for a moment. "What's going on, Mindy? Why are you marrying a man you obviously don't love? Is he blackmailing you into it? Did you do something foolish with drugs?" She'd heard horror stories about foreign prisons. Could that be Roberto's hold over her?

"Good Lord, no!" Mindy's unguarded response was reassuring. "I might do a few crazy things now and then, but I'd never mess with that stuff. You ought to know me better than that."

"Then what reason would you have for marrying Roberto?"

Mindy walked over to the window and stared out. "He's really a super guy. Roberto isn't exactly warm, but he's somebody you can count on. I admire him a lot."

"That's no basis for marriage."

Mindy turned around. "I'm not asking you to understand, only to trust me. I've done some irresponsible things in the past, but I've grown up. I intend to marry Roberto, with or without your blessing, but I hope you'll stand by me. I need you, Chelsea, more than I've ever needed you before."

Chelsea was struck by the new maturity in her sister's face. Something had happened to change her, something that couldn't be solved with a check to cover an outrageous extravagance. If only Mindy would confide in her. Since she wouldn't, Chelsea could only offer her support.

Mustering a smile, she said, "Hey, what are sisters for? My maid-of-honor dress better be smashing, or you'll never hear the end of it."

Mindy threw her arms around Chelsea's neck. "You're the greatest! I never came right out and said so, but I love you, Chelsea."

Chelsea held her tightly. "I'm fairly fond of you, too."

Mindy drew away self-consciously. "I really am sorry about tonight, but don't expect me to sprout instant wings and a halo."

Chelsea laughed. "I never did believe in miracles. But I do expect you to promise me something."

"What?" Mindy asked cautiously.

"I want you to go easy on the liquor from now on."

Mindy's tense figure relaxed. "You've got it. I don't even like the stuff. I guess I was a little hyper tonight. I know you don't approve of Roberto, and I was afraid you two might clash head on."

"I can't pretend I think he's right for you, but you should have known I wouldn't do anything embarrassing."

"Too bad it doesn't run in the family," Mindy said ruefully. "Roberto was pretty steamed at me. I'm not looking forward to seeing him in the morning."

"I don't blame you. He's rather formidable. I'd never in a million years expect you to be attracted to such an imperious man."

"You have to admit he's a real hunk."

"I suppose so," Chelsea agreed grudgingly.

"Actually he's more your type than mine. Roberto knows all about books and the theater and high finance—your world."

Chelsea raised an eyebrow. "That's curious. You've never been particularly interested in my world."

"He can also be very charming," Mindy said hastily. "You didn't see him at his best tonight. Believe me, by the time the next two weeks are over, you're going to feel completely different about Roberto."

"I hope you're right." Chelsea didn't see any point in prolonging the discussion, since Mindy couldn't be swayed. Not yet, anyway. "Well, it's been a long day. I'm going to bed."

Chelsea was tired but not sleepy. She got undressed, wondering what magic words would bring Mindy to her senses. Nothing had worked so far. Would it help to try and reason with Roberto again? The memory of his cool stare and lordly manner discouraged that idea.

As she mulled over the problem, sounds below her window told her the party was breaking up. A wide driveway at the side of the house led to a former stable that had been converted to garages. Slipping into a robe, Chelsea walked over to the window and looked out.

Miguel drove away first in a powerful sports car that shattered the stillness of the summer night. He was long gone by the time the old aunties were settled in the back seat of Ramón's sedate Rolls-Royce. The del Machado family interests were obviously very profitable, whatever they were.

Roberto had accompanied them outside and was patiently helping the elderly ladies into the car. When the Rolls had driven away he remained in the driveway, watching the receding taillights. Even after the red glow had disappeared he stood motionless, gazing down the road.

A short time later, headlights appeared in the distance. A red convertible approached and turned into the driveway. Then Chelsea realized what Roberto had been waiting for. A woman with long blond hair braked to a stop and jumped out of the car, calling to him joyfully. She was wearing a very short glittery sheath that showed off a magnificent figure.

Fury engulfed Chelsea as the woman flung her arms around Roberto's neck. Instead of embracing her in the same manner, he held her by the waist. Their bodies didn't touch, but that didn't appease Chelsea. He obviously knew how visible they were.

Chelsea couldn't hear their conversation because Roberto had ordered the blonde to lower her voice, which she did at once. Women seemed to comply instantly with his every wish, Chelsea thought angrily.

After a short discussion during which the blonde appeared to be pleading with him, Roberto helped her into the passenger seat of the convertible. As Chelsea watched with mounting indignation, he got into the driver's seat and drove away.

Chelsea paced the floor, trying to stifle her wrath so she could think clearly. It was unthinkable to allow the wedding to take place. If Roberto was cheating on Mindy while they were engaged, what would her life be like after they were married? But would Mindy believe her? Roberto would deny it, of course, and he had Mindy hypnotized. That was another concern. If Chelsea did manage to convince her, she would be terribly hurt by his infidelity.

Chelsea got into bed finally, but she didn't fall asleep for a long time. It was quiet enough outside. If Roberto returned that night, it was many hours later.

As a result of her troubled night, Chelsea didn't waken until almost noon, and then immediately worried about disrupting the household routine. That was the disadvantage of being a houseguest.

After a quick shower she dressed hurriedly in cream-colored silk pants and a matching blouse. Mindy's bedroom door was still closed when she passed it on her way downstairs.

The downstairs rooms were empty, although faint sounds came from the back of the house where the kitchen was located. Chelsea was dying for a cup of coffee. As she was wondering if it would be proper to go into the kitchen and request one, a car door slammed outside. A few moments later the car drove away and Roberto entered the house. He was wearing the same clothes he'd worn the night before.

After greeting her without any sign of embarrassment, he remarked, "I hope you slept well."

"Fairly well after you and the others drove off," she answered icily.

He returned her gaze steadily. "I'd forgotten your room was above the driveway. I'm sorry if we disturbed you."

"I'm more than disturbed, I'm furious!" Chelsea decided to confront him. He couldn't very well deny the obvious fact that he'd been out all night. "You have the morals of a tomcat! How could you spend the night with another woman when you're supposed to marry my sister in just two weeks?"

"What makes you think I spent the night with a woman?"

"Do you think I'm simpleminded? I *saw* you drive away with that sexy blonde."

"So you automatically assumed we wound up in bed."

"It was rather late for a movie, and she didn't look like the type who enjoys discussing current events," Chelsea replied witheringly.

"Do you always make these snap judgments about people?" he asked.

"My opinions are beside the point. What matters is your shameful behavior. What do you think Mindy would say if I told her?"

"Why don't you try it and find out?" he drawled.

"Don't overestimate your charm," Chelsea said grimly. "Mindy wouldn't put up with your transgressions."

"*If* she believed you," he answered mockingly.

"I fully expect you to deny everything, but Mindy isn't as naive as you think. She just might start to see through you."

"I don't intend to deny anything. I did leave here with a woman, and I *was* out all night, but I didn't spend it in the lady's bed."

"You honestly expect me to swallow that?"

"Frankly, Miss Claiborne, it doesn't matter to me if you do or don't. Now, if you'll excuse me, I'm going to shower and change clothes."

Chelsea stared after him impotently. Roberto's automatic assumption of invincibility was maddening. She had him dead to rights, and his confidence wasn't even shaken. Chelsea was forced to suppress her rage when his mother joined her.

After they exchanged a few words, Dolores said, "You must be hungry. Would you prefer to eat indoors or out?"

"Whichever is more convenient. I hope I didn't upset your schedule by coming down so late."

"Not at all, my dear. We're quite flexible about breakfast and lunch. Dinner is the only time we gather together. Just tell Luis what you'd like, and Consuela will prepare it for you. I hope you'll excuse me for not joining you. I have an appointment."

"That's quite all right," Chelsea assured her.

Before leaving, Dolores summoned Luis. As she was going out the door, Dolores turned back to Chelsea. "Will you give Roberto a message for me? Tell him Carlos called. Roberto left his signet ring on the nightstand in the guest room last night."

Chelsea stared at her. "Did you say Carlos?"

"He's one of Roberto's old friends." Dolores's smooth brow furrowed in a slight frown. "What on earth was Roberto doing at Carlos's last night? Ah, well, who can keep up with him?" She shrugged. "Just be sure to give him the message. The ring belonged to his father. Roberto would be very upset if he thought it was lost." With a wave of her hand, Dolores left.

Chelsea didn't know what to think. Was it possible Roberto had told the truth? That didn't seem likely when all the evidence pointed in the other direction. He *had* left here with that woman. Chelsea suddenly realized Luis was talking to her.

"It is a beautiful day, *señorita*. Would you like me to set the table in the courtyard?"

"Yes, that would be lovely," she answered absently.

The pots of flowers were especially vivid in the brilliant sunshine. It was a picture-perfect day, with a clear blue sky and enough breeze for comfort. Luis set the round glass table with heavy silverware on an appliquéd organdy place mat, then left to convey Chelsea's simple request for toast and coffee to Consuela in the kitchen.

Under ordinary circumstances Chelsea would have delighted in the luxurious accommodations, but worry over Mindy made that impossible. She was toying with her toast when Roberto made an unexpected appearance.

His late and presumably eventful evening hadn't taken any toll. He looked vital and well rested, also extremely attractive in white slacks and a navy shirt. The outfit emphasized his broad-shouldered, lean-hipped physique.

"Will I spoil your breakfast if I join you?" he asked. "It seems rather ludicrous for us to eat in separate rooms."

"That would be uncomfortable," she agreed. "Especially since we're going to be stuck with each other for the next two weeks. Unless I can change your mind about marrying my sister."

"Why don't we simply try to make the best of it?" he replied, turning to the manservant who had appeared at his side.

"What can I bring you, *señor?*" Luis asked.

Roberto eyed Chelsea's plate. "That looks fine. But I'll have some fresh fruit as well."

After the man had left, Chelsea remembered to give Roberto his mother's message.

"That's a relief," he remarked calmly, pouring himself a cup of coffee from the silver pot on the table. "I'd feel badly if I lost it. The ring is a keepsake."

"So your mother said," Chelsea murmured.

"I don't suppose it changed your mind about my whereabouts last night," he commented ironically.

"It doesn't really prove anything. You could have gone to your friend's house after..." She stumbled to a halt.

Roberto chuckled unexpectedly, a deep masculine sound. "Poor Chelsea, what unromantic lovers you must have had. Did they creep out in the middle of the night like little boys with a curfew?"

"My private life is none of your concern," she snapped.

Chelsea was annoyed at herself for the sudden warmth in her midsection. She began to understand Roberto's success with women. When his gaze rested on her mouth she could almost feel his lips moving over hers, coaxing, teasing, until they parted willingly.

He was watching her with a tiny smile. "I was merely inquiring into your American customs. In Spain, a man is not so easily satisfied when he has a beautiful woman in his bed."

"Or *her* bed."

"As the case may be," he conceded with a mischievous twinkle in his eyes.

"So your defense is that if you had been with that woman, you would have stayed all night?"

"Most assuredly." He was wearing a broad grin now.

"I don't find this as amusing as you do," Chelsea said coldly. "You've conveniently skimmed over the fact that you had a late date. Our American customs are obviously different from yours. We frown on that sort of activity when a man is engaged."

"And rightly so. I did not have a late date, or any other kind."

"You were simply waiting outside for her to deliver the morning paper?"

"I wasn't waiting for anyone. I was merely enjoying the peace and quiet, and doing a little thinking," Roberto answered patiently. "I don't usually feel compelled to explain my actions, but in the interest of better relations between us I will make an exception this time. The woman you saw, Claire Vanderlip, was someone I knew before your sister came into my life."

"From the way she threw her arms around your neck, I gathered you were acquainted," Chelsea commented coolly.

He gave her a quelling look before continuing. "Claire had been to a party where she had a lot to drink. It suddenly seemed like a good idea to come and visit me."

Chelsea's mouth thinned disapprovingly. "To relive the good old days?"

"The reason isn't important," he replied impatiently. "What matters is that it was dangerous for her to drive down the mountain in her condition. I took her home and left her there. Since it was late and I didn't relish the trip back at that hour, I went to my friend's house for the night."

Roberto's terse explanation had the unmistakable ring of truth. Chelsea was reminded of the way he'd held the woman off. If he'd shared her passion, the risk of being seen wouldn't have bothered him. Chelsea had a feeling Roberto took what he wanted and dealt with the consequences later.

"You have a rather unpleasant habit of driving women to drink," she grumbled, in an ungracious acceptance of his story.

"Claire is one of your people," he said dryly. "American women are a great deal more uninhibited than Spanish women."

"That doesn't seem to disturb you."

"You're mistaken. A man likes to do the pursuing."

"What a hypocritical thing to say," Chelsea flared. "You seduce women, and then complain because it's too easy."

"I have never seduced a woman," he said evenly.

"How about my sister?"

His expression hardened. "That includes your sister. I have never touched her."

Chelsea stared at him incredulously, but Roberto returned her gaze without blinking. Was it possible? Or was she being taken in like all his other deluded women?

"Will you tell me why on earth you're marrying Mindy?" The words burst out of her.

"That's a strange question. Your sister is a beautiful girl."

"Exactly. She's only a girl, and you're a man—a very experienced one. Mindy can't possibly measure up to the women you've known. If sex isn't the attraction, what is?"

He smiled thinly. "Perhaps I'm charmed by her naïveté."

"For one evening, possibly. Level with me, Roberto."

"You must have asked Mindy the same question. What does she say?"

"That she's in love with you. I didn't believe *her*, either."

He shrugged. "I don't know what to do to convince you."

"A show of affection might help, for starters. You don't put your arm around her or hold her hand. You don't even smile at her."

"The Spanish have great reserve in public. Privately, we turn into veritable tigers. Would you like a demonstration of my passionate nature?"

"Not personally," she said stiffly, aware that he was laughing at her.

"Too bad it isn't possible under the circumstances." His eyes moved from her classic features to the creamy skin of her throat. "You and your sister are amazingly lovely, in very different ways."

"Our taste in men is different, too," Chelsea answered tartly.

"What sort of a man appeals to you, Chelsea?"

"Someone who doesn't regard women as a hobby."

Roberto smiled. "Is that a criticism of me or an indictment of the men you've known?"

"I've never had a bad experience," she answered primly.

He gazed appraisingly at her pink cheeks. "I wonder just how much experience you have had."

Chelsea was furious at herself for letting him rattle her. She was usually coolly poised with men, but she'd never met one like Roberto. His magnetism was a little frightening. She felt herself reacting to his masculinity, and she didn't even like him!

"I'm a guest in your house, so I don't wish to be rude, but my sex life is none of your business," she said angrily.

"You're right, of course." He seemed to lose interest in the subject. "What are you and Mindy going to do today?"

"There won't be much of the day left by the time she gets up. I wonder if I should go and check on her."

"Luis will do it." Roberto rang a crystal bell, and the servant appeared almost immediately. "Will you knock on Señorita Mindy's door and ask if she wishes breakfast?"

Chelsea glanced at her watch as the man left. "It's afternoon already. Your days begin and end so much later than ours. We didn't finish dinner last night until after eleven. I could never get used to that on a regular basis."

"If you lived here for any length of time it would soon seem natural. We live a more leisurely life."

"Evidently. When do you go to work?"

"I don't have specific hours, but I work very diligently at times."

"I wouldn't know what to do with myself if I didn't go to the office every morning."

Roberto smiled. "Perhaps we will teach you how to relax and enjoy yourself."

Luis returned with a message. "The *señorita* says she doesn't feel well. She intends to stay in bed all day."

Chelsea was immediately concerned. Had her sister managed to sneak a few drinks while Roberto wasn't looking?

"I should go to her." She sighed.

"She might have gone back to sleep," Roberto said quickly.

Chelsea considered the matter. If her sister had a hangover, this was no time to talk to her. "You're right, I'll check on her later."

"What would you like to do today?"

"I thought I'd take a walk through some of those little winding streets. They look fascinating."

"They are. I will show you some of our historic places."

"You intend to go with me?" she asked in surprise.

"Don't you want me to?"

How could she say no? "It's kind of you to offer, but I'm sure you must have things to do."

"Nothing pressing. I'd enjoy showing your around."

Chelsea was certain that he merely felt obligated, but having a guide always made sightseeing more interesting.

As they strolled down the narrow streets, Roberto told her a little about Ronda's long history.

"In spite of our natural fortification, many battles have been fought for control of the city. At one time or another through the ages it was ruled by Celts and Visigoths, caliphs and kings. The monarch Fernando visited here with his queen, Isabella, in the early 1500s. During more recent times, Bizet was inspired by one of our local women. He based his opera *Carmen* on her."

Roberto stopped in the middle of a stone bridge and pointed into the chasm that plunged hundreds of feet to the river below. "The setting for the thieves' den in *Carmen* was suggested by these cliffs."

Chelsea stared at the sheer sheets of rock on each side, broken only by the dark openings of caves that seemed inaccessible. At the bottom, turbulent water rushed over jagged rocks. It was a wild and awesome sight.

"How did anyone ever get up here?" she marveled.

"The southern side of town is the only natural access. It was well fortified, and guarded by the Almocábar Gate. Come, I will show you."

Roberto continued his bits of information as they walked. "Ronda was a favorite of your countrymen. Ernest Hemingway once called it his favorite Spanish town, and Orson Welles shared that admiration. His ashes are buried near here."

"I can't believe I'd never heard of this place before," Chelsea said.

"You're not alone." He smiled. "Perhaps it's just as well, or we'd be overcrowded. People fall in love with Ronda and want to stay."

"Is that what happened to Mindy?"

His expression changed. "No pressure was put on her, I assure you."

Chelsea was sorry she'd mentioned her sister. Roberto had been a charming companion until then, and she'd been enjoying herself. Now the atmosphere between them was charged with tension again.

She followed him in subdued silence as he pointed out the wrought-iron balconies that were a product of Ronda, and told her about other industries the town was noted for.

Roberto's warmth didn't return until they reached a beautiful garden called the Alameda. He was pleased by her obvious delight in the lush flowers and splashing fountains.

"You might be interested to know that not one penny of government money was spent on this," he remarked.

"Was it a gift from someone?"

"From a lot of people." He grinned. "The work was paid for by fines levied on people who had either been obscene or provoked scandal on the streets. That was the official language of the edict."

"I'm glad to hear it. I was beginning to think you were a city of saints," she teased.

"That's because I didn't tell you about the more colorful figures in our past, like José Ulloa, a skilled bullfighter. He was married to a gypsy girl whom he adored. One day he left for Málaga to perform in the bullring, but on the way he fell off his horse and broke his arm. Since there was no point in going on, he returned home late at night."

"I have an awful feeling that he should have stopped at a pay phone and called ahead." Chelsea smiled.

"An incident like this might have been what inspired your Alexander Graham Bell to invent the telephone."

"What happened? Was his wife entertaining a gentleman friend?"

"She had been. The man was hiding in a huge oil jar. He was the sexton from a neighboring parish, but José didn't approve of the kind of guidance he was giving. José became one of our more noted outlaws because of the ensuing disagreement."

"I suppose the lesson to be learned from that story is, don't ever hide in an oil jar."

"It wouldn't be my first choice, but the occasion isn't likely to arise," Roberto said.

"Because oil jars are scarce these days?"

"No, because I've never been involved with a married woman."

That left plenty of single ones, Chelsea reflected as they walked along the cobblestone path. Suddenly her heel caught in one of the crevices between the stones and she stumbled.

Roberto caught her before she fell, but she was hopelessly off balance. Her body was a deadweight against his, forcing him to hold her tightly.

As she struggled to right herself, Chelsea was acutely conscious of every hard male angle of his lithe body. Her breasts were crushed against his broad chest, and her nose was buried in his neck. Even their thighs were glued together.

The incident lasted only a few moments, but that was long enough to make her heart race. The instant physical reaction of her body appalled Chelsea.

Her cheeks were flushed when she finally managed to pull away. "I was...I'm so sorry," she stammered. "I'm not usually this clumsy."

"It was my fault," he answered gallantly. "I should have warned you to be careful on these uneven paths. Let me help you with your shoe."

Her heel was wedged so tightly that her shoe had come off completely. Roberto crouched down to free it. As he clasped his hand around her ankle and lifted her foot, Chelsea was forced to hold onto his shoulder to steady herself. The intimate feeling of his shifting muscles under the silk shirt didn't add to her peace of mind.

"That's better." He stood up and smiled at her. "I'll keep a closer eye on you from now on."

Roberto didn't seem at all affected by the mishap, but Chelsea couldn't dismiss it that lightly. What kind of a person was she? This was the man her sister was going to marry!

"I think we'd better start back." She didn't trust herself to look at him. "I'm worried about Mindy."

"I'm sure she's all right, but you've probably had enough sightseeing for one day. We'll save the bullring and the Giant's House for another time."

Chelsea had no intention of repeating today's experience, but she nodded silently.

When they reached the house, Chelsea left Roberto and went upstairs immediately. Music blasting from Mindy's bedroom told that she had recovered. Chelsea knocked on the door and went in.

Mindy was sitting at a dressing table, putting bright red polish on her nails. Her head bristled with fat pink curlers. She turned around and waggled her fingers, either in greeting or to dry her nails.

Chelsea turned down the CD player. "I gather you're feeling better."

"First-rate and raring to go. Sorry I flaked out on you today, but I felt like the way the bottom of a bird cage looks."

"I'm not surprised."

Mindy changed the subject hastily. "Luis told me you went out with Roberto. You two must have found a lot in common."

"Why do you say that?" Chelsea asked warily.

"You were gone all day."

"We didn't start out until afternoon. He showed me some interesting places and told me stories about Ronda."

"Isn't it a nifty little town? Did you poke around in any of the shops?"

"No, we went sightseeing."

Mindy looked critically at Chelsea's feet. "Those aren't the right kind of shoes for walking on cobblestones. Didn't you bring any flats?"

"Yes, but I...I didn't realize how bumpy the pavement would be." Chelsea had trouble looking at her sister. She still felt guilty about that moment in the park, even though it had been an accident.

"You could take a nasty fall in those skinny heels."

"I won't wear them again, okay?" When Mindy showed surprise at her sharp tone, Chelsea asked more mildly, "What did you do all day?"

"After I finally got around to feeling human again, I washed my hair and went through my pitiful wardrobe, looking for something to wear tonight." Mindy's face was discontented. "Cinderella had a better selection."

"I suppose that means you want me to be your fairy godmother," Chelsea said dryly.

"You catch on fast." Mindy laughed. "Marbella has great stores, but that won't help me tonight. Do you have anything smashing I can borrow?"

"What's so special about tonight?"

"Didn't Roberto tell you? One of his friends is giving us an engagement party. Her name is Veronique Broussard, and she lives in one of those big houses on the side of a hill. I think she and Roberto had a thing going once, but evidentally it's all over."

Chelsea's eyes narrowed. "Does she have long blond hair?"

"No, she's a brunette."

At least Roberto hadn't been lying about the blonde, Chelsea thought. So far he'd told her the truth—as far as it went.

"Veronique was a French movie star at one time," Mindy continued enthusiastically. "She quit to marry some fabulously wealthy older man, only he isn't around anymore. I don't know if he died or she left him. Anyway, it's going to be a sensational party. All of the jet set will be there. What are you going to wear?''

''I'm not invited.''

''Of course you are. You're my sister, and I'm the guest of honor. Well, along with Roberto.''

''I think I'll pass. I didn't bring anything dressy enough for a big bash, and I wouldn't know a soul there.''

''You *have* to go,'' Mindy insisted. ''It wouldn't look right if you didn't. The Spanish are very big on keeping up appearances.''

''I won't reflect any glory on them in a little black dress,'' Chelsea protested.

''You can borrow something of mine.''

''I thought you were threadbare.''

''Relatively speaking.'' Mindy grinned. ''Let's see what we can find for you. This will be one party you won't forget in a hurry.''

Chapter Three

Mindy had completely understated the condition of her wardrobe. The closet was packed with outfits for every occasion from casual to chic. All of them were flamboyant, a reflection of her personality.

"Where did you get all these things?" Chelsea gasped. "They must have cost a fortune."

"Not when you know where to shop. Dawn and I found a couple of terrific outlet shops."

"I've been meaning to ask what happened to Dawn."

"Later." Mindy pulled out a short black dress printed all over with large red, yellow and green hearts. It had a low neck and a pouf on one hip. "How about this?"

"Good Lord, no! Not for me," Chelsea exclaimed. "Or you, either."

Mindy held the dress against her body. "It doesn't look bad on. Still, maybe it *is* a little too wild. Okay, what about this one?" She held up a backless white sheath with a gold lamé sash trailing from the waist to the brief hemline.

"Give it up, Mindy. Nothing of yours is going to be right for me."

"You're too conservative. You've got a great body. Why not show it off?"

"Because that isn't my style. I don't care to call attention to myself."

"All right, but you're going to wind up an old maid with only a cat for company," Mindy warned.

"I'll take my chances, if this is the alternative." Chelsea smiled. "I'd better see if my black dress needs pressing."

"No, wait, there must be something here that won't give you a panic attack." Mindy snapped her fingers. "Got it!" Delving into the back of the closet, she came out with a lavender chiffon gown. The sleeveless crystal-beaded tank top was attached to a skirt made of floating petal-shaped layers. "Tell me there's something wrong with this one," she crowed.

"It doesn't look like you," Chelsea admitted.

"It isn't. I don't know why I ever bought it. This isn't my color, but it will look sensational with your auburn hair."

"It's kind of short," Chelsea said tentatively.

"Get real. Queen Victoria is dead."

"All right, already! Get off my case. I'll wear the dress and I'll come on to all the men at the party. Will that satisfy you?"

Mindy smiled mischievously. "It won't do a lot for me, but it might change *your* life."

"I like my life just the way it is," Chelsea said in annoyance. "I'll see you later. I'm going to my room."

Luis was coming up the stairs as Chelsea started down the hall. "You have a telephone call, *señorita*," he told her.

"It must be for my sister."

"No, the *señora* asked for you. There is a telephone in your room if you would prefer to speak there."

"Yes I would. Thank you, Luis." The call had to be from her mother, and Chelsea didn't want anyone to overhear the conversation.

Doris Claiborne didn't waste any time on preliminaries. "Why haven't you called me?" she demanded.

"I just got here yesterday."

"What have you been doing since then? You've had plenty of time to straighten things out. Did you tell Mindy we absolutely forbid her to get married?"

"We both know how far that would get me."

"Well, what *have* you done?"

"I tried to reason with her, but so far I haven't gotten anywhere."

"How could you fail us like this, Chelsea?" Doris wailed. "We depended on you."

"I can't work miracles," Chelsea protested. "Mindy is determined to get married. Only God knows why, and He isn't sharing the information."

"Is the man truly dreadful?"

"No, he . . . he's not so bad in some ways."

"What does that mean? Does he have a decent job? Who are his friends? Has he ever been in trouble with the law?"

"How would I know all those things, Mother? I'm not a detective."

"That's a good idea! I want you to go to an agency and have them prepare a complete dossier on this Roberto person. He could be a very unsavory character."

"I doubt if there are any detective agencies in Ronda, and even if there were, an investigation would take too long. The wedding is in two weeks."

Doris gave a wounded cry. "How could she do this to us? Mindy knows we've always planned on having a formal wedding with bridesmaids, and all our friends attending."

"Cheer up, Mother. Maybe I'll make it to the altar some day," Chelsea said ironically.

"Don't digress," Doris told her sharply. "Are you just going to throw up your hands and let your sister ruin her life?"

"All I can do is try to persuade her to postpone the wedding. Mindy gets fired up about things, but her enthusiasm doesn't usually last long. Time is on our side, if I can convince her to wait."

"And if you can't?"

"What else would you suggest?" Chelsea asked helplessly. "It might make you feel better to know that Roberto isn't some sleazy creep. His family is both wealthy and influential. They trace their lineage back hundreds of years. The family portraits are all over the house."

"You sound as if you approve of the man," Doris said indignantly.

"Not for Mindy. Their marriage would be a disaster. He's a sophisticated man and she's still a kid."

"How do *you* get along with him?" Doris's voice held speculation.

"So-so."

"What does that mean?"

"Roberto is a very complex man," Chelsea answered slowly. "He can be terribly autocratic, but he can also be very considerate. He took me sightseeing today, and he was quite charming.''

''That's wonderful. I think you've found the solution to all our problems.''

''I must have missed something,'' Chelsea said blankly.

''It's so simple. You get him to switch his affections to *you*. That shouldn't be too difficult. You're so much more mature and experienced than your sister.''

''I can't believe you'd even suggest such a thing!''

''I'm not advising you to...um...become *familiar* with the man. I merely want you to flirt with him. You're a beautiful woman. You could make him give up Mindy if you put your mind to it. Then afterward you could simply say you were sorry if he misunderstood.''

''Roberto is not a man you play games with,'' Chelsea said grimly. ''Besides, Mindy would never forgive me, and I wouldn't blame her. That would be a really shabby thing to do.''

''It's for her own good,'' Doris insisted.

''Forget it, Mother. Roberto has his pick of women. If he chose Mindy, it must be because he loves her.''

Doris argued heatedly, but Chelsea was adamant. The older woman gave up reluctantly. ''At least promise you'll think about it.''

''No, I won't. We'd better hang up now. This call is costing a fortune. Give my love to Dad, and try to keep a good thought. I'll phone you in a few days.''

''Wait, Chelsea. I have something else to tell you. Dawn's mother telephoned this morning. As furious as I am at that girl, I have to feel sorry for her mother. Dawn has disappeared.''

''Disappeared!''

''Well, they haven't heard from her in a couple of weeks, and they can't get in touch with her. Mrs. Renzler asked if you can find out what happened to her and either have Dawn phone home or call yourself."

"I'll ask Mindy if she knows where she might be, but other than that I wouldn't know where to look. Does her mother want me to contact the police?"

"Not unless you think it's necessary."

"How can I tell? That's a decision her parents should make."

"Well, I can't help you. I'm half out of my mind with worry about *one* teenager."

"I'm glad I didn't expect this trip to be a vacation." Chelsea sighed. "Tell Mrs. Renzler I'll see what I can do."

After hanging up, Chelsea went back to Mindy's room and told her about Dawn. "Do you know where she is?"

"I haven't talked to her since I moved up here to Roberto's."

"Isn't that rather casual? You two were traveling together."

Mindy shrugged. "We didn't report to each other."

"Or anybody else. Neither of you qualify for merit badges. Dawn's parents are very worried. They haven't heard from her in weeks."

"That's a real bummer," Mindy agreed, frowning. "It isn't like Dawn, either. She was always sending picture postcards home." Her face cleared. "That's probably it. You know how postcards always arrive a month after you get back from vacation."

"Maybe, but we'd better go to Marbella tomorrow and see if we can find her."

"That would be fun. We'll plan on it."

Since there was nothing she could do until the next day, Chelsea had to settle for that. Between Mindy and Dawn, she was going to need a real vacation when she went home.

* * *

That evening, Chelsea sprayed herself with perfume, looking in the mirror incredulously. She almost didn't recognize herself. Mindy's dress was the sexiest thing she'd ever worn, although she had to admit it was in good taste. The low, square-cut neckline revealed just a hint of cleavage, enough to be enticing without being blatant. But Chelsea had never gone in for seductive clothes. The figure-molding bodice and short, flirty skirt made her feel vulnerable, somehow.

"This will be tame compared to what the jet set has on," she assured her image in the mirror. "Nobody will even notice me."

Mindy let out a whoop of delight when Chelsea joined her and Roberto in the living room. "You look sensational," she exclaimed. "Roberto, take a look at my sister. Isn't she gorgeous?"

He had been adjusting his cuff links, but he glanced up dutifully. For one unguarded moment his expression was predatory as he gazed at Chelsea's lovely face and alluring body. Her pulse quickened, but the brilliant light in his eyes was extinguished almost immediately.

"I don't know what you were complaining about." Mindy looked her over critically. "That skirt could even be a little shorter."

"For a tennis dress, maybe." Chelsea was uncomfortably aware that Roberto's eyes had moved automatically to her legs.

"We'll leave it up to Roberto," Mindy said.

He smiled. "You both look charming."

"That's no answer," she complained.

"It can't get me into any trouble." He laughed.

"That's right, play it safe. You and Chelsea were made for each other," she said disgustedly.

"What time are we leaving?" Chelsea asked quickly.

"We should start now," Roberto answered.

"Wait a minute. You forgot your earrings," Mindy told Chelsea.

"I don't have anything suitable," she replied.

"Why didn't you say so? I have the perfect pair." Mindy sped out of the room.

Chelsea turned to Roberto with a rueful expression. "As you must have guessed from her proprietary interest, I'm wearing Mindy's dress."

"It's very becoming on you." He made a lingering inspection. "Actually it doesn't look like anything I've ever seen her in."

"This isn't really my style, either. I usually wear very simple, understated clothes."

"Why?"

"Partly because of my work, I suppose. The people I associate with are mostly stockbrokers and bankers." She smiled wryly. "They're a rather sober lot."

"So I've found. But what about your social life? Surely you don't see those same people at night?"

"We have a lot in common," she answered defensively. "I didn't mean to indicate they were dull, only conservative."

"Where do you go on a date?"

"Different places. Out to dinner and the theater, or perhaps a gallery showing."

"And then what?"

Chelsea couldn't believe he was inquiring into her personal life. "I'm not sure I know what you mean," she said warily.

"Do you ever stroll through the flower mart in the early hours when the vendors are setting up their stalls? Or stop in a bakery for hot rolls to eat as you wander the city and watch the sun come up?''

''People don't walk the streets of New York at night for pleasure.''

''How sad. The nights are meant to be enjoyed in many ways.''

His low, musical voice was like a siren song, throbbing deep inside her. Chelsea drew in her breath sharply. ''You and Mindy are better matched than I thought. She loves to do zany things like that.''

A look of shock came over his face, as though he'd forgotten Mindy's existence. He moved away and looked at his watch. ''I wonder what's keeping her?''

Mindy appeared a moment later and handed Chelsea a long, dangling pair of crystal earrings. ''I had a devil of a time finding these. Some day I'll have to get organized.''

Chelsea smiled. ''You know you won't.''

''The possibility is remote,'' Mindy admitted, watching Chelsea clip on the earrings. ''Wow, sexy! You'll be a smash at the party, won't she, Roberto?''

''Undoubtedly.'' He flicked the merest glance at Chelsea. ''Can we please go now?''

Roberto was very quiet in the car, but Mindy monopolized the conversation, so his silence wasn't noticeable. She was fizzing with excitement at the evening ahead.

Chelsea wasn't really looking forward to it, but she was pleased to see her sister so happy. Mindy was like a little girl, unpredictable and thoughtless at times, but warm and loving underneath. Chelsea was especially touched by Mindy's generosity toward her, and by her pride in Chelsea's appearance.

The house where the party was being held was halfway down the mountain. Perched on a plateau, it had a stunning view of Marbella below and the Mediterranean in the distance. A wide brick driveway was already crowded with expensive cars, and the sound of many voices came from the brilliantly lit house.

"We seem to be late," Chelsea commented.

"It doesn't matter," Mindy said. "These things go on all night."

The prospect didn't delight Chelsea, but she followed them into one of the most glamourous homes she'd ever seen. While the del Machado house was quietly luxurious with an old-world ambience, this one was strictly modern.

The white marble floor in the entry had an inlaid sunburst design of contrasting black marble at its center. Overhead, a crystal chandelier picked up the colors of the Impressionist paintings on the walls, and sparkled like a rainbow.

Before Chelsea could make a closer inspection, their hostess appeared. Veronique Broussard was almost as interesting as the artwork. She was a gorgeous woman in her thirties, with lustrous dark hair framing a face like a painting on porcelain. Her figure in a form-fitting black satin gown was lush.

Roberto's tastes were eclectic, Chelsea thought acidly. Claire Vanderlip was a blond, Veronique, a brunette, and Mindy, a redhead. She watched as Veronique kissed Roberto on both cheeks. Mindy got only a pinch on the cheek.

"The little one looks *ravissant,*" Veronique said to Roberto. "She must have had her nap today."

Instead of getting angry, Mindy laughed. "As a matter of fact, I did."

"Allow me to present Chelsea Claiborne, Mindy's sister," Roberto said. If the French woman's comment bothered him, it didn't show.

Veronique inspected Chelsea closely, appraising her flawless skin and thickly fringed blue eyes. "Did you know the child had a sister like this?" she murmured to Roberto. "Welcome to Spain, Miss Claiborne." Her greeting to Chelsea held amusement.

"Thank you," Chelsea replied stiffly. "It's nice of you to include me at the last minute this way." She was furious over the dig at Mindy, but Roberto was the one who should have said something.

"The unexpected is always the most interesting." Veronique smiled mischievously. "Come, you must have a drink and meet everyone."

She led the way into a living room of gigantic proportions. The wall facing the water was made of glass. When the sliding doors were open, as they were now, the wide terrace became an extension of the living room. A bar was set up out there, and a group of musicians were playing at an ear-splitting level.

"I can't believe it!" Mindy gasped. "That's Slaves of Love, my very favorite group. Come dance with me, Roberto."

"We can't leave Chelsea alone," he objected.

"Go ahead, don't worry about me," Chelsea said.

"I will take care of Miss Claiborne," Veronique assured him.

As Mindy pulled Roberto toward the terrace, a waiter came up to Veronique. "The caterer would like a word with you, *señora.*"

She nodded and beckoned to a man standing in a group nearby. "Clive, come here. I want you to meet someone."

"Please don't bother, I'll be fine," Chelsea said, but it was too late. The man came over to them.

"Clive Forsythe, meet Chelsea Claiborne," Veronique said. "She is the sister of Roberto's little bride-to-be."

He was a man about Roberto's age, deeply tanned and athletic looking, but with subtle lines of dissipation in his face. His eyes glowed as he gazed at Chelsea. "Roberto was always a lucky man."

"Take care of her, Clive." With an airy wave, Veronique left them.

He smiled intimately at Chelsea. "My stars are definitely in the right orbit."

"You're English, aren't you?"

"From jolly old London. What gave me away?" He was joking, since his accent was unmistakably British.

Chelsea glanced around the room. "I haven't seen people from so many different countries since I was at the United Nations last."

"We're a merry mix," he agreed.

"How did you all meet?"

"We gather at the same spots and go to the same parties."

"Is that all you do, party?"

"Certainly not. We ski in the winter and sail in the summer, among other strenuous activities."

"Don't any of you work?"

"Frightfully hard." He laughed. "You know how rigorous wind surfing is."

"So I've heard," Chelsea said, wondering just how much of this was a put-on.

Another man joined them, looking at her admiringly. "Where did you find this ravishing creature, Clive?"

"Go away, Maurice. She's all mine. Veronique gave her to me in a burst of generosity," Clive declared.

"Veronique always has such clever party favors. What did she give Daphne?" the man asked mockingly.

"Why don't you go and find out, while Chelsea and I dance?" Clive replied. The loud music had given way to something more mellow after the rock group took a break.

"Who is Daphne?" Chelsea asked as they walked outside.

"My wife," he answered, taking her in his arms and holding her closely.

That was the last thing Chelsea expected. His behavior certainly didn't give any indication. "How long have you been married?" she asked.

"Four or five years," he replied indifferently. "You'd have to ask Daphne. Women keep track of those things." His expression changed. "Has anyone ever told you your eyes are the color of the Aegean Sea off Crete?"

"Not recently." She tried to put distance between their molded bodies. "I thought Englishmen were supposed to be reserved."

"A dastardly rumor I'd be happy to disprove."

"Don't bother. I'll just check with Daphne."

"Why do you keep dwelling on her?" he asked plaintively. "She isn't being neglected, I assure you. Several men here tonight are madly in love with her."

"That doesn't bother you?"

"Not at all. She's a very beautiful woman."

"Why did you get married?" Chelsea asked bluntly.

He shrugged. "For the same reason we all do, sooner or later. When a man reaches a certain age he has to show a little responsibility—produce an heir and all that sort of thing. The family name must continue, don't you know."

"So love had nothing to do with it?"

"Oh, I wouldn't say that. Daphne and I are remarkably compatible. We understand each other." He drew Chelsea against him once more, his eyes kindling. "Now let's talk about you. I want to know everything about you."

"Later." The music had stopped, and Chelsea took advantage of the momentary pause before the next selection. She stepped back saying, "I must tell my sister something."

Without giving him a chance to protest, she went inside and threaded her way through the crowded room, then slipped into the garden beyond the terrace. It was dark there, and she felt the need to be alone.

Chelsea was appalled by the revealing conversation with Clive. Was that why Roberto was marrying Mindy? To produce an heir to carry on the family name? Ramón and Rosa had only girls, and the youngest brother wasn't married. Did Roberto feel it was his obligation?

She could sketch in the details Clive had omitted. A wife was a convenience. Someone to run a man's home and be his hostess. She must be decorative but not demanding. In return, he provided the good life and allowed her to indulge in her own little flings.

Had Roberto spelled this out for Mindy? Was that why they didn't display undue affection for each other? Mindy was clearly enamored of his life-style, yet Chelsea couldn't believe her sister was so dazzled that she'd agree to such an arrangement. Still, what other explanation was there for all the puzzling undercurrents Chelsea had felt since her arrival?

The sound of voices made her retreat hastily behind a large bush. Two women and a man were drifting across the lawn in her direction.

"I still say it's a strange choice," one of the women was saying.

"She's adorable," the man answered indulgently. "You ladies just can't forgive her for being so young."

Chelsea stiffened to attention as the second woman said, "Roberto is a man of the world. He'll tire of that child in a month."

"But, ah, what a month it will be," the man said with a chuckle.

"And then what?"

"They'll settle down like everyone else. Claire and all the rest will be waiting to supply Roberto with the more adult pleasures, and the bride will find someone who shares her enthusiasm for the youthful pursuits."

"Claire wants more than a few romantic interludes," the first woman remarked. "She's telling everyone Roberto is the love of her life."

"He would never have married her," the man said. "Claire has loved not wisely but too well."

"What a delicate way of putting it, darling." The second woman laughed.

Their voices drifted off as they returned to the house. Chelsea shivered and wrapped her arms around herself. What horrible people! They were like piranhas, waiting to rush in and feed on her sister's misery.

Chelsea was so steeped in her own unhappiness that she didn't notice a man approaching. She jumped when Roberto spoke to her.

"I've been looking for you. What are you doing out here by yourself? Is something wrong?" he asked.

"How clever of you to notice," she answered bitterly.

"I'm sorry you were left alone. I thought Veronique would take care of you."

"She did. I'm here because I want to be."

"What happened, Chelsea?" Roberto asked quietly.

"I don't fit in with your jet-set friends, that's all."

He frowned. "Was someone unpleasant to you?"

"No, just truthful. I met a man who gave me an eye-opening version of your way of life, and it horrified me."

Roberto took her arm and led her to a garden bench, in spite of Chelsea's efforts to pull away. "I think you'd better tell me why you're so upset."

"Gladly! I realize your customs are different than ours, but marrying for the sake of convenience is totally unacceptable in *my* family."

"Who told you that's one of our customs?"

"Clive Forsythe."

"What would he know about us? He's an Englishman!" Roberto exclaimed.

"Maybe so, but he's one of your group, and he indicated it's a common practice in your set. And that isn't even the worst of it! I overheard some more of your friends speculating on how long you'd be faithful to Mindy. Does that give you a slight indication of why I'm upset?"

"To begin with, you're confusing acquaintances with friends," Roberto said in a voice filled with disgust.

"Do you expect me to believe that? They're here at your engagement party. They know everything about you, who you had affairs with, when you broke up."

"I had no control over the guest list, and you overheard gossip, nothing more," he said firmly.

"They mentioned your blond friend, Claire, so they weren't making things up," Chelsea insisted.

"I don't know what stories are going around about Claire and me, and chivalry would prevent me from denying them, anyway. But in any event, that's all part of the past."

"How about the future? According to Clive, the main requisite for a good marriage is to have an understanding wife."

"Clive is a dilettante with too much money and a pea-sized brain," Roberto answered in a clipped tone. "You're the first person who ever took him seriously."

"I found it difficult not to when he came on to me on the dance floor, after freely admitting he had a wife."

"I'm not surprised. Clive has made a career out of women, since he doesn't have a talent for anything else."

"None of you people work," Chelsea said scornfully. "If you ever put in an honest day's labor, you might have higher standards."

"You've accused me of that before. Tomorrow I'll drive you down to the valley and show you exactly what I do."

"That isn't what concerns me right now. Mindy thinks your life is glamourous. She doesn't see any of the sordidness and intrigue. When she finds out what really goes on, it will blow her mind. If you have an ounce of decency, you'll call off the wedding before you destroy her."

"I can't," he said heavily. "I gave my word."

Chelsea stared at him in disbelief. "Are you trying to tell me *she* pressured *you* into marrying her?"

"I didn't say that," he answered carefully. "I asked Mindy to marry me, and she accepted. I understand your concern, but I assure you it's misplaced. Honor is sacred in my family. I will never be unfaithful to your sister, nor will I ever intentionally cause her pain."

His voice held such sincerity that Chelsea was impressed in spite of herself. She wanted to think he was telling the truth, but the things she'd heard that night couldn't be dismissed.

"You're asking me to believe you're different from these people," she said slowly.

"Yes. You can't be expected to know that on such short acquaintance, but I hope you'll be reassured in the days to come."

"I hope so, too," she murmured, gazing searchingly at him.

The moonlight cast harsh shadows across Roberto's face, emphasizing his high cheekbones and turning his eyes into fathomless pools. Could she trust him? Chelsea honestly didn't know.

"Will you at least keep an open mind?" he asked.

"I'm trying to, for Mindy's sake. You two don't seem to have anything in common, but maybe love is enough. I wouldn't know," she said helplessly.

"You've never been in love?"

"Not really." Chelsea sighed. "Maybe there's something wrong with me."

Roberto chuckled unexpectedly. "If there is, it isn't visible."

The frank admiration in his eyes pleased and bothered her at the same time. She glanced away. "I guess we'd better go back to the party before somebody starts a rumor that we're showing undue interest in each other."

"That might not be all bad." He rose, gazing at her enigmatically. "Then you'd learn not to believe everything you hear."

Roberto was mistaken if he thought she was won over. Chelsea was still wary as she accompanied him back to the house.

Mindy's bright coppery curls and gold lamé mini-dress made her easy to spot in the crowded room. She was surrounded by a group of admiring men, her cheeks flushed with excitement at all the attention.

Chelsea slanted a swift glance at Roberto's austere face. "Mindy likes to be the center of attraction," she said hastily. "It doesn't mean anything."

"She certainly isn't pining," he answered coolly. "Shall we dance?"

Roberto's apparent jealousy was reassuring, Chelsea thought as she followed him out to the dance floor. That meant he cared. Maybe he was simply one of those men who found it difficult to be demonstrative in public.

When he took her in his arms, Chelsea stopped trying to figure him out. Their bodies conformed automatically, as if through prior acquaintance. He didn't hold her tightly, but she was aware of his arm circling her waist and the width of his shoulders. The subtle scent of woodsy cologne and clean masculine flesh filled her nostrils like an intoxicant.

Chelsea drew in her breath sharply. She was behaving like a school girl discovering the opposite sex for the first time. She raised her head abruptly to say something, anything to ward off Roberto's attraction.

The swift movement had disastrous results. Her lips brushed across his mouth as he gazed down at her. For one electric moment his arms tightened and their eyes held in unmistakable awareness of each other.

Chelsea's flaming cheeks were the visible sign of the heat inside her. "I'm sorry," she said struggling for composure. "I'm afraid I got lipstick on you." She reached up to wipe away the smudge, then jerked her hand back.

"You see how appearances can be deceiving?" He smiled.

"I'm sure this is the first time the circumstances were so innocent."

"They wouldn't be if I'd met you at a different time."
He trailed a forefinger across her cheek in a caress that
was tantalizing yet chaste.

"But you didn't," she answered flatly.

"That's true." he released her. "Would you like some
champagne?" Roberto was once more conventionally
polite.

As they reentered the living room, Veronique was clap-
ping for attention. She beckoned to Roberto and Mindy
to join her.

Roberto stifled a sigh. "Will you excuse me?" he asked
Chelsea.

"Certainly." She drifted to the back of the room as the
others surged forward.

Veronique linked arms with Roberto and Mindy. His set
expression contrasted with their smiles. "You all know
why we're here tonight," Veronique announced.

"Because we never turn down a party," someone
shouted.

"Behave yourself, Victor, or you won't be invited
back," she reproved him.

"Is this really necessary?" Roberto asked in a low
voice.

"Of course it is, *mon amour.* If you insist on getting
married, you have to pay a price." She turned a laughing
face to her guests. "I want to propose a toast to the loving couple. May they have all the happiness they deserve."

"I'll drink to that," a man called.

"You'll drink to anything," someone answered to general laughter.

Veronique took a glass of champagne from the tray a
waiter presented. Raising her glass she said, "This is your

last chance, ladies. Make the most of it. In two weeks Roberto will be off limits. Isn't that right, *chéri?*"

"That's correct." His eyes searched the crowd, looking for Chelsea. Their gaze met and held until someone moved and blocked her view.

As the hilarity rose in volume Chelsea slipped outside, unwilling to take part. She was plagued by something far worse than doubt now. For one shattering moment when Mindy had given Roberto a secret smile, she'd felt a pang of jealousy—toward her own sister! What kind of monster was she?

Chelsea stared moodily down at the city lights, trying to put things into perspective. Was it really so unnatural to be attracted to someone as wildly charismatic as Roberto? She was a normal, healthy woman, and he was a superb male in his prime. No emotions were involved. The sparks that sometimes ignited between them were purely due to chemistry.

There was nothing to feel guilty about. She would certainly never do anything to jeopardize Mindy's happiness. Nor would Roberto, to be perfectly fair. At least not with her. He was even quicker than she to erect a wall between them before they got too personal.

The situation was uncomfortable, though, in spite of being perfectly innocent. The only solution was to avoid Roberto whenever possible. That would be easier if she could move to a hotel, yet how would she explain the reason? Chelsea sighed deeply. It was going to be a long two weeks.

Chapter Four

The party lasted until the small hours of the morning. Chelsea and Roberto were ready to go home much earlier, but Mindy refused to leave. As a result, Chelsea slept later than she intended the next day.

After rushing around to dress she went to Mindy's room, only to find her sister still curled up in bed. When Chelsea shook her, Mindy burrowed deeper into the pillows.

"Go away," she grunted.

"Do you know what time it is? You can't sleep all day."

"You want to bet?"

"You have to get up, Mindy. I want to get to Marbella. I promised Mother I'd find out what happened to Dawn."

"Get off her case. She's probably in Gibraltar or Tangier, having a ball."

"I don't doubt it, but I have to report to her parents."

"Good luck," Mindy mumbled.

"I need your help," Chelsea exclaimed in frustration. "I don't even know where she was staying."

"My address book is on the dresser."

Chelsea knew she was fighting a losing battle. Mindy was convinced that Dawn was having the time of her life in some glamorous locale. That was the most logical explanation, but Chelsea was charged with the responsibility for making sure.

"Why me, oh Lord?" she muttered as she rummaged through the clutter on the dresser top.

Mindy's address book was crammed with names of both men and women. How had she met so many people in such a short time? Some of the addresses were crossed out several times and changed to new ones. Her friends seemed to have a habit of drifting from one place to another like feathers on a breeze. No wonder Mindy wasn't worried about Dawn.

Chelsea's jaw set grimly. Locating Dawn was apt to take a lot of legwork. She put the address book in her purse and went downstairs to confer with Dolores.

Luis directed Chelsea to a sunny room looking out onto the courtyard. It was smaller and cozier than the formal living room. The couch and chairs were covered in a cheerful blue-and-green print, and one wall was lined with bookcases. Dolores was sitting at a small, beautifully carved desk, writing notes.

She glanced up with a smile. "I didn't expect to see you so early."

"This is scandalously late for me, even on weekends. But at home I don't usually stay out all night."

"Roberto's friends are prone to excess," Dolores remarked dryly. "Did you enjoy the party?"

"It was very...interesting."

Dolores looked at her shrewdly, but her reply was conventional. "I'm sure it was. Did Mindy have a good time?"

"We could barely drag her away. Of course she's young and has more stamina."

"You're scarcely the next generation," Dolores commented. "But you're right about the very young. They haven't learned moderation." She glanced unconsciously at an oil painting on the wall.

Chelsea noticed it was a portrait of Dolores and her three sons. "What a handsome family you have." She walked over for a closer look. "This must be Jorge."

"Yes, that is my youngest son," Dolores answered.

The family resemblance to Roberto was unmistakable. Jorge had his older brother's darkly handsome face, but his eyes held a mischievous twinkle. From his picture, and the little Chelsea had heard about him, she guessed that Jorge had given his mother a few gray hairs. Like Mindy had given *their* mother.

"You mentioned that he's still in college. What is he majoring in?" Chelsea asked.

"Jorge wishes to be an architect, and I think he will be a good one. His grades are excellent and he gets along well with everyone."

"I don't doubt it. He looks as if he has a good sense of humor."

"Yes, Jorge is always entertaining. Too bad we see so little of him." Dolores's voice was ironic.

"Judging by my sister's address book, people their age move around a lot. That's what I wanted to talk to you about. Would it be possible for me to borrow your car to go into Marbella? I really hate to ask, but it's rather urgent." Chelsea explained about Dawn.

"Her poor parents." Dolores sighed. "Of course you must go. Perhaps Roberto will take you."

"Oh, no, I couldn't ask him."

"Nonsense. If he isn't busy, Roberto will be happy to do it."

As Chelsea was renewing her protests, Roberto came into the room. "What are you volunteering me for?" he asked with a smile.

After Dolores told him, Chelsea said, "I just want to borrow a car, unless there's some other way I can get to Marbella."

"None that's very convenient, but I'd be happy to drive you."

"That's really isn't necessary," Chelsea insisted. "I'm sure you're busy, and it would be terribly boring for you."

He gazed at her without expression. "You're not familiar with Marbella. How do you expect to find your way around?"

"Maybe I could buy a map someplace," she said tentatively.

"Your success in locating the young woman will be a lot greater if you have Roberto along," Dolores urged. "He knows Marbella well."

Chelsea realized she didn't have a choice. Her resolution to avoid Roberto was still valid, but her obligation to Dawn's parents took precedence. They must be frantic, and without someone to guide her around the chance of finding Dawn was slim. Unfortunately, the only "someone" was Roberto. Chelsea's affection for her sister was seriously strained at that moment.

"If you're sure you won't mind," she told him halfheartedly.

"Not at all. Are you ready?" he asked.

"Yes, I'd really like to get this over with."

"I'm sure everything will turn out fine," Dolores soothed, misunderstanding the troubled look on Chelsea's face.

Chelsea was surprised when Roberto backed a white Ferrari down the driveway instead of the expected Bentley. It suited him a lot better.

When she commented on the fact he laughed. "I only drive Mother's car when I need more room, since this is a two-seater. Driving a Bentley and steering a hippopotamus must have a lot in common."

"I'm constantly seeing a new side of you," Chelsea said. "I think you and your brother are a great deal alike."

Roberto turned to look at her with a raised eyebrow. "Ramón?"

"No, Jorge."

"What do you know about Jorge?"

"You didn't want me to guess your secret, did you?" she asked lightly.

Roberto concentrated on the hairpin turns he was navigating. "What secret is that?"

"How many do you have?"

"Will you kindly tell me what you suspect me of, Chelsea?"

She was taken aback by the roughness in his voice. "I was only joking," she faltered. "Everyone was talking the other night about Jorge's life-style. I simply meant you liked some of the same things."

Roberto's grim jaw relaxed, but his voice was still cool. "A lot of men like fast cars. That doesn't make them irresponsible. Jorge is a different matter."

"I suppose that's true," Chelsea murmured.

She privately thought Roberto was too hard on his brother. Jorge was in college, getting good grades, so what was so terrible about cutting loose a little in the summer? Roberto had almost certainly done the same things when he was that age. She didn't want to provoke an argument by pointing that out, however. The atmosphere between them was already strained, and they'd only been alone for ten minutes.

He finally broke the silence. "I'm surprised Mindy didn't want to come with us today."

"She was tired after the party last night."

He turned his head to give her an appraising look. "You were up just as late."

"I'm not used to sleeping in the morning. Mindy would have come along if I'd waited till later, but I didn't want to waste any time. Dawn's parents are waiting to hear from her."

"Do you have her last known address?"

"Yes, and the names of some of her friends." Chelsea took Mindy's address book from her purse. "There are quite a lot of them, so I'm sure we'll find her."

"Unless she doesn't want to be found." Roberto's mouth curved sardonically.

Their first stop was the *pensión* where Mindy had stayed with Dawn. It was a tall, narrow home that had been converted to a rooming house. Loud music blared from many of the open windows, different rock groups that merged together into one discordant sound.

The door was opened by an austere-looking Spanish woman. Behind her, young people were running up and down the stairs, calling to each other. The scene was as frenetic as it had sounded from outside. The landlady didn't ask them in.

"I have no vacant rooms," she announced.

"That isn't why we're here," Chelsea said. "I'm looking for a girl who was staying with you, Dawn Renzler."

"She moved out."

"Did she leave a forwarding address?"

The woman shrugged. "They come, they go. Who can keep track of them?"

"It's very important that I get in touch with her," Chelsea persisted. "Her parents are worried about her."

"I rent rooms," the woman answered curtly. "I don't get involved in their lives."

"All I'm asking for is a phone number, or someplace where she can be reached." Chelsea was becoming increasingly frustrated. "Where do you send her mail?"

Roberto had stayed in the background until then. Now, he took a folded bill out of his pocket and flicked it back and forth across his chin reflectively. "We'd be very grateful for any information you can provide. Perhaps you might remember something if you tried very hard."

The woman's truculence vanished as she eyed the bill. "I don't know where she is," she said regretfully. "She left when I told that boy he had to go. I put up with their noise and their crazy hours, but there are some things I don't allow. Never have I had trouble with the police."

"The police were here?"

"No, and I don't *want* them here, asking a thousand questions. As if I had any control over those delinquents!" The woman's indignation burst forth. "It was different in my day, I'll tell you. Young people didn't run wild then."

Roberto guided her back to the subject. "You thought the police might be after Señorita Renzler's friend?"

"He is a bad seed, that one," the woman said darkly.

"So you told him to leave, and the *señorita* went with him?" Roberto asked.

"They left together. Whether they are still together, who can tell?"

"What is the boy's name?"

"Sancho Rodriguez."

Roberto handed her the bill. "Thank you, *señora*. You've been very helpful."

When they were back in the car, Chelsea turned a troubled face to him. "Now I'm really worried. Mindy was sure Dawn merely took off for someplace new, and I thought so, too."

"That's still possible."

"But she's with a little thug!"

"We don't know what he did," Roberto soothed. "The landlady didn't actually make any charges. She's simply down on youngsters, in general. That was pretty obvious."

Chelsea bit her lip. "Why do you think she threw him out?"

"It could have been for any number of reasons," he answered evasively.

"The one I'm worried about is drugs."

Roberto reached over and squeezed her clenched fingers. "Don't borrow trouble. We'll talk to some of her friends. Chances are she's already dumped the boy and simply moved to another place."

"I hope you're right."

Roberto's calm was reassuring. His strength seemed to flow into her. Instinctively, Chelsea turned her hand palm up and linked fingers with him.

"You were wonderful with that woman," she said gratefully. "I would have been lost without you."

His clasp tightened and he gazed at her with a little smile. "I'm glad you're starting to see my good points."

Chelsea was aware of a lot more than his competence. Her voice was a little unsteady as she said, "Well, I guess we'd better start tracking down Dawn's friends."

It wasn't an easy task. Some had moved, some had left town, and the ones who still lived at the same addresses weren't at home. Finally they managed to locate a young woman who could tell them something, although it wasn't encouraging.

Lauren Westbrook didn't mince words. "Sancho Rodriguez is bad news. I told Dawn that, but she said everybody was just down on him. She wouldn't believe he was dealing drugs."

Chelsea's heart plunged as her worst fears were realized. "Does Dawn . . . ?" she asked tentatively.

"No way! We all have sense enough to stay away from that stuff."

"You're saying Dawn didn't know this Sancho was involved with drugs?" Roberto asked.

"She knew he was using, but he kept telling her he was going to stop. She actually fell for that," Lauren said scornfully. "Everyone knows guys like him never change."

"Drug dealers usually have a lot of money," Roberto said. "Why was he living in an inexpensive boarding-house?"

"Sancho is just a two-bit pusher. Whatever he makes goes up his nose."

"Do you know where they are now?" Chelsea asked.

Lauren shook her head. "When it all hit the fan at the boardinghouse several of us tried to talk Dawn out of going with Sancho, but she told us to butt out. None of the old crowd have heard from her since."

Lauren couldn't tell them any more than that. As they walked back to Roberto's car, Chelsea was more concerned than ever.

"We simply have to find her," she said. "But how?"

"Do you want to go to the police?"

"I can't! Suppose Sancho convinced her to try drugs? If the police picked her up, they'd throw her in jail."

"The longer she stays with the boy, the more chance there is of his making a convert of her," Roberto said quietly.

"I realize that, but it's such a risk. She's only a kid who used bad judgment. What if I'm responsible for sending her to prison?" Chelsea started to tremble. "I want to do what's best for her, but I don't know what that is."

Roberto put his arms around her and gently urged her head onto his shoulder. "Don't upset yourself, *querida*. We'll find her."

"Suppose we can't?"

"Trust me." His lips brushed her temple as he smoothed her hair.

His low voice was soothing, and his embrace comforting. Chelsea wanted to stay in Roberto's arms and shift all her burdens to his broad shoulders. He was the kind of man she'd always been looking for and didn't think existed. Too bad he was off limits.

Drawing away self-consciously, she managed a small laugh. "I'm sorry. Nobody who knows me would ever believe I fell apart like that."

"It isn't shameful to need someone to lean on now and then," he said gravely.

"I guess it comes as a surprise. I never did before." She turned toward the car. "Where do we go from here? Do you have any ideas?"

"One, to start with." He helped her into the car and walked around to the driver's side. "I have a friend who owns a disco. He hears about everything that goes on in Marbella."

"But Sancho is just a little fish. Surely your friend wouldn't know anyone that insignificant."

"What Carlos doesn't know, he can find out."

Carlos Perez lived in the penthouse of a gleaming white building overlooking the sea. The apartment was decorated elegantly, and the view from the floor-to-ceiling windows was stunning. Blue sky and golden sand framed darker blue water tipped with gold by the late-afternoon sun.

Carlos wasn't classically handsome the way Roberto was. His face would be described as interesting rather than arresting. He had Roberto's self-assurance, though; the confidence that came from centuries of breeding and wealth.

His first glimpse of Chelsea brought admiration mixed with speculation. The second emotion was quickly masked as he greeted Roberto. "*Hola, mi amigo.* This is a pleasant surprise. What brings you back so soon? Don't you trust me with your father's ring?" he joked.

"I am rather anxious to have it back, but that isn't the reason for this visit. Permit me to present Chelsea Claiborne, Mindy's sister."

"Ah, I see." Carlos inspected her with even more interest. "You have come for the wedding."

"Well, I . . . yes," Chelsea answered lamely.

"As Roberto's oldest friend, may I tell you that your sister is getting a fine man."

"I'm trying to convince her of that," Roberto said dryly.

"You have doubts, *señorita?*"

"No, I'm sure he's everything you say. I ... my family and I would just prefer to have the wedding in New York."

"A problem," Carlos conceded. "But I'm forgetting my manners. What may I offer you to drink?"

"I'd rather have something to eat," Roberto said. "We left in a bit of a hurry today and didn't stop for lunch."

Chelsea suddenly realized that she was hungry, too. She hadn't had lunch *or* breakfast.

Carlos looked dubious. "My housekeeper has gone for the day. We'll have to go out, unless you would like me to phone for something to be sent in."

"That always takes so long," Roberto objected.

Chelsea felt the same way. Now that she was reminded of it, she was starving. "Would you like me to fix something here?"

Both men looked at her in surprise. "You can cook?" Carlos asked.

"Of course I can cook. What kind of helpless women do you know?"

"This one is a jewel." Carlos smiled. "Perhaps you're marrying the wrong sister."

Chelsea didn't look at Roberto. "If you don't mind, I'll see what's in your refrigerator."

"Follow me."

Carlos led the way to a large, modern kitchen equipped with every imaginable convenience. In addition to a double oven and microwave, one wall held a built-in barbecue. Gleaming copper utensils were hung from pegs on another wall, and at the far end of the room was a round marble-topped table and four chairs.

In contrast to the lavishly appointed kitchen, the refrigerator was almost bare. Champagne and bottles of white wine were stacked on the bottom shelf, and the top shelf held milk, cream and orange juice. In between were a carton of eggs, a lump of Parmesan cheese and a few jars containing olives, pickles and various condiments.

"You don't eat at home much, do you?" Chelsea commented to Carlos.

"I'm afraid not. Let me telephone the restaurant across the street."

"No, this just calls for a little Yankee ingenuity."

Roberto peered over her shoulder at the sparse provisions. "You have a very optimistic nature. Nobody could make anything out of what's in there."

"You want to bet?" she challenged.

"I mean real food, not some olives and a pickle on a toothpick."

Chelsea opened one of the vegetable bins and looked speculatively at the contents, a few scallions, a couple of tomatoes and a green pepper. They didn't seem to offer much promise, but she wasn't daunted.

"I'm not talking about pickles and olives. If I can produce a meal in fifteen minutes, will you apologize for doubting me?" she asked.

"I'll do better than that. I'll accept your bet. What would you like to wager? A hundred pesos?"

"An apology will be sufficient. I don't want to take your money."

"All of a sudden you're not so confident," Roberto crowed.

"Stop trying to goad me into something. It wouldn't be fair to bet on a sure thing."

"You're right. I don't want to take *your* money."

Carlos had been listening with a smile to their good-natured bickering. "A bet doesn't have to involve money. Why not make the forfeit a kiss?"

"That's not much of a reward," Chelsea said.

"I don't believe Roberto would feel cheated."

"What do I get if *I* win?" she asked, wondering why she was going along with the absurd suggestion.

Carlos's eyes twinkled mischievously. "The payoff is the same for both of you. Isn't that the way it works when money is involved?"

"What he's proposing is, heads I win, tails you lose," Roberto commented dryly.

"Not at all." Carlos laughed. "I'm suggesting a solution that will satisfy both of you."

"If I don't get started, nobody will win." Chelsea reached into the vegetable bin. "Will you gentlemen kindly remove yourselves so I can go to work?"

They retreated, but only as far as the other end of the room. While Chelsea filled the electric coffeepot and then rummaged in the cupboards for various necessities, the two men sat at the table and chatted idly.

Roberto's eyes strayed often to Chelsea as she diced the green pepper and scallions and cut the tomatoes into small chunks. After melting butter in a frying pan, she added the peppers and onions, then turned the heat down low.

While the vegetables were sautéing, she searched the pantry shelves. They yielded a box of round crackers. She spooned mayonnaise into a small bowl, added a generous amount of grated Parmesan cheese and mounded the mixture liberally on the crackers. A sprinkling of paprika and dill weed decorated the top of each one.

When they were lined up in neat rows on a cookie sheet, Chelsea located silverware in one drawer, and napkins and place mats in another. She carried them to the table.

"Will you join us?" she asked Carlos. "I'm making enough for three."

He sniffed appreciatively. "How can I refuse? Something smells wonderful."

"That's only the coffee," Roberto said.

"You're going to eat those words," Chelsea warned.

Roberto grinned. "They'll probably be as filling as your lunch."

"You have five more minutes of feeling superior," she said as she went back to the stove.

After lighting the broiler she broke eggs into a bowl and beat them with a wire whisk. Before pouring the mixture into the frying pan she slid the crackers under the broiler. While they slowly turned a golden color, she stirred the eggs with a wooden spoon.

When the eggs were a creamy consistency, Chelsea took the pan off the fire and folded in the vegetables. By that time the crackers were puffed up and toasted on top. She divided the eggs between three plates, and arranged the crackers on a small platter.

"Here you are," she announced as she set a steaming dish in front of each man. "Not a pickle or an olive in sight."

"I'm speechless." Roberto stared at his plate.

"I thought you would be," Chelsea answered smugly as she went to get the crackers.

Carlos sampled his eggs. "Mmm, this tastes even better than it looks."

"Try one of these." She held out the platter. "You didn't have any bread so I had to improvise."

He bit into one of the rich morsels and groaned in appreciation. "Ambrosia! Would you consider coming to work for me?"

"I can't think of an easier job. I'll bet you haven't had a meal here in a month."

A little smile curved Carlos's mouth as he gazed at her. "I haven't had this incentive."

"Maybe you need to hire a better cook," she said lightly.

"The position is open, any time you're interested."

"I'll definitely keep you in mind," she promised.

Roberto rose abruptly. "I'll get the coffee."

Chelsea could tell by his austere face that he was annoyed. But why? She would never get used to his lightning change of moods.

After Roberto had poured the coffee he said to Chelsea, "Don't you think you'd better tell Carlos why we've come?"

She sighed. "I'd almost forgotten."

"Evidently." Roberto frowned.

"Is there a problem?" Carlos asked.

"A big one." Chelsea told him about Dawn, and the little they'd found out. "Roberto said you might be able to help me find her."

"Surely her own friends would be a better source of information."

"She's broken with all of them. Apparently this Sancho has her mesmerized. If we could locate him, we'd find her."

"Why couldn't you ask for something easy, like the winning numbers of the lottery?" Carlos shook his head. "There are so many of these misguided youngsters throwing their lives away."

"That's what I'm trying to prevent Dawn from doing," Chelsea said anxiously. "Will you help me?"

"Gladly, *señorita,* but you have to realize the odds you're facing. Marbella is a relatively small place, but someone who wants to disappear can usually manage to— at least temporarily."

"Listen to the man," Roberto said somberly.

"Are you telling me it's hopeless?" Chelsea faltered.

"Not at all. That's just the worst scenario," Carlos said soothingly. "I'm only saying I can't promise anything."

"I understand." Her shoulders slumped. "I shouldn't have gotten my hopes up. You'd scarcely come in contact with anyone like Sancho Rodriguez. It was probably a waste of time to come here."

"I'd be very sorry if you considered the afternoon wasted." His eyes were compassionate.

"I didn't mean that the way it sounded. It was very rude of me. Especially after you've been such a splendid host." She mustered a smile.

"I'm the one who is indebted to *you*. Did you enjoy your meal, Roberto?"

"It was excellent," Roberto answered.

"Then you won't mind paying off on your bet."

Roberto's expression changed to a smile as he turned his head to gaze at Chelsea. "I suppose it would be the honorable thing to do."

"I proved my point," she said hastily. "That's all that mattered to me."

"I believe you were the one who instigated the bet," Carlos said mischievously.

"It was just a figure of speech," she insisted.

"How could that be when the payment was agreed upon?"

"That was *your* idea. Roberto and I didn't agree."

Roberto smiled. "I'm afraid we did give tacit agreement."

She knew both men were teasing her, but it was impossible to match their light tone. Any physical contact with Roberto—even the thought of it—was unnerving!

"We've milked this gag for all it's worth." She stood and picked up her plate. "I'm going to do the dishes."

Roberto rose swiftly and took the plate from her. "A matter of honor is no laughing matter," he said with a grin. "You must allow me to pay my debt."

When he framed her face between his palms, Chelsea felt a slow tide of warmth begin at her toes and travel upward. She stared into the fathomless dark pools of his eyes, unable to move away.

"This is crazy," she whispered.

"Probably," he murmured as his head descended.

His lips merely grazed hers for a tantalizing instant, as though that was all he planned. Chelsea sighed unconsciously. In spite of her protests, she wanted him to kiss her.

Suddenly, Roberto fulfilled her wish. A ripple of excitement coursed down her spine as his mouth took dominant possession of hers. She swayed and put her arms around his waist because her legs felt boneless. As their bodies met, Roberto clasped her closely, wrapping his arms so tightly around her shoulders that her breasts were crushed against his hard chest.

When Chelsea thought about it afterward—a lot more often than she cared to—Roberto's kiss seemed to have lasted an eternity. She'd been aware of the tensile strength of his lean torso, the muscularity of his rigid thighs. She'd even had a fleeting prescience of the way he'd make love, masterfully, yet with great care and tenderness.

In reality, the kiss lasted only a few moments. As soon as their bodies met, they were both jolted into an awareness that the joke had gotten out of hand.

Carlos watched them enigmatically, although he acted afterward as though nothing cataclysmic had happened.

When they drew apart he said, "Well, that's over with. Don't you feel better now?"

"Compared to what?" Roberto asked sardonically.

Chelsea turned away. "I have to do the dishes."

"Leave them," Carlos said. "My housekeeper will clean up tomorrow."

"I'll just put everything in the dishwasher." Chelsea was glad to have something to do.

"If you insist. Come into the guest room, Roberto. I'll give you your ring."

"I'm glad you reminded me." Roberto followed Carlos out of the room.

When the two men were alone, Carlos asked without preamble, "Is the wedding still on?"

"Of course. Why would you think otherwise?"

"I wondered if you were having second thoughts," Carlos answered slowly. "Marriage isn't a step to be taken lightly."

"I'm well aware of the consequences." Roberto's face appeared carved from stone.

"That's a strange way of putting it."

"What do you want from me, Carlos?" Roberto asked impatiently.

"It's what I want *for* you, old friend. We've known each other a long time. I want you to be happy."

Roberto jammed his hands into his pockets and turned aside. "Happiness is measured by many standards."

"Some men take their marriage vows lightly, but you and I are different," Carlos said quietly. "That's why we've waited so long—for the right girl."

Roberto attempted a smile. "Don't get discouraged. Yours will come along."

"Are you sure yours has?"

"Do you think I would get married otherwise?"

Carlos hesitated. "I'll admit I'm puzzled. At the risk of making you angry, I have to say I'm surprised at your choice. Mindy is adorable, but she's a child. You're used to... more complexity," he finished helplessly.

"Perhaps I find her refreshing."

"Doesn't it bother you that she hasn't blinded you to other women?"

"What are you implying?" Roberto demanded. "I haven't touched another woman since I asked Mindy to marry me."

"That doesn't surprise me. But can you say you haven't desired one?"

"You're straining the bonds of friendship," Roberto warned.

"I'm willing to take that risk if it means saving you from making a serious mistake."

"I had no idea that you had such a low opinion of my fiancée," Roberto said stiffly.

"Don't be an idiot," Carlos answered impatiently. "Mindy would be ideal for your kid brother, but her sister is more your type. Now *there* is a gorgeous woman."

"I noticed you were attracted to her," Roberto said coldly.

"I noticed the same thing about you. That wasn't a familial kiss you gave her."

"You started the whole stupid thing."

"Admittedly, but I didn't realize how explosive the situation was. She's attracted to you, too."

"That's nonsense! Chelsea doesn't even approve of me as a brother-in-law. We argue a good part of the time."

"Frustration has that effect," Carlos murmured.

"You're way off base." Roberto restrained himself with an effort. "I'll admit she's a beautiful woman. Being engaged doesn't deaden the senses. But if you think either Chelsea or I would stoop to anything so—''

"Hold it." Carlos raised both hands. "I wasn't suggesting anything of the sort. I know you better, and even on short acquaintance I can tell Chelsea is our kind of people."

"Then what the hell is this all about?"

"I'm telling you not to rush into anything. If you can kiss another woman with that much feeling, you're not ready for a lifetime commitment."

"A man would have to be dead not to react to Chelsea," Roberto muttered. "But it won't happen again, I assure you."

"You think that's going to solve everything?"

"I know it will. Now, if you'll give me my ring, I want to start home."

A glance at Roberto's hard face told Carlos the subject was closed. He silently opened a drawer in the nightstand and handed Roberto his father's ring.

Chelsea was in the living room, standing by the window looking out at the glorious view. She turned when the two men joined her.

"I thought you'd deserted me."

Carlos smiled. "I don't imagine that's ever been one of your problems."

"Are you ready to leave?" Roberto asked her curtly.

"Any time you are," she answered in a muted voice.

Roberto's remote expression promised an uncomfortable ride home. How could a man change moods so swiftly? Not long ago he was kissing her with barely restrained passion. Did he regret it so much that he couldn't be civil? Well, Roberto might be sorry, but he was no sorrier about the tasteless incident than she was.

Carlos was the only one who managed to act normal. "It has been such a great pleasure meeting you." He took Chelsea's hand and kissed it. "You will be hearing from me soon."

"Do you really think you might be able to find out something about Dawn?"

"What is your expression? I will put my ear to the floor."

Chelsea laughed. "That's close enough. I'll be forever grateful to you."

"That in itself will be an incentive."

"Can we go now?" Roberto asked abruptly. His mouth was a tight line.

Carlos walked them to the door, giving no indication that he felt his friend's tension. After they left, however, he sighed.

"Roberto, Roberto," he murmured. "What pact have you made with the devil?"

Chapter Five

Roberto helped Chelsea into the car, but with restrained impatience. He strode around to the driver's side and slammed the door with a jarring crash.

Chelsea fastened her seat belt without comment. She was torn between wanting to clear the air between them and reluctance to get into yet another argument with Roberto.

As he drove through the small charming town of Marbella, Chelsea looked longingly at the mellowed brick houses. Many had window boxes along their second stories, filled with colorful flowers that cascaded down the fronts of the buildings.

She would like to have strolled through the winding streets where rows of shops crowded the narrow sidewalks. They looked fascinating, but she caught only the merest glimpse as Roberto raced by. Asking him to stop—or even slow down—was out of the question. One of these days she'd return with Mindy for a leisurely visit, if she could ever get her sister out of bed before noon.

Roberto stopped reluctantly for traffic signals, but when they reached the cutoff to Ronda he trod on the gas pedal. The powerful Ferrari surged forward like a wild stallion released from restraint.

He drove competently, with complete mastery over the car, but a lot faster than Chelsea was comfortable with. It wasn't so bad when they were on the lower slopes, but when the road rose steeply, she was glad they were on the inside next to the mountain, rather than on the cliff's edge. Still, as they rounded a curve with squealing tires, Chelsea gave an audible gasp.

Roberto became aware of her, seemingly for the first time. He slowed down immediately. "I'm sorry. I didn't mean to frighten you."

"This road is rather scary."

"I'm so used to it that I forget other people aren't." Noticing her knuckles were white where she was gripping the seat, he said gently, "Relax, I'll get you back safely."

"You should have told me you were in a hurry. We could have left sooner."

"You seemed to be enjoying yourself."

"I was. Carlos is a charming man."

Roberto stared at the road. "A lot of women think so."

When the conversation seemed in danger of drying up, Chelsea said hastily, "I was thinking about something. If Carlos doesn't come up with any leads on Dawn, maybe I could hire a private detective."

"Give him a week first."

"I only have a little more than that, myself."

"You've only been here a few days."

"It seems longer. Time flies when you're having fun," she said ironically.

Roberto slanted a quick glance at her. "I'm sorry about today, Chelsea."

She wasn't sure what he was apologizing for, but it was best not put into words. Before he could explain she said, "I'm the one who should be sorry. I took you on a wild-goose chase, trying to track down someone you don't even know. I'd say you've been remarkably patient."

"That's never been one of my virtues," he said wryly. "I've been acting abominably because I was annoyed at Carlos, but that's no excuse for taking it out on you."

Chelsea was relieved that she wasn't involved. "What did he do? I didn't notice anything?"

"It isn't important." Roberto shrugged. "He means well."

"That sounds like my mother," Chelsea remarked. "She has my best interests at heart, too, but she drives me up a wall."

"Mothers are like that."

"Not yours. I'll bet Dolores doesn't tell you how to run *your* life."

"You might be surprised."

They were driving through rolling fields that circled the mountaintop. Ronda was a stone fortress at the crest, overlooking the peaceful pastoral land below. On both sides of the road, orchards were laid out in rows, and precise lines of vegetables gave a quilt-like effect.

Roberto turned off the highway onto a dirt road. "I promised to show you what I do for a living."

"Do we have time?" Chelsea asked doubtfully. Although it was still daylight, the sun had set and twilight was approaching.

"Plenty of time," he assured her. "That's the pleasure of dining late."

"I'm getting to like it. Where are we going?"

"We're already here." Roberto waved an arm at the fields that stretched to the horizon. "This is del Machado property."

"All of it?" Chelsea gasped.

"What you can see from here."

"You must employ hundreds of workers," she exclaimed. "Everything looks so well kept up."

"In feudal days the fields were worked by virtual slaves. As I mentioned once, the land grant has been in my family for centuries. Even in relatively modern times, peasants put in long hours for very little pay. But my father and I changed all that. Amassing money for its own sake makes no sense."

"What did you do?" Chelsea asked curiously.

"We formed a cooperative. All of our farmers have a stake in their own labor. They choose their crops, and when it's time to harvest them I arrange for the sale. By combining their output, I can negotiate a higher price. I also take care of all the boxing and shipping."

"That's a tremendous job!"

"It's not work for a dilettante," he said dryly.

"I deserve that. I really misjudged you."

His dark eyes searched her face. "Does that mean I've finally gained acceptance?"

Chelsea didn't meet his eyes. The more she discovered about Roberto, the more she admired him. Which made her feel uneasy.

She was saved the necessity of a reply when a man ran out of a small house they were passing. He waved his arms, and Roberto stopped the car.

"I am so glad to see you, *señor.*" The man smiled widely. "Surely you were not going to drive by without saying hello?"

"I didn't want to bother you, Pedro. This is your time with your family."

"You are always a welcome guest," the older man said. "Will you and the *señorita* honor me by accepting a glass of wine?"

Roberto's glance at Chelsea was apologetic, telling her the invitation couldn't be refused. She didn't mind in the least. This was what she'd hoped for, a chance to meet the real Spanish people, not just a bunch of peripatetic jet setters.

Roberto was greeted by loud cries of joy from Pedro's wife and several small children. Two little boys vied for his attention, while a toddler tugged on his trouser leg.

Roberto swung the tot into his arms. "What a big girl you're getting to be. I can hardly lift you," he told the delighted youngster.

One of the boys pulled on his arm. "I'm getting big, too."

"Indeed you are, and Fernando, also." Roberto smiled at the child attached to his other arm.

"Soon we will be big enough to ride a horse. You promised to teach us, remember?"

"I haven't forgotten," Roberto assured him.

"When will that be?"

"Stop pestering the *señor*," their mother scolded. "Has he ever broken a promise? *Vamos,* all of you! Leave us to visit with the *señor* and his lady."

As the children trooped out reluctantly, Roberto introduced Chelsea to Pedro's wife, Ana.

"You must excuse the little ones," Ana apologized. "They adore the *patrón*."

"He's certainly good with children," Chelsea remarked. That was something she never would have expected from someone as moody as Roberto.

"Ah, what a father he will be! May the good Lord bless him with many babies," the other woman beamed.

"All in good time," Pedro chuckled. "Where is the wine? We must offer our guests some refreshment."

While Ana got out her best glasses and a carafe of homemade wine, Pedro said to Roberto, "It was very kind of you to advance Garcia Escobar more money for seed."

Roberto shrugged. "He had a run of bad luck."

"That is the life of a farmer, but not many *patrónes* are so understanding. The *señor* is a saint," Pedro told Chelsea.

Roberto laughed uncomfortably. "I'm afraid she wouldn't agree with you, my friend, and she would be right."

"Don't be too sure," Chelsea said. "I'm beginning to see a new side of you."

"*Bueno,* here is Ana with the wine. We are in for a treat." Roberto was relieved to avoid further discussion of himself.

They sipped their wine and discussed the state of the crops and market prices. Pedro and Ana were eager to sing Roberto's praises to Chelsea, but he headed them off every time they tried to relate one of his generous acts.

After a suitable period, Roberto and Chelsea left, with many courteous speeches on both sides. She thoroughly enjoyed the courtly old-world ritual of good manners.

When they were in the car starting back, Chelsea said, "I'm really glad we stopped. I enjoyed meeting them."

"Pedro and Ana are good people."

"They certainly think a lot of you. Why does it embarrass you to hear them say so?"

Roberto frowned. "Because they don't owe me anything. Nobody deserves praise for not exploiting his fellow man. That should be the rule, not the exception."

"But it isn't. You're a very remarkable man," Chelsea said softly.

He hid his gratification under a joking tone. "Does that mean I'm forgiven for my bad temper earlier?"

"I'm getting used to it," she teased.

"I could promise it won't happen again, but I'd probably break my word."

"Then for goodness sake don't promise." Chelsea laughed. "I know how much honor means to you."

They had arrived home, and Roberto pulled into the driveway. His expression changed as he stared at the family coat of arms over the venerable portal.

"Yes, honor rules my life," he answered tonelessly.

Mindy pounced on them the minute they walked in the door. "Where have you been all day?" she demanded.

"We went to Marbella," Chelsea answered. "Roberto drove me. I told you where I was going."

"I didn't expect you to be gone this long. I've been hanging around all afternoon with nothing to do."

"You could have come along," Chelsea pointed out. "I asked you to."

"Well, it's too late now. Did you find Dawn?"

"Not a trace of her, unfortunately. She's simply dropped out of sight."

"There's a lot of that going around," Mindy said sarcastically.

"If you'll excuse me, I must see about something." Roberto left them alone.

Chelsea scarcely noticed. She was bewildered by the undertone of anger in her sister's voice. "Do you know something you're not telling me?" she asked uncertainly.

"Not a thing." Mindy's brow creased in a frown. "I really thought Dawn would have left a message for me. Did you ask the landlady?"

"I didn't think of it, and she didn't mention any. But I believe the chances are slim. Dawn quarreled with all her other friends."

"Over what?"

"She apparently took up with a boy none of them approved of, Sancho Rodriguez. Do you know him?"

Mindy searched her memory, then shook her head. "She must have met him after I split. What's wrong with him?"

"He's a dope pusher," Chelsea answered succinctly.

"Oh, wow. That's a bummer."

"My sentiments exactly."

"It isn't like Dawn to get mixed up with a junkie. She could get in a lot of trouble." Mindy was genuinely concerned. "Can't you do something, Chelsea?"

"I'm trying. Roberto took me to a friend of his, Carlos Perez. Have you met him?"

"Yes, he's a really neat guy. Carlos can scare up tickets to sold-out rock concerts, and he always gets the best tables in restaurants. He has a lot of clout and he knows everybody." The strain vanished from Mindy's face. "If Carlos is on her case, Dawn is as good as found."

Chelsea envied Mindy's ability to shift her burdens. "I wish I had your confidence."

"Everything will turn out fine with Roberto and Carlos on the job." When Mindy caught sight of Roberto entering the hallway she ran to him and threw her arms around his neck. "You're a love for helping Dawn. I won't forget it."

As his arms circled Mindy's waist, Chelsea turned toward the stairs. "I'll see you at cocktails," she said over her shoulder.

"Chelsea, wait! Let's go out to dinner," Mindy said. "Can we, Roberto?"

"Not back to Marbella," he groaned.

"Why not? You love to drive," she wheedled. "Let's take Chelsea to that place on the dock where everybody hangs out."

"Not tonight," Chelsea declined.

"Don't be that way. You'll love it. The Delfin is Roberto's favorite restaurant."

"Then you two go. I've had it for today."

"How can you say that? You're not going to be here very long. I should think you'd want to see as much as possible."

It was a logical assumption. Yet how could Chelsea explain something she didn't understand herself? She was upset that Roberto and Mindy didn't display any affection, yet when they did she found it difficult to watch.

"You don't need a third wheel along," Chelsea mumbled.

"That's just plain dumb. Tell her so, Roberto." Without giving him a chance, Mindy added plaintively, "We haven't spent any time together at all."

"We will tomorrow. How about a trip to Torremolinos? We'll make a whole day of it. Just the two of us," Chelsea added without looking at Roberto.

Mindy brightened. "That sounds great. Can we take the Ferrari, Roberto?"

"No, you may not. It's much too fast for you." When he became aware of Chelsea's ironic stare, Roberto said, "You have to know how to handle a car that powerful."

"Men are so macho about their silly cars," Mindy grumbled. "You put one piece of gum in the ashtray and they have a nervous breakdown."

"I don't care about the car, I care about *you*. I don't want anything to happen to you. Or Chelsea," he added.

"Well, there goes our trip to Torremolinos," Mindy sighed.

"Not necessarily. You can take the Bentley. Ramón or I will take Mother anywhere she has to go."

"I guess I've had worse offers." Mindy grinned.

Chelsea was up early after a restless night. She'd gone to bed at a reasonable hour, but she was still awake when Mindy and Roberto came home, well after midnight.

She showered and dressed, resigning herself to a long wait. After her late night, Mindy wouldn't be up for hours. As Chelsea passed her room on the way downstairs she was pleasantly surprised to hear sounds coming from inside. She rapped softly and went in when Mindy answered.

"I didn't expect you to be up yet," Chelsea said happily. "I appreciate the sacrifice. Now we have the entire day ahead of us."

"If I live through it," Mindy groaned.

A closer look showed that her face was pale and she was perspiring. "You look terrible," Chelsea exclaimed. "What's wrong?"

"I must have gotten a bad clam last night."

"You poor kid. I'll tell Roberto to call a doctor."

"Don't do that. I'll be okay."

"Food poisoning is nothing to fool around with. Are you in pain?"

"Not really. I just feel yucky."

"Well, he can give you something for that."

"No, I'll feel better after I have something to eat."

"You feel like eating?" Chelsea asked incredulously.

"Just some dry toast. Will you ask Luis to bring it, and a pot of hot tea."

"I'll go get it myself." Chelsea gave her a worried look. "Are you sure you don't want Roberto to at least get you a prescription for something?"

"I'll be fine, honestly," Mindy said wearily.

Chelsea met Roberto in the downstairs hallway. "*You* look okay, anyway," she said.

He smiled as his eyes traveled over her slim figure. "You look more than just okay."

His smile vanished when she told him about Mindy's food poisoning. "I'd like to call a doctor, but she insists she doesn't want one," Chelsea said. "Maybe you can convince her."

"Why don't we wait and see if she feels better?"

Chelsea thought that was rather unfeeling, but she couldn't argue with both of them. "She wants some tea and toast. I'm going to get it for her."

"That should make her feel better. I'll go up and sit with her."

When Chelsea returned with a tray, Roberto was sitting on Mindy's bed, holding her hand. Chelsea's hostility vanished at the sight. Roberto did care for her sister. The proof brought a lump to her throat.

"Consuela sent some butter and marmalade, in case you felt like it," she said.

Mindy grimaced. "Take it away. I'll be lucky if I keep the toast down."

Chelsea and Roberto stared at her as she broke a piece of toast in half and took a tiny bite. Her expression was dogged as she chewed and swallowed.

When she became aware of their fascinated regard, Mindy said tartly, "Why don't you come back in half an hour? I'm even more entertaining when I drink tea."

They left meekly. Outside the door Chelsea said, "I guess she can't be too sick if she's that testy."

He laughed. "You're right. The time to worry is if she turns saintly."

When Chelsea returned a little later, she was amazed to hear her sister singing in the shower. "What are you doing?" she asked as Mindy emerged from the bathroom and started opening dresser drawers.

"I'm getting dressed," Mindy answered calmly. "We're going to Torremolinos."

"Are you out of your mind? Get back in bed. You're sick!"

"Not anymore. That clam is history." She looked Chelsea over approvingly. "I see you have on sensible shoes this time."

"Be reasonable, Mindy. You're in no condition to go running around."

"Says who? I was thinking about a change in plans, though. There really isn't that much to see in Torremolinos except the Spanish Steps, and we can do those on the way back. I thought we'd go to Fuengirola instead. The flea market is on today. Then afterward we can drive up the mountain to Mijas. It's a neat little town."

"You really feel up to all this?" Chelsea asked helplessly.

"You don't think I got up for nothing, do you?"

Chelsea could only marvel at the recuperative powers of a nineteen-year-old.

When Mindy asked Roberto for the car keys, he cupped her cheek in his palm and gazed at her searchingly. "Are you sure you feel all right?"

"You know me, pal." She smiled. "I'm a survivor."

"Take care of yourself," he said gently.

Mindy drove because she knew the way. "Stop watching the road and look at the scenery," she ordered.

"Between you and Roberto, I'm getting gray hairs," Chelsea remarked.

"He's something else, isn't he?" Mindy chuckled.

"Yes, he is," Chelsea answered quietly.

Mindy glanced over at her. "You've changed your mind about him, haven't you?"

Chelsea paused to frame her answer carefully. "I'll admit my first impression wasn't exactly...accurate. But I still think you ought to wait and get to know each other better."

"Do you ever really know someone?" Mindy's eyes darkened as she stared at the winding strip of road. "You think you do. You think he loves you as much as you love him, and then suddenly you find out it was just a slick line."

"Every woman runs across a creep now and then," Chelsea said dismissively. "You just have to chalk it up to experience and forget about him."

"What if you can't forget?"

"Are you referring to anyone in particular?" Chelsea asked uncertainly.

Mindy's intensity lightened. "Well, there was Johnny Madison. That was a night to remember."

He was the boy who had deserted her at her senior prom. They argued over something, and he left with another girl. It had been one of Mindy's few humiliating experiences.

"You weren't in love with Johnny. The only thing he damaged was your ego," Chelsea said. "And Troy Levitt boosted that in a hurry."

"Wasn't he gorgeous? Too bad he was about as interesting as a houseplant."

They talked about Mindy's friends, and hilarious events from the past. Chelsea hoped the reminiscences would make Mindy homesick, but she didn't like to push the point. It was so nice to spend this time alone with her little sister.

Fuengirola was a small, bustling city. Office buildings and banks lined the main street, and people were dressed in business clothes rather than resort wear.

The city atmosphere vanished abruptly when the street dead-ended in a rural area of packed dirt and patches of scraggly grass. Rows of makeshift tables were set up inside the flea market, forming lanes that wandered off in every direction. The stalls offered a variety of merchandise, from clothing and jewelry to housewares and children's toys.

Chelsea and Mindy joined the crowds, strolling leisurely and stopping often to inspect the wares. But when Chelsea picked up a cheap necklace, Mindy shook her head.

"Wait till we get to Mijas. They have pearls that you'd swear were real. If you'll make me a temporary loan, I'd like to get a strand to wear with my wedding dress."

"You've picked out your wedding gown?" Chelsea asked slowly. Of course she must have, with the event so imminent. "You never mentioned it."

"I didn't want to start the argument all over again, but I've been dying to show it to you. It was Roberto's grandmother's. The bride of the oldest son always wears it when she gets married. I only hope I don't spill something and spoil the family tradition." Mindy giggled nervously.

Chelsea was engulfed by a feeling of hopelessness, but she had to make one last try. "Are you *sure* this is what you want to do?"

Mindy's merriment fled as she met her sister's eyes steadily. "Very sure."

After a searching look, Chelsea forced a smile. "Maybe I've just been selfish. I don't want to lose you."

"You won't. You'll come and visit us often."

"That's a thought," Chelsea said noncommittally, turning to pick up a pottery bowl.

The vendor approached when he saw her intent stare. "That is a very beautiful piece, no? A real find."

"What? Oh, yes," she answered vaguely.

"It has a chip on the edge," Mindy objected.

"A small thing." The man shrugged. "Not even noticeable, but maybe I can do better on the price."

"We'll think about it." Mindy dragged her sister away. "You need a keeper. That stuff was junk. Let's go see what they have over there."

During their wanderings they came across an area selling produce. Among the eggplants, strings of garlic and red peppers, there were large containers of pine nuts and pistachios.

"Let's get a bag of each," Mindy suggested.

"Do you think you should?" Chelsea asked. "Your stomach was queasy just a few hours ago."

"I've forgotten all about that. Come on, my treat." Mindy grinned mischievously. "You can buy the pearls."

"Like that old joke about the two Texans who go in to buy a Cadillac?" Chelsea asked dryly.

"Exactly. One paid for the car because the other had bought lunch."

With a warm feeling of companionship, they ambled along eating nuts and bantering back and forth.

Beyond the food section was an area devoted to flowers and plants. Large bunches of daisies, hyacinths and tulips made bright spots of color in tin pails. But what drew Chelsea's attention were the rosebushes. Each was several feet high and covered with exquisite blooms.

"I've never seen such gorgeous roses," she exclaimed. "Look at this cream-colored bud with pink around the edges."

"It's pretty, but I like the scarlet ones," Mindy said.

"I'd buy one for Dolores, but I don't know about carting it home in the Bentley." Chelsea looked dubiously at the trickle of mud seeping out of the can's drainage holes. "Wouldn't it be beautiful, though, espaliered against a wall in the courtyard?"

"Don't you have to put nails in the plaster? She might not go for that. The del Machados are very large on keeping everything the way it's always been. Not that I'm complaining. I've gotten used to being waited on," Mindy joked.

"Are you going to live there after you're married?" Chelsea asked with a curious reluctance.

"I guess so. There's plenty of room. Roberto and his mother each have their own suites. You should see his bedroom. It's tremendous."

Chelsea didn't want to hear any details. "We've covered everything here and I'm getting hungry. Let's go to Mijas."

Mijas was a scenic little town atop a mountain. Not as high up as Ronda, but elevated enough for a panoramic view of several villages below.

They stopped for a late lunch in a small café, then made a walking tour of the city. The whitewashed houses reminded Chelsea of Greece, and the winding streets were typical of any ancient European hamlet.

Although they'd recently finished lunch, Mindy stopped to buy *churros* from a curbside vendor. The twisted, doughnut-like confections were warm and dusted with sugar. About a dozen of them filled the paper cone the man handed her.

"How do you have room for those?" Chelsea protested. "I'm still stuffed from lunch."

"Try one." Mindy extended the cone. "They're habit-forming."

Chelsea had to agree. She ate her share as they rambled along the picturesque streets. Near the summit was the bullring. The only square one in Spain, Mindy informed her, built during Arab domination.

"See how broadening travel is?" Mindy bragged. "And you thought I was just an airhead."

"No more."

As Chelsea walked over to peer through the slits in the thick stone walls of the bullring, Mindy burst out laughing. Turning to see what was so funny, Chelsea noticed a small white poodle trotting down the middle of the road. The wind blowing up the steep hill was so strong that his floppy ears were standing out horizontally.

"If he runs a little faster he'll take off and fly to Fuengirola," Mindy chortled.

"To the flea market?"

Mindy groaned. "You can do better than that."

"Maybe it's the altitude. Let's go shopping. That's a cure for everything."

They discovered a lovely jewelry store filled with every size of pearls. Glass cases displayed a wide variety of necklaces, bracelets and earrings.

An elegant young woman with dark hair and eyes came forward to greet them. "May I help you?"

"We want to see some necklaces," Mindy answered.

"We have a large selection. What length would you prefer?"

Chelsea stared at the woman curiously. "Where did you learn to speak English so perfectly? You don't have a trace of an accent."

The saleslady smiled. "I was born in Chicago."

"How did you wind up in a little town in Spain?" Chelsea exclaimed.

The woman shrugged. "The usual story. I met a man."

"This must be quite a change for you," Chelsea remarked slowly.

Was she happy? Had her life turned out as she hoped? Those weren't questions one asked a stranger, but Chelsea was burning to find out. She did discover that the young woman still had a keen interest in her own country. She asked about everything from the current fashions to the latest movies. But she also spoke pleasantly of Spain and its attractions, so Chelsea didn't come to any real conclusion.

While they talked, Mindy prowled around the store examining everything. Finally she called, "Can you tell me how much this one is?"

The saleslady opened the case and removed an opera-length necklace. "These are lovely."

Chelsea gazed admiringly at the strand of lustrous pearls that seemed to glow from within. "You have excellent taste, but I don't know if I can afford them," she told her sister. "They must be real."

"I told you that you wouldn't be able to tell the difference," Mindy said.

"Surely those are cultured," Chelsea said to the saleslady.

The woman shook her head. "They're the finest simulated pearls in the world, made by a secret process. Each piece is registered, and guaranteed for ten years."

When she quoted the price, Chelsea said, "That's hard to believe."

"Can I have them?" Mindy asked. "I'll pay you back out of my next allowance."

"You don't have to. Consider it your wedding present."

Mindy threw her arms around her sister's neck. "You're a doll! This sure beats heck out of a toaster oven."

While the woman was filling out a certificate of authenticity and putting the pearls in a red velvet box with a satin lining, Chelsea picked out a pair of pretty earrings for their mother.

"That ought to soften her up," Mindy remarked.

"It's going to take more than a pair of earrings to make her happy," Chelsea said quietly. "She looked forward to seeing you get married one day."

Mindy's laughing face sobered. "Things didn't work out the way I planned, either."

"They still could."

"Leave it, Chelsea. It's been such a great day."

Mindy seemed subdued when they left the jewelry shop, and Chelsea regretted her last ditch efforts. She knew by now they were doomed to failure, so why spoil what little time she and Mindy had left? Who knew when they'd be together like this again?

Mindy was uncharacteristically silent as they walked down the hill. When the town square was in sight Chelsea said hesitantly, "Don't be angry with me. I might be as annoying as a cold sore, but it's only because I care about you."

Mindy flashed her a warm smile. "How could I be mad at my favorite sister?"

"You're awfully quiet."

"I guess I'm running out of steam."

That wasn't like Mindy. She was always full of energy. Chelsea looked more closely at her, noticing the shadows under her sister's eyes.

"Don't you feel well?" she asked anxiously. "I knew you shouldn't have eaten those *churros.*"

"My stomach is fine. I'm just a little tired, that's all. Will you drive home?"

Chelsea was even more concerned when Mindy slumped down in the seat, put her head back and closed her eyes. "Do you mind if we skip Torremolinos?" she asked.

"Of course not. We have to save something for another day."

"Right," Mindy murmured. "Maybe tomorrow." Before they reached the broad highway leading to Marbella, she was asleep.

Chelsea worried about her sister all the way home. She'd seemed to bounce back from her attack of food poisoning, but obviously it was still in her system. Chelsea blamed herself for not insisting they postpone their sightseeing, yet when had Mindy ever listened to reason?

She awoke when Chelsea pulled into the driveway and turned off the motor. "Are we home already? That was fast."

"You slept all the way back."

"Sorry I conked out on you." Mindy yawned.

"That's unimportant. Go upstairs and get into bed," Chelsea ordered. "I'm going to find a thermometer and take your temperature."

"I'm not sick. Stop fussing over me like a mother hen," Mindy said irritably, but she went to her room.

Roberto came into the hall when he heard their voices. "Did you have a good time?" he asked.

"Yes, it was a lot of fun, but I'm worried about Mindy."

His smile faded. "What's the matter?"

"We shouldn't have gone. She said she felt better, but she doesn't."

Roberto frowned. "Did she get sick again?"

"No, just tired. By the end of the day she was dragging her anchor."

He seemed relieved. "That doesn't sound very ominous. You were gone a long time."

"Mindy never gets tired. I've known her to stay up most of the night and then go out to play tennis the next morning."

"Aren't you making a lot out of nothing? Everyone gets tired now and then."

"I think she should see a doctor," Chelsea said stubbornly.

"By all means—if that's what she wants."

"That's the whole problem. She doesn't."

"Then I suggest you respect her wishes."

"*I* care what happens to her," Chelsea answered stiffly.

"So do I." Roberto's dark eyes were unfathomable as they held hers.

She could scarcely doubt his statement. Chelsea remembered how solicitous he'd been toward Mindy that morning. Roberto was undoubtedly right. She was making a big deal out of nothing. Was she grasping at straws? Looking for any reason that could cause a delay?

Up until that point, all of Chelsea's energies had been directed toward preventing the upcoming wedding. Suddenly she wished it was over. Then she'd be free to go home and forget all about Roberto del Machado.

Chapter Six

Mindy knocked at Chelsea's door fairly early the next
morning. "Are you up?" she called.

Chelsea opened the door. "For ages, but I was going to
let you sleep."

"That's all I've been doing. You and Roberto wouldn't
let me go out last night," Mindy grumbled.

"A good thing, too. You look much better today."

"I was fine yesterday," Mindy answered peevishly.
"Will you kindly get off my back?"

"Okay, okay. I won't mention it again."

"Good. Let's go down to breakfast."

Roberto was sitting at the table in the courtyard, reading a newspaper. He rose politely when they joined him.

"Is that the financial section?" Chelsea asked as she sat
down.

"Yes. Would you like to see it?" He offered her a section of the paper.

"I guess I should check on how the stock market is doing."

"Why?" Mindy asked. "I never could understand why people get all bent out of shape when a stock goes up or down an eighth of a point."

"It makes a lot of difference to my clients—if I still have any when I get back," Chelsea said ruefully. "I said I'd only be gone a few days."

"You won't lose your job. Although it might be the best thing that could happen to you. All you ever meet at work are those button-down type men."

"What's wrong with that? I'm a button-down type myself."

"You've just answered your own question." Mindy stared critically at her sister's classic white camp shirt and tailored beige pants. "Roberto, you're a man. Would you look twice at a woman who was dressed like that? You'd never guess what a sensational figure she has."

His dark eyes moved over the curves of Chelsea's breasts, then lingered on the creamy skin revealed by the V neck of her blouse. "A man likes a little mystery in a woman." He smiled.

"That's what they *say*, but it's the bimbos in miniskirts they turn around to look at," Mindy declared.

"Only men without a true appreciation of women." He turned his attention to Chelsea again.

She could feel the heat rising to her cheeks, but she tried to appear unaffected. "Don't bother defending me. The only way I could win Mindy's approval would be to have a flaming affair with a bullfighter."

"Right on! Do you know any you could introduce her to, Roberto?"

"One or two, but I don't think they're Chelsea's type."

"What is my type?" Chelsea challenged. Did he agree with Mindy's assessment of her as prim?

"Someone who appeals to the intellect as well as the senses."

"We're back to the Wall Street guys again," Mindy said derisively. "Chelsea needs to meet a man who's good in the bedroom, not the boardroom."

Roberto looked amused. "The two talents aren't mutually incompatible."

"Do you have anyone in mind?" Mindy asked hopefully.

"Unfortunately, no." He reached for a small crystal bell on the table. "I wonder what's keeping Luis?"

Chelsea welcomed the diversion, knowing her sister would have worried the subject like a dog with a favorite bone. By the time Luis had appeared and taken their breakfast orders, Mindy's attention had turned to plans for the day.

"What shall we do?" she asked.

"We could drive to Gibraltar," Roberto suggested. "Chelsea might find that interesting."

"We went sightseeing yesterday," Mindy objected.

"I wouldn't mind going again," Chelsea said.

"We can do that later in the week. Let's go shopping instead. You have to get a dress for the wedding."

"I suppose you're right," Chelsea murmured, unable to conceal her lack of enthusiasm.

"Chelsea is going to be my maid of honor," Mindy informed Roberto.

"I'm delighted," he answered, although he didn't look it.

"Will it be a big wedding?" As long as she was committed, Chelsea felt she should show some interest.

"Quite large. All of my relatives are coming, and of course many friends."

"Who is taking care of all of the arrangements?"

"My mother and Rosa."

"These things require a lot of preparation. Aren't there going to be rehearsals?"

"I presume they're scheduled for next week, along with numerous parties." Roberto repressed a sigh.

Chelsea hoped his reaction was simply a man's normal aversion to all the hoopla. But Mindy didn't seem to be in a white heat of anticipation, either. She was gazing at Roberto with the most curious expression. It could almost be described as sadness. Chelsea told herself she was being fanciful. They both wanted this marriage. No one was forcing them to go through with it.

They were almost finished eating when Luis came to the table. "You have a telephone call, Señorita Claiborne. Would you like me to bring you the phone?"

"Yes, thank you, Luis. It must be mother again," she said as the man left. "I should have called her, but I didn't have anything good to report—about Dawn," Chelsea added as Roberto turned a sardonic gaze on her.

"We'll have to call Carlos this morning. He's probably found her already," Mindy said.

"Let's wait till we're sure. I don't want to get her mother's hopes up."

"Lighten up, Chelsea. Why are you always so pessimistic?"

"Because I live in the real world—unlike you." Luis returned with a cordless phone which Chelsea held out to her sister. "Here. It's your turn to take a little flak."

"You're so much better at it," Mindy wheedled, shaking her head.

With a sigh, Chelsea put the phone to her ear. She was relieved when the voice that greeted her was Miguel's. She was more receptive than she might have been. "It's nice to hear from you, Miguel."

"I gave you time to be with your sister, now I hope you can spare some time for *me*," he answered in a dulcet voice. "I thought we might go for a sail on my boat today."

"Oh, I'm sorry. I've already made plans with Mindy."

"Where does he want you to go?" Mindy asked.

"Sailing," Chelsea replied briefly.

"That sounds like fun. Ask him if we can come along."

"I'd prefer not to," Roberto said.

"Why not? You like sailing."

At the same time, Miguel was saying, "Can't you change your plans? I'd very much like to see you."

"Excuse me a minute." Chelsea put her hand over the mouthpiece. "Could you keep it down? I can't hear."

"Let me talk to him." Mindy reached out and took the phone. "Hi, Miguel, it's Mindy. Does your invitation include Roberto and me? We can drive Chelsea down there. That way, you won't have to come all the way up here to get her."

"That's very thoughtful of you," he answered tepidly.

"Glad to do it. Are you having a big group?"

"I might as well." His voice held irony.

"Great! What time shall we be there?"

"Why did you do that?" Chelsea asked in annoyance after Mindy had hung up. "Roberto doesn't want to go, and I'd just as soon have gone shopping."

"We can do that any time, and Roberto doesn't have to go if he'd rather not."

"I suppose I'd better come along to make sure you don't fall overboard," he said a trifle grimly.

"You'll enjoy yourself," Mindy said pushing back her chair. "I'm going upstairs to change."

"You're very patient," Chelsea remarked when she and Roberto were alone.

He shrugged. "If these little things make her happy, why not?"

Much as she loved her sister, Chelsea couldn't help being impatient. "Because sooner or later she has to learn that everyone doesn't necessarily do what she wants them to."

"I think she's already learned that," he answered quietly. Before Chelsea could ask for examples, Roberto excused himself to make some business calls.

Chelsea expected a modest sailboat, but Miguel's boat was a virtual yacht. It was equipped with a motor for alternate power, and had a luxurious salon furnished with couches, chairs and even a television set. Beyond the salon was a galley fitted with every modern appliance. Below decks were the master cabin and several staterooms.

The *Claro Mar* was docked at Puerto Banús among similarly expensive craft from many parts of the world. Several had parties going on while they remained moored to the long pier that stretched into the sea.

A party was in progress on Miguel's yacht, too. Music came from the salon, mixed with the sound of laughing voices. Their host greeted them from the top of the gangway with a glass in one hand.

"Welcome aboard," he called. "We're ready to cast off."

"I never expected anything this grand." Chelsea gazed around at the teak decks and gleaming brass railings. "I wore my bathing suit under my clothes because I expected to help crew."

"You might have to." Miguel smiled. "My captain is down with the flu."

"Do you think we should go out, then?" Roberto asked.

"Why not? I'll simply use the motor instead of the sails."

"Someone has to stay at the helm," Roberto pointed out.

"I'll take her into deep water and anchor there. It won't exactly be a cruise, but this gang won't even notice," Miguel laughed. "Let me get you a drink," he said to Chelsea.

The large cabin was filled with many of the same people who had been at Veronique Broussard's party. Chelsea was less than thrilled and Roberto didn't look overjoyed, but Mindy was in her element. She plunged into the group, greeting everyone with enthusiasm. Chelsea was gratified to note that Mindy had fully recovered from her little upset the day before.

Adding to the party atmosphere were two young men in white coats who circulated among the guests, bringing drinks or offering platters of hors d'oeuvres from the galley. Although it was a beautiful, cloudless day, no one seemed interested in going on deck. Miguel was correct in his assumption. They didn't care if they were at sea or ashore as long as the liquor supply held out.

Chelsea had no intention of staying in the cabin. "I'd like to look around," she told Miguel.

"I'll give you a guided tour." He took her hand and held onto it as he led her toward the stern of the ship. "I'm delighted that you're here, but this isn't the kind of day I was hoping for," he remarked ruefully.

"What more could you ask? There isn't a cloud in the sky."

"I was hoping to spend the day alone with you." His voice deepened.

"You must have invited all these people," Chelsea said lightly, finally managing to free her hand.

"Only after I discovered Roberto was coming. My dear cousin doesn't approve of me, so I avoid being in small groups with him."

"It's too bad you don't get along. You would seem to have a great deal in common."

"That's the problem. We don't. Roberto has all these radical ideas about the virtue of honest labor and equal opportunity for the working classes."

"Since I'm a working woman myself, I tend to agree with him," she said evenly.

"That's different. I admire women who take an interest in things. Lady Ashborne designs jewelry, and Pepe Moran's wife is on the board of the Cultural Center."

"I wonder how they find the time," Chelsea murmured.

When they reached the pilot house, Miguel said, "I guess we might as well get started. Come inside with me while I start the motors."

"You go ahead. I'm going to look around some more," she told him.

Chelsea wandered back to the stern and watched the dock recede as the *Claro Mar* slowly glided away from it. When they picked up speed, a breeze sprang up and the calm water became choppy. Chelsea was a good sailor so she hunched over the railing, enjoying the wind in her face.

Suddenly a wave slapped the side of the boat. The force sent a geyser cascading over her when she was leaning against the side. Her T-shirt was drenched and water trickled inside her jeans.

After the initial shock, she inspected herself ruefully. The sun would dry her clothes, but they felt clammy so she stripped them off. She was wearing a one-piece blue bathing suit underneath, cut high at the thighs but otherwise fairly chaste. At least compared to a bikini.

Chelsea was bending over, draping her jeans across a lounge chair when Roberto came around a corner past the furled mizzenmast. Pinpoints of light flared in his eyes as they rested on her cleavage. The fullness of her breasts was emphasized by the form-fitting suit. His reaction was masked by the time she straightened up, but he continued to gaze at her slender figure.

"I see you decided to get some sun," he remarked pleasantly.

"Of necessity." She laughed. "I got clobbered by a wave."

"Luckily you were wearing a bathing suit underneath."

"My clothes are no problem, but look at my hair." She combed her fingers through the long strands that were already turning into an untamed auburn cloud.

"I like it that way. You look like the star of one of those sexy Italian movies." He smiled.

"Really? I've never been accused of being sexy." She tugged at her suit nervously, which had an unwanted effect. Roberto's attention transferred to her long, slim legs.

"It wasn't an accusation. I meant it as a compliment."

"Well, thanks." She managed a slight laugh. "We've certainly come a long way in a few days, haven't we?"

"What do you mean?" he asked warily.

"We could scarcely be civil to each other when I first came here."

"I'm glad we've gotten past that stage."

"I am, too," she admitted.

"We still haven't achieved the relationship I'd like, though."

"I'm not sure I know what that is," she answered carefully.

"I was referring to your automatic reaction when we're alone together."

"Nothing could be farther from the truth," she flared. "Besides the fact that you're engaged to my sister, you aren't my type at all."

He stared at her in surprise. "I meant you always seem uneasy around me. Is that why you tense up whenever I get near you? You don't trust me? What kind of man do you think I am?"

"I don't know," she mumbled, feeling like a fool. How could she have thought Roberto was coming on to her? His incredulity at the very idea was proof that he never considered such a thing.

"Well, you damn well *should* know by now! When have I ever given you reason to doubt my commitment to Mindy?"

"Maybe I was wrong." She turned away, unable to face him.

"*Maybe?*" He grabbed her arm and whirled her around. "Is that the best you can do?"

"She's my sister." Chelsea gazed intently at his tanned throat. "Naturally I want to be sure you love her."

"So you decided to test me yourself," he said grimly.

"No!" She looked up wide-eyed. "I wouldn't do a thing like that. I told my mother—" She stopped short.

"So I was right! Just tell me one thing." He snaked an arm around her waist and jerked her against his taut body. "How far were you prepared to go? Was I at least going to get some reward before you ran to tell little sister what a heel she picked?''

"You're wrong." Chelsea tried to pull away, but Roberto's arms were like iron bands, welding her to his hard frame.

He ignored her protests, running his hand down her back to cup her bottom and draw her hips against his. The more Chelsea struggled, the more aware she became of his potent masculinity.

"Why don't you show me what I'm missing?" he taunted. "I might change my mind."

"Stop it this instant! You must be—"

Chelsea's words were cut off as Roberto's mouth closed savagely over hers. After prying her lips apart, his tongue plunged deeply, again and again. The veneer of civilization was stripped away as he plundered her mouth and explored her body. She pounded his shoulders with her fists when Roberto's hand curled around her breasts, but he merely made a low sound deep in his throat. She was helpless in his embrace, overwhelmed by the sheer male power of him.

The frenzy passed when Chelsea's strength failed and her tense body had to acknowledge his superior strength. Roberto's punishing grip loosened as she relaxed against him in exhaustion. His mouth softened and his hand cradled the back of her head, supporting it gently.

This was almost worse than his primitive onslaught. She could fight that. His switch from force to seductiveness produced a frightening reaction. Suddenly, every instinct urged her to respond to his sensual kiss, to twine her arms around his neck and give in to the raging desire he was creating.

She traced the straining muscles in his shoulders restlessly. They were like steel coils, as taut as the rest of his body. The heat of his rigid thighs made her own passion flame with the same urgent demand for fulfillment. Nothing else seemed of any importance at that moment.

Sanity returned when Roberto buried his face in her hair, murmuring her name over and over. With a supreme effort of will, Chelsea dug her nails into his shoulders and pushed him away. His hands tightened on her waist for a moment, as though he didn't intend to let her go. Then the intensity in his face died. It was replaced by shock.

"I'm sorry, Chelsea. I never meant to—"

"Just go away and leave me alone." She wrapped her arms around her trembling body.

"I have to explain."

"I'd prefer not to talk about it."

"We *have* to talk. What happened just now was...an aberration. I've never acted like that in my life."

"Lucky me," she answered bitterly. "I got to see a side of you no one else ever has."

"You were partly responsible," he said quietly. "I thought you respected me, no matter what other reservations you might have. How do you think I felt when I discovered you've been trying all along to trick me?"

"That isn't so! I'll admit my mother suggested it, but I told her in no uncertain terms that I wouldn't consider such a thing."

"But suddenly you decided it wasn't such a bad idea, after all."

"No! You have to believe me."

He smiled without humor. "How does it feel to be blameless, and still have someone doubt you?"

"You weren't so blameless a minute ago," Chelsea muttered.

"I deeply regret the incident. I don't even know how it happened." Roberto ran rigid fingers through his thick hair. "It's no excuse, but sometimes things build up until you can't take it anymore. Then you vent your frustration on an innocent person."

What he called an "incident" had left her moved and shaken. She could still taste Roberto's kiss on her lips. Her body still bore the imprint of his. For one wild moment she'd wanted him to make love to her. Chelsea's indignation died when she realized she was at least as guilty as he.

She turned away, shivering as the sun was obscured by a black cloud. Even the elements were frowning on her. An imminent storm darkened the sky and sent gusts of wind howling through the furled masts.

"Can't you understand and forgive me?" he pleaded.

"Yes, it's all right."

He stared uncertainly at her straight back. "My rotten temper got the better of me. I never would have touched you otherwise."

Chelsea lowered her head and walked toward the rail. "Go back to the others, Roberto. I'll be along in a minute."

"*Chelsea!*"

She turned around at the urgency in his voice, just in time to see him make a flying leap at her. She fell backward under his weight and landed flat on the deck with Roberto on top of her. She was momentarily dazed when her head thumped against the wooden boards, and the breath was knocked out of her.

"Are you all right, *mi corazón?*" Roberto was tenderly smoothing the tumbled hair away from her face. When she couldn't answer, he gently probed the top of her head. "Speak to me angel. Did I hurt you?"

She stared at him in confusion, convinced that she was imagining his tenderness. Adding to the unreality was something swinging back and forth overhead, making a grating sound.

"Why did you do that?" she asked faintly.

"The sail broke loose. You could have been killed."

In his relief, Roberto gathered her tightly in his arms. Her face was buried in his neck, and their bodies were so closely joined that she was almost a part of him. Chelsea's head hurt and Roberto's hipbones were digging into her, but she'd never felt better in her life.

When she shifted to ease the pressure on her thighs, he immediately released her and levered himself up. Helping her to a sitting position he looked at her anxiously. "Are you all right?"

She smiled tremulously. "Now I know how a quarterback feels when he gets sacked."

"I'm sorry. There wasn't time to do anything else."

"I wasn't complaining. I'm grateful to you for saving me from broken bones at the very least."

"Does that make up for...my tasteless behavior?"

Her smile faded. "We had a misunderstanding all around. I want to forget it as much as you do."

"I'm sure you do." He gazed at her without expression. "At least some good came of it. We corrected any misconceptions between us."

"Yes." Chelsea's lashes feathered her cheeks.

Roberto got to his feet and helped her up. Gathering her jeans and T-shirt, he handed them to her. "You'd better get inside. It's going to pour at any moment."

"Aren't you coming?"

"I have to secure that sail first."

Chelsea slipped into her clothes before entering the salon. She also tried to tame her windblown hair. But no one was interested in either her appearance or her activities for the past hour. The unexpectedly turbulent sea had cast a pall over the party.

"This isn't amusing anymore," Veronique said petulantly.

"I'm with you," Mindy stated. "Why doesn't Miguel turn this tub around?"

"One of the sails broke loose," Chelsea said. "It has to be tied down first."

Mindy stared at her. "Where have you been and what happened to you?"

"What do you mean?" Chelsea asked warily.

"Your hair is a mess."

"A storm is blowing up," Chelsea answered vaguely.

"We won't be stuck out here, will we?" asked Clive Forsythe, the amorous Englishman from Veronique's party.

His wife, Daphne expressed the same alarm. "That would be dreadful!"

"I'm sure there's no danger on a ship this size," Chelsea said reassuringly.

"That's not what I'm worried about. We're invited to a party at Lady Ashborne's tonight."

"Cheer up, she might not even miss you," Chelsea told her ironically.

Mindy laughed as Daphne bridled indignantly. "I can't take you anywhere," she murmured to Chelsea.

"Is that a promise?" Chelsea murmured back.

A small cheer went up as the motor throbbed to life. The rocking motion stopped and the *Claro Mar* cut through the water on its way back to port.

Rain was pelting down when they reached shore. It was greeted by cries of dismay from the ladies concerned about their hairdos.

"Don't worry, I have plenty of umbrellas," Miguel said. "This doesn't have to spoil the party. We'll simply move to my apartment and pick up where we left off."

"Face it, Miguel. Everybody's out of the mood," Mindy told him.

"You'll come, won't you?" he appealed to Chelsea.

"No thanks, I'll go with Mindy," she answered.

"Aren't you carrying this sister act a little far?" he sneered.

Mindy's eyes narrowed. "Do you have a problem with that?"

"The children's hour is over," he drawled. "It's time for the adults to play."

Roberto's face was expressionless. "The lady gave you her answer."

"Don't be a dog in the manger, cousin," Miguel taunted. "You have your girl. Chelsea made a date with *me*."

"It's over," Chelsea replied curtly.

As they walked to the car, Mindy remarked, "I'm disappointed in Miguel. I thought he had more class."

"Your perception is improving." Chelsea shot Roberto an apologetic look. "I'm sorry. I forgot he was family."

"I can't be blamed for that." He smiled.

"Well, what shall we do now?" Mindy asked when they'd settled into the car.

"I don't know about you two, but I'd like to go home and get cleaned up," Chelsea said.

"Sounds good to me," Roberto remarked. "Mindy?"

"I guess we might as well," she agreed, to Chelsea's surprise.

Dolores came to greet them when they returned to the house. After they told her about their outing, she said to

Chelsea, "I'm glad my son is taking care of you. I'm afraid I've been neglecting you shamefully."

"Not at all," Chelsea answered. "You've been more than hospitable. I didn't expect to be entertained."

"You're very generous, my dear. I do wish we could spend more time together, but I've had my hands full with the wedding."

Chelsea found it difficult to muster any sympathy. Dolores could have avoided all that by having the wedding in New York. But what was the point of bringing it up now?

"I suppose there are a lot of details to take care of," she remarked politely.

"An unbelievable amount. I'd like to discuss them with you when you have a moment."

"With me?" Chelsea asked in surprise.

"I'm sure you have some suggestions."

"Not really. I don't have any experience with this sort of thing."

"That goes for Roberto and me, too. We'll just have to wing it." Mindy grinned.

"Aren't you going to have a rehearsal?" Chelsea asked in alarm. Mindy was unpredictable enough without letting her improvise.

"That's what I need to confer with you about," Dolores said. "Can you spare me a couple of hours tomorrow afternoon?"

"Mindy will *make* time," Chelsea said firmly. "But you don't need me." She wanted as little to do with the proceedings as possible.

"You're the maid of honor," Dolores pointed out. "You're part of the wedding procession."

"A very unimportant part. Couldn't someone else stand in for me?"

"I suppose so if you have other plans," Dolores answered reluctantly.

"You didn't say anything to me." Mindy looked at her sister curiously. "Where are you going?"

"Well, I...uh...I thought I'd better go shopping for a dress." That was as good an excuse as any. Actually it was a valid one. Chelsea hadn't wanted to admit the wedding was going to take place, so she'd refused to discuss it. Now she was forced to. "What color are the bridesmaids wearing, and where did they get their gowns? Mine will have to coordinate with theirs."

"Only with Rosa's. You two are the only attendants. It's going to be a short procession." Mindy's smile had a fixed quality.

"Rosa will be the matron of honor. Mindy said she didn't want bridesmaids," Dolores explained.

"Who would I ask? Roberto's old girlfriends? That would make quite a crowd." Mindy's voice was brittle.

"How about some of the friends you made over here this summer?" Chelsea asked hastily.

"They're just acquaintances, except for Dawn, and now I don't know where she is." Mindy's mouth drooped. "I really wanted her at my wedding."

"I'll call Carlos and see if he has any news," Roberto said gently. "I have to phone him anyway."

"I'll go with you," Mindy said. "I want to hear what he has to say."

After they left the room, Dolores said apologetically, "I'm afraid Mindy is disappointed at not having her friends here."

"It isn't the kind of wedding any of us had planned." Chelsea was too angry to care if she sounded curt. Her heart had twisted at the forlorn look in her sister's eyes.

"I'm sorry," Dolores said simply.

"It isn't too late to do something about it." Chelsea couldn't stop trying. "You have children. You must know what our parents are going through."

"I feel deeply for them. I would change things if I could, but some events are beyond my control," the older woman answered quietly.

Chelsea had the familiar feeling of being run down by a juggernaut. Nothing she did was going to stop it. "Can you tell me about Rosa's gown, or should I check with her?" she asked tonelessly.

Dolores didn't allow sympathy to show in her voice. "My dressmaker made both our dresses. Come into my office and I'll show you the sketches. If you like her work, perhaps she can run up something for you."

"At this late date?" Chelsea asked, following the other woman to her sitting room.

"She's very accommodating."

Dolores rummaged through the top drawer of her desk and brought out some drawings. The dresses were simple yet elegant, what Chelsea would have expected her to choose.

"Rosa's gown is peach-colored organza," Dolores said. "If you like the style, perhaps yours could be done in a shade of apricot. It would be lovely with your auburn hair. You and Mindy have such beautiful coloring."

"It's hereditary. Our father is a redhead, and our grandfather was, too. It runs in the family in varying degrees."

"That means we can look forward to having our own little coppertops." Dolores smiled. "That will be quite a novelty."

"Yes...well...about the dress..." Chelsea stared down at the sketch she was holding.

"Will something like that satisfy you?"

"It would be lovely."

"Then I'll call Señora Melendez and have her here tomorrow. Don't worry about a thing. Your gown will be ready in plenty of time."

"Men have it easy. They already own tuxedos."

"That's true. And they look so nice in them. It will be a beautiful wedding," Dolores said placatingly.

"I'm sure it will." Chelsea managed a smile. "People only look at the bride, anyway. They won't even notice that there aren't any bridesmaids or ushers."

"Except for Carlos. Ramón will act as Roberto's best man, but Carlos will stand up with him, too."

"I realize he's Roberto's best friend, but won't that make things a little lopsided?"

Dolores looked puzzled. "In what way?"

"I mean, with Rosa and me one one side, and Roberto's two brothers and Carlos on the other."

"Jorge will not be there."

"Surely he wouldn't miss his brother's wedding!" Chelsea could hardly believe that, knowing the importance the del Machados placed on family.

"It's unfortunate," was Dolores's only response.

Chelsea knew that Roberto disapproved of his youngest brother, but there must be a real rift between them for Jorge to be banished from the occasion. How could Roberto be so inflexible? His mother was obviously upset over the situation. Dolores's eyes held deep sadness, but her reserved manner didn't invite further discussion.

"Well, if everything's settled, I'm going to wash my hair," Chelsea said awkwardly.

She met Mindy in the hallway and they walked upstairs together while Mindy gave her a report on Dawn.

"Carlos hasn't heard anything yet, but it's only been two days. He told me to relax."

"I wish *I* could." Chelsea sighed. "Mother will be phoning again at any moment, and I don't know how long I can stall her. I don't even know if I should."

"What's the point in stirring everybody up over nothing?"

"I wouldn't call Dawn's disappearance nothing," Chelsea answered sharply. "Who knows what that little creep is persuading her to do right this minute?"

"I know Dawn better than you do. Trust me. She's too smart to do anything that stupid."

"She hasn't displayed much intelligence so far," Chelsea said disgustedly. "Everybody warned her against the boy. Why couldn't *she* see through him?"

"Love isn't only blind, it's deaf and dumb, too," Mindy remarked sardonically.

"That doesn't exactly cheer me up."

"Have faith. I just hope she turns up in time for my wedding," Mindy said wistfully. "Dawn is like family."

Chelsea was reminded of her conversation with Dolores. "Did you know that Roberto's brother, Jorge isn't going to be there?"

Mindy paused at the entrance to her room. "Who told you that?"

"His mother. She's very unhappy about it."

Mindy shrugged. "He's probably made her unhappy before."

"That's remarkably unfeeling, even for you! I think you should talk to Roberto."

"About what?"

"I don't know what he argued with Jorge over, but now is the time to make up. Roberto is older and more mature. It's up to him to make the overture."

Mindy's soft mouth thinned. "Roberto has done more for Jorge than he deserves."

''Naturally you're on Roberto's side. You should be. But weddings are supposed to be happy events. This is a perfect opportunity for them to patch up their differences.''

''You don't even know what they are. Why do you automatically assume that Roberto is at fault?'' Mindy demanded.

''It's never solely one person's fault,'' Chelsea answered patiently. ''I'm merely saying he could make this a happier occasion for his mother.''

''Why don't *you* try telling him that?''

''I'm strictly an outsider,'' Chelsea protested.

''Exactly,'' Mindy answered coolly. ''But if you think I'm going to argue with Roberto about Jorge, you're out of your gourd.''

After Mindy had closed her door firmly, Chelsea went on to her own room. Maybe she was wrong to meddle. It would be ironic if she alienated her sister while trying to get Roberto and his brother together.

The only positive sign was Mindy's spirited defense of her finacé. Chelsea treasured every evidence of devotion on either side, since their marriage didn't seem to be generating much joy.

Chapter Seven

Chelsea had a lump in her throat as she watched her sister walk down the aisle the next day, even though Mindy didn't look like a bride, dressed as she was in jeans and running shoes.

Carlos was watching Chelsea. "The maid of honor isn't supposed to cry," he teased gently. "That's reserved for little old ladies in the audience."

"I always cry at weddings." She gave him a watery smile.

"But this is only a rehearsal."

"I know. I'm afraid I'll disgrace myself at the real thing."

"No, you won't. I'll make funny faces if I think you're in any danger."

"Promise?" Chelsea raised a smiling face to him.

He gazed down at her. "My solemn word."

"Chelsea! Carlos! If you can tear yourselves away, will you get over here so we can finish this thing before midnight?" Roberto called sarcastically.

"Do you detect a slight case of jitters?" Carlos asked Chelsea in a low voice as they moved toward the group at the altar.

"It's no wonder. Things are a little chaotic," she said.

Rosa had brought her two daughters, although only one was required. Melia, the older, was slated to be the flower girl. Her sister, Carmen, had been whining about it intermittently—between running up and down the aisles and climbing over the pews. Rosa's attempts to control the girls were minimal at best.

When Chelsea and Carlos joined the others, Melia and Carmen were having a tug of war over a straw basket.

"It's mine," Melia grunted. "You can't play with it."

"Yes, I can, too!"

"I'll buy you a different one, mother's angel," Rosa said mildly. "Melia needs that for her rose petals."

"All right, take it! I don't like it anyway. It's ugly." Carmen thrust the basket at her sister so violently that Melia sat down with a thump and started to cry.

"Those kids are a strong argument for birth control," Carlos murmured in Chelsea's ear.

"Or a straitjacket, at least." She laughed.

Roberto scowled at them. "I'm glad *someone* finds this amusing."

"Come with me, children." Dolores's tone was uncompromising, and the little girls followed her meekly. She led them outside, and returned alone.

"What did you do with them?" Rosa asked anxiously.

"Put them in separate cages, if she's smart," Roberto muttered.

As Rosa gave him an indignant look, Dolores said, "They needed to run off their excess energy."

"Can we get started now?" the priest asked patiently.

He explained the procedure, when they should respond and at what point Ramón would hand Roberto the ring. When he'd finished, they all went into the vestibule to practice the march down the aisle.

As the organist struck up the opening chords of the wedding march, Carlos chucked Chelsea under the chin. "You're on your own until you get to the altar," he said.

She noticed the stormy look Roberto gave him as the three men went to take their places. What had Carlos done to arouse Roberto's wrath? Nothing that she could tell. Wasn't the bride the one who was supposed to be jumpy? She glanced at her sister, but Mindy was enjoying all the excitement.

It grew a little stale as they repeated the procession over and over. Small interruptions kept the ritual from going smoothly—an urgent telephone call for the priest, a stuck pedal on the organ.

"I think we've all gotten the idea," Roberto declared, when Rosa had to go outside in response to a demand from Carmen. "Let's wrap this up."

"We haven't had one smooth run-through," Dolores objected.

"The marriage will be just as binding if Carlos drops the ring or Mindy stumbles coming down the aisle," Roberto answered grimly.

"Did you have to say that?" Mindy made a face.

"I think we could all use a little break," Carlos remarked tactfully.

"Yes, that's a good idea," Dolores agreed, slanting a look at her son.

"If Carlos hadn't suggested it, I was going to," Mindy whispered to Chelsea. "Let's find a ladies' room."

"Is Roberto feeling all right?" Chelsea asked as they walked to a small room off the entry.

"As far as I know. Why?"

"He seems so tense."

"I didn't notice." Mindy went into the bathroom.

Chelsea combed her hair while she waited, dismissing her uneasiness. Roberto always disturbed her, in one way or another. Today was bound to be even worse.

Mindy returned, fastening her belt. "I feel better now."

"Ready to walk down the aisle another couple of dozen times?" Chelsea smiled.

"Dolores is a real perfectionist, isn't she?"

"You'll be grateful when everything goes off without a hitch on the big day."

"I guess so." Mindy leaned forward to look in the mirror while reaching for her purse. When it fell to the floor she gave an exclamation of annoyance that turned to dismay. Her jeans had ripped up the back when she bent over.

Chelsea inspected the split seam. "You really did a number on yourself. Why do you have to wear your jeans so tight?"

"This is no time for twenty questions. What am I going to do?"

"Well, if I can locate about a dozen safety pins, I can keep you decent."

"Forget it. I'm not walking down the aisle with everybody's eyes riveted on my rear."

"What's the alternative?"

"I'll just have to go back to the house and change."

"I guess that makes better sense," Chelsea conceded.

"Tell everyone I'll be back as soon as I can."

Dolores looked harried when Chelsea conveyed the news. "Oh dear. Father Cuervas has to leave in fifteen minutes, and things aren't going at all as I hoped."

"The next rehearsal will be smoother," Chelsea soothed.

"It's so difficult to get everyone together." Dolores gazed speculatively at her. "Let's run through it one more time. You can stand in for Mindy."

"I couldn't possibly!" The very idea upset Chelsea.

"I know this is getting tedious, dear, but you'd be doing your sister a favor."

"*She's* the one who needs to rehearse."

"Actually, Mindy knows her part better than the men. This sort of thing seems to come naturally to women." Without giving Chelsea a chance to protest further, she clapped her hands. "All right, everybody, we're ready." As the music started she nodded to Rosa.

Chelsea watched the others go through their stylized motions. But when her turn came, she was frozen in place. A little push from Dolores propelled her down the aisle where Roberto waited at the altar. Chelsea was acutely aware of the stunned look on his face. She had to force herself to move with measured steps so this torture wouldn't have to be repeated. His eyes remained on her all the way down the aisle.

When she reached him, Chelsea said haltingly, "Mindy had to leave for a few minutes. I'm taking her place."

The priest was only anxious to finish up. "Join hands please," he instructed.

Chelsea's cold hand was enveloped by Roberto's warm one. He continued to stare at her while the priest gave a capsule version of the marriage ceremony.

"This is where where I will say, place the ring on her finger." The priest looked expectantly at the best man.

Ramón held the gold circlet on his outstretched palm, but he had to nudge Roberto to get his attention. Roberto stared at the ring for a moment, then slipped it on the third finger of Chelsea's left hand, gazing at her with an unfathomable expression.

She couldn't meet his eyes. A feeling of horror chilled her as she realized why the thought of this moment had panicked her. She wanted it to be real, not make-believe. She'd suppressed the knowledge, refused to admit even the possibility, but it was true. She was in love with Roberto—her sister's fiancé.

Gradually the world stopped spinning and the priest's words penetrated. "Very good. Now I'll tell you to kiss the bride."

Chelsea wanted to stiffen away, but she was powerless to resist when Roberto slipped his arm round her waist. She turned toward him like a flower to the sun, and her body was pliant in his arms.

Almost in slow motion, Roberto's head descended to hers. His warm breath feathered her parted lips and her lashes fluttered down in anticipation. Father Cuervas broke the spell.

"You don't have to rehearse the kiss." He chuckled. "Especially since the *señorita* is only a substitute."

Chelsea drew in her breath and quickly removed the ring. She handed it back to Roberto, steeling herself not to flinch when their fingers touched.

"I never knew getting married was such hard work," she commented in a brittle voice. "I'm glad it's Mindy and not me."

"You'll change your mind when the right man comes along." The priest gave her a benevolent smile. "Now, if you'll all excuse me, I have another commitment."

As everyone started to mill around, Roberto turned on Chelsea. "Whose idea was this little charade?" he demanded. "Yours or Mindy's?"

"Don't bother to thank me," she answered tautly. "I was happy to step in."

"I'll just bet you were," he muttered. "Anything to make my life miserable."

"Listen to me, pal! I was simply doing your mother a favor. I don't care if your wedding gets the blooper-of-the-year award."

Chelsea's angry response covered profound misery. It was bad enough to be riddled with guilt over her treacherous feelings. But Roberto's annoyance at her for taking Mindy's place added salt to the wound. The fact that he wasn't similarly affected by her should have been a relief, but it wasn't.

Carlos stepped in before the argument could escalate. "I think our efforts deserve a drink." He put his arm around Chelsea's stiff shoulders and led her toward the door.

When they were outside the church she said, "I don't really want a drink, but thanks for getting me out of there. I'd just about had it!"

"I could tell. Does a stroll around the square appeal to you?"

"Yes, I'd like that."

After they'd walked silently for a few moments, Carlos remarked casually, "It's curious the way wedding preparations tend to make people tense."

"I'm sorry for making a scene," Chelsea said in a subdued voice.

"That was only a minor flare-up. Roberto is the one who was ungracious."

"It's a good thing I live thousands of miles away. We don't get along very well."

"You haven't reconciled yourself to their marriage, have you?"

"I can't say I approve, but I've accepted it."

"Are you sure?" Carlos asked quietly.

She gave him a startled look. "What makes you doubt it?"

"You're not good at concealing things. If I can sense that you have reservations, Roberto certainly can, too. Maybe that's why sparks fly when you're together."

"I haven't voiced my objections lately. Roberto simply takes offense at everything I do or say. He just doesn't like me."

"I'm sure you're wrong. In fact, there have been times when—"

"When what?" she prompted after he didn't continue.

Carlos shrugged. "It isn't important. I'm undoubtedly wrong. I should stop trying to figure Roberto out. He's a very complex man."

"That's a polite term for autocratic, ill-tempered and infuriating," Chelsea said grimly.

"Maybe it *is* a good thing you'll have an ocean between you." He laughed.

"That doesn't help right now. I dread having to spend the evening with him, in the mood he's in."

"I can solve that problem easily. Have dinner with me, just the two of us."

"You're very kind, but I don't want to saddle you with my problems."

"I'm not being kind. I'd really like to be with you."

"If you're sure," she said hesitantly. "It would be a blessing to get away from here for a while."

"Consider yourself blessed. My car is parked in front of the rectory."

"I'll have to go back to the house first to change."

"If you like, although you look charming just the way you are."

Unlike Mindy, Chelsea had dressed for the rehearsal. She was wearing a soft yellow silk dress with a full skirt. The sleeveless scoop-neck top was smocked, and the waist was cinched in by a wide white belt that matched her high-heeled sandals. She would have chosen something more sophisticated for a dinner date, but the chance to make a quick exit from Ronda was more attractive.

"I'll tell Dolores and leave word for Mindy," she said.

When they reached the church, Mindy had already returned. After Chelsea told her where she was going, Mindy said, "That sounds like fun. Can Roberto and I come, too?"

"No, you may not." Carlos's smile and teasing tone took the sting out of his refusal. "When a man has a date with a beautiful woman, he wants to be alone with her."

"I guess I can understand that, but no funny business." Mindy grinned.

Carlos's eyes glinted with amusement. "I assure you my actions won't be designed to provoke laughter."

"I think you latched onto a live one," Mindy told Chelsea. "Just promise you won't talk stocks-and-bonds and ruin everything."

"Goodbye, little sister," Chelsea said firmly.

Carlos was a delightful and amusing companion. In spite of her troubles, Chelsea found she was enjoying herself. His attention was flattering and he made her laugh.

When they reached Marbella, Carlos said, "Would you mind if we stopped off at my apartment first so I can pick up my phone messages? I've been out of touch all day."

"I don't mind at all."

It was funny, Chelsea reflected. If Miguel had suggested the same thing, she would have vetoed the idea emphatically. But Carlos didn't have to resort to deviousness to try to seduce a woman. He could accomplish that with his considerable charm. Carlos was not only attractive, he was intelligent and possessed magnetism as well. Women must find him irresistible.

So why didn't she feel the leaping excitement that someone special brings? Chelsea wondered somberly. Why did it have to be Roberto who made her joyous and miserable at the same time?

"Well, here we are." Carlos opened the front door of his apartment. "I'll fix you a drink and then, if you'll excuse me, I'll turn on my answering machine."

"Go ahead. I'll wait and have a drink with you when you're through."

"Can I get you the newspaper or a magazine?"

"No, I'll just look out at the view and unwind."

He patted her hand. "Don't let Roberto get to you. He's all the things you said, but he's also the finest man you'll ever meet. You'll learn to love him."

Chelsea stared out at a brightly lit ship chugging out of the harbor like a fluorescent bug skimming the dark water. Love wasn't a fatal disease, she told herself—it just felt like one. But she'd recover. And no one would ever know she'd been stricken.

Carlos's messages went on and on. Small beeps punctuated men's and women's voices. He really did have a wide circle of acquaintances.

He returned full of apologies. "I'm sorry. Most of the calls could have waited, but a few were important."

"That's perfectly all right," Chelsea assured him.

"You're very understanding."

"Perhaps because I'm a working woman. I'm a slave to the telephone, too. Especially in my business."

"Do you actually understand all those numbers and symbols on the stock-market pages?" he asked curiously.

She laughed. "I really do, but Mindy told me not to talk about it. She says real men aren't interested."

Carlos smiled. "What's her definition of a real man?"

"Nothing I'd care to discuss in mixed company."

He shook his head in rueful amusement. "I hope this doesn't make me sound ancient, but these kids today are shortchanging themselves. They know everything about sex and nothing about romance."

"Like Dawn." Chelsea nodded. "I don't suppose any of those calls pertained to her, or you would have told me."

Carlos walked over to a built-in bar and began to mix them each a drink. "If her boyfriend was a big-time operator it would be relatively simple to locate him. But the Costa del Sol is full of youngsters living on the fringes."

"You think it's hopeless?" she asked soberly.

"Not at all. I have a lot of people looking for her." He handed Chelsea a glass and sat down on the couch beside her. "But tonight you're only going to worry about enjoying yourself."

"That's easy." She smiled at him gratefully. "I already am."

Chelsea wasn't merely being polite. It was pleasurable to have a drink in Carlos's luxurious apartment and bask in his unobtrusive admiration.

Later they went to an elegant restaurant for a delicious dinner. People were waiting in the crowded bar, but the maître d' greeted Carlos like a cherished guest. They were led to a choice table, although he could scarcely have made a reservation.

"You're a good man to know," Chelsea remarked.

"If you ate out as much as I do, you'd get preferential treatment, too," he answered deprecatingly.

Chelsea knew that wasn't so, but she didn't make him uncomfortable by pursuing the subject. "You don't have to tell me how often you eat out. The reason you don't have mice in your apartment is because they all died of malnutrition."

"You made a gourmet meal out of the contents of my refrigerator," he protested.

"Only because I'm a genius."

"I guessed that the minute I saw you."

"It's nice to be appreciated." She smiled.

"I'm sure you get lots of that."

"Guess again," she answered wryly.

"You must be very fussy—as you deserve to be." Carlos looked at her consideringly. "Hasn't any man ever tempted you to make a commitment?"

Chelsea concentrated on the bread crumbs she was rolling into a ball. "I guess I'm hopeless." She glanced up. "How about you. How have you managed to escape unscathed?"

"Not by choice. Every rational person wants love, but it's hard to find."

"The kids don't seem to have that trouble. They fall in and out of love every week."

"That isn't for me, and I don't think it's for you, either."

"No," she answered sadly.

''Perhaps we're overlooking a possibility that's right under our noses.'' His eyes wandered over her lovely face.

''I'm not a good prospect, Carlos,'' she said gently. ''I'll be going home soon, and we probably won't ever see each other again.''

''I'd be very sorry to believe that.''

''You're just feeling a little insecure because Roberto's taking the leap and you're still clinging to the cliff,'' she teased.

''You could be right.'' He relaxed in his chair. ''But if *your* grip on the mountain ever loosens, keep me in mind.''

''I can't think of anyone I'd rather call,'' she answered sincerely.

''Well, in the meantime, how would you like to go dancing?''

They went to several nightclubs, and at each one people gathered at their table. The time passed swiftly for Chelsea, between dancing and interesting conversation.

Their last stop was the disco Carlos owned, a lively, noisy club filled with a diverse crowd. The dance floor was packed and the noise level was horrendous. When Carlos tried to tell her something, Chelsea had to ask him twice to repeat it. Taking her by the hand, he led her to a flight of stairs next to the bar.

Carlos's office on the second floor was relatively quiet after the din downstairs. It was also luxuriously furnished, more like a living room than a place of business, except for the desk and filing cabinets.

''Is this better?'' he asked.

''Much. I couldn't hear a word you were saying.'' She glanced around at the thick carpeting and deep, wide couch. ''What a lovely room. It's like a home away from home.''

"I spend so much time here that I decided I might as well be comfortable. If you'll excuse me for a few minutes, I have to speak to my manager. And then I guess I'd better take you home."

Chelsea glanced at her watch and gasped. "I had no idea it was so late!"

"That's a compliment. It means you enjoyed yourself."

"Tremendously."

"I did, too." He smiled. "There are some magazines on the table, but I won't be long. We'll leave as soon as I return."

"If only Ronda wasn't so far. I hate to make you take that long trip up the mountain and back at his hour," she fretted.

"Tonight was worth it," he assured her.

"You're very gallant, but I still feel guilty. You won't get home until almost daylight."

"I honestly don't mind, but if it really bothers you, you can stay at my apartment overnight. I'll take you home in the morning."

"Oh…well…I don't think that would be such a good idea."

"I was offering you the guest room," he said gently.

"I knew that," she answered quickly.

"Not that I wouldn't prefer a more romantic arrangement," he teased. "I've never entertained such a beautiful woman so platonically."

"That's just the point, Carlos. Nobody would believe it. I know you're sincere in your offer, but I wouldn't want Dolores and the rest to get the wrong idea."

"That would bother you? Even though it wouldn't be true, we *are* adults."

"Who fell into bed on their first date? What does that do for my image?"

"I see what you mean. All right, I have another suggestion. You stay in the guest room and I'll sleep here."

"I couldn't ask you to sleep on a couch," she objected.

"I've done it many times when I've worked late. It's very comfortable."

"I have a better idea. *I'll* sleep here."

"Chelsea, my sweet, if we keep arguing over logistics, morning will be here and *neither* of us will get any sleep. It's all settled," he said firmly.

When they reached Carlos's apartment, he gave Chelsea a new toothbrush and the top of a pair of his pajamas. "Is there anything else I can get for you before I leave?" he asked.

"I can't think of anything." She walked him to the front door. "It's been a wonderful evening. The best time I've had since I came to Spain."

That was true. The time she spent with Roberto was always filled with excitement. Every nerve in her body came alive when she was with him. But guilt and frustration were the price she had to pay.

"We'll do it again soon," Carlos promised.

He leaned forward and kissed her cheek. When she smiled up at him, he curved one hand around the nape of her neck and kissed her on the lips. Chelsea didn't pull away, but she tensed unconsciously.

Carlos drew back immediately and patted her cheek. "Good night, Chelsea. I'll see you in the morning."

She went into the bedroom and got undressed, suddenly realizing how tired she was. It had been a long, enjoyable evening, thanks to Carlos. His admiration was soothing without being insistent, and he hadn't made her feel guilty for not responding to him. Carlos was too secure to take her rejection personally. Chelsea was smiling as she climbed into bed.

The strident ringing of the telephone shattered the silence of the dark bedroom. Chelsea surfaced from a deep sleep, reaching out blindly in the unfamiliar surroundings. Her fumbling hand knocked the phone to the floor. She reached down to retrieve it, only half-awake.

"Hello," she mumbled.

"Chelsea? Are you all right?"

"Yes, I just knocked the telephone off the nightstand. Roberto? Is that you?"

"I'm surprised you recognized my voice," he answered sarcastically.

"Is anything wrong?" Chelsea was gripped with sudden apprehension.

"Apparently not. I was worried when you didn't come home. I've been trying to locate you for hours."

Her tense body relaxed. "Is that all? I was out with Carlos. You knew that."

"You mean, I shouldn't have expected you to come home? You'll have to excuse me. I'd forgotten how persuasive he can be—if persuasion was called for."

"Just exactly what are you implying?" she asked angrily.

"Give my apologies to Carlos for calling at such an inopportune time."

"For your information, Carlos isn't—" Her words fell on empty air. Roberto had hung up.

Chelsea got out of bed and paced the floor furiously. Roberto's suspicions were all too obvious, but what right did he have to be annoyed? Her personal life had nothing to do with him. Why should he care if she did sleep with Carlos?

Chelsea got back into bed eventually, but she didn't go back to sleep for a long time.

Chelsea didn't tell Carlos about Roberto's phone call when he came over the next morning. She didn't want to cause a rift between the two men, nor did she want Carlos to tell Roberto the truth. He could think whatever he liked.

She declined Carlos's invitation to stop for breakfast. Knowing a confrontation with Roberto was inevitable, she wanted to get back and have it over with. When Carlos pulled up in front of the del Machado house, her nerves were on red alert.

He didn't seem to notice. "Wasn't this a better idea than dragging up here in the middle of the night?" he asked as he opened the car door for her. "This way, we both got a good night's sleep."

She hoped *he* had, anyway. "Thanks for all your hospitality, Carlos."

"*De nada*. Say hello to the family for me."

"Would you like to come in?" She was almost forced to ask.

"Not this time." He got back into the car and waved. "See you soon."

Chelsea didn't have long to be apprehensive. Roberto pounced on her as soon as she was inside the front door, and it was quite evident that his temper hadn't improved.

"This is a pleasant surprise." His voice dripped with acid, belying the words. "I didn't expect you out of bed this early."

Her temper rose to match his, but she decided to use restraint. "Why does that surprise you?"

"I know what a strenuous evening you must have had," he sneered.

Chelsea gave up on restraint. "That's your whole problem. You think you know everything, but you don't."

"I'm well acquainted with the way Carlos operates," he said grimly.

"He was a perfect gentleman. I had a marvelous time."

Roberto gave a bark of cynical laughter. "I'm not surprised. He seldom gets complaints."

"You could learn a lot from Carlos," she said defiantly, refusing to set the record straight.

Roberto moved closer, menacing her with his taut body. "Shouldn't you have all the evidence before you make comparisons?"

"That won't be—" She stopped as Luis approached them.

"Will you and the *señorita* want breakfast, *señor?*" he asked.

"Not right now," Roberto answered without consulting her.

"*Sí, señor.*" After a look at his employer's tight-lipped face, Luis beat a hasty retreat.

Chelsea resumed hostilities as soon as they were alone again. "You have no right to subject me to this inquisition."

"As long as you're under my roof I'm responsible for you," he answered stiffly.

"I wasn't under your roof," she taunted.

"I'm well aware of that." His face darkened. "My error was in being concerned about you."

Chelsea's anger evaporated somewhat. Perhaps staying out all night *had* been thoughtless. "I would have called to say I wasn't coming home, but it was too late by the time I decided to stay over."

"Was there ever any doubt?"

Her jaw clenched. "Not in your mind, anyway."

Dolores came into the hall scanning some papers in her hand. "Roberto would you look into this bill from the plumber? It seems excessive." She glanced up and saw Chelsea for the first time. "Good morning, my dear. Did you sleep well?"

It was clear her question was merely a polite inquiry to a guest. Dolores obviously had no idea that Chelsea was just getting home.

"I slept very well, thank you," Chelsea answered with a challenging look at Roberto.

"That's nice." Dolores handed her son a piece of paper before returning to her office.

Chelsea decided nothing would be gained by prolonging the argument with Roberto. She turned toward the stairs, but he stopped her.

"We haven't finished our discussion," he said coldly.

"We have as far as I'm concerned. You might be my host, but you're not my keeper. I'm sorry if I worried you by staying out all night, but your reaction is out of all proportion to my supposed crime."

"Why did you have to pick Carlos?" he asked in a low voice.

"Would you rather I chose your cousin, Miguel?"

He advanced on her furiously. "I ought to—"

Once again Luis interrupted them, this time with trepidation. "There is a telephone call for you, *señor*."

"Tell them I'll call back," Roberto grated. "This place is worse than an airline terminal," he muttered between clenched teeth. Clamping his fingers around Chelsea's wrist in a vise-like grip, he jerked her toward the staircase.

"What do you think you're doing?" she demanded. "Let go of me this instant!"

He continued to drag her up the steps without bothering to answer. At the top of the stairs he turned right, toward the wing of the house where the master bedroom was located.

"Where are you taking me?" Chelsea asked, although she already guessed.

Roberto pulled her inside his room and slammed the door shut. "Maybe now we can talk without interruption."

"We have nothing more to say to each other." She tried to brush by him, but he held her by the upper arms.

"You think you can torment me, and then just walk away?" His grip tightened almost painfully. "Do you know what I went through last night, picturing you in Carlos's arms?"

Chelsea's breath caught in her throat. "Why would you care?"

"I know I don't have a right to," he groaned. "I've told myself often enough, but you're like a fever in my blood."

"Roberto, no," she whispered.

He drew her toward him for an electrifying moment. Then her words penetrated and he turned away. "Forgive me. I guess I went a little crazy for a minute. I don't blame you for despising me."

"I don't hate you," she said in a choked voice. "I understand."

"How can you, when *I* don't even understand? I've always prided myself on being an honorable man, but all I can think of, night and day, is making love to you. I want to kiss your breasts and the soft skin behind your knees. I want to explore all the secret places that bring you pleasure."

Chelsea could almost feel his seductive hands arousing her unbearably. "You musn't say things like that," she murmured desperately.

Her plea didn't seem to penetrate. "I've dreamed of possessing you completely, of losing myself in your beautiful body and bringing us both the greatest joy a man and woman can share." His hand curved around her neck and his thumb circled the throbbing pulse in her throat. "Now you know why I went through hell last night."

Chelsea gazed up at him steadily. "Carlos didn't stay with me. He slept in his office."

Roberto's hand fell away. "You don't have to lie to me. It only makes me more ashamed. Carlos has a right to make love to you. I don't."

"That's true, but it didn't happen."

"Are you telling me the truth?" he asked, examining her face intently.

"Why would I lie?"

"I don't know." He sighed. "I don't know anything anymore."

Chelsea hesitated, wanting to be sure of her motives before pointing out what had to be said. Roberto was very graphic about wanting her. He didn't mention love, but even if desire was all he felt, that was reason enough for calling off the marriage. Chelsea knew it wasn't self-interest that prompted her. There could never be anything between herself and Roberto. Not at her sister's expense.

"Under the circumstances, you can't go ahead with the wedding," she said quietly.

"I understand your revulsion, but I can only assure you that nothing like this will ever happen again."

"I believe you, but that's not the important thing. Mindy deserves a man who loves her wholeheartedly."

"I told you before, I intend to do everything in my power to make her happy," he answered tonelessly.

"Why are you so adamant?" Chelsea exclaimed in frustration.

"I have no choice," he said simply. "I made a promise."

"She'd release you from it if she knew all the facts."

"I hope you won't feel obligated to tell her."

"How can I? You have me neatly boxed in."

Roberto smiled without humor. "You have a lot of company."

"Isn't there anything I can do to change your mind?" she asked without any real hope.

"You've already created havoc in my life. Isn't that enough?"

"What do you think you've done to mine?" she asked sadly.

He touched her hair so lightly that it was like a soft breeze. "I wish I could have played some part in your life."

So do I, Chelsea answered silently. No purpose would be served by telling Roberto she was in love with him. The knowledge would only make it harder for both of them.

"I can't expect you to forget what happened today, or even to forgive me." He put his hand on the doorknob. "All I can do is apologize."

What could she say? That it didn't matter? That would be ludicrous! But Chelsea couldn't bear to see this strong man humbled.

"Nothing happened between us," she said gently. "I provoked you into saying things you didn't really mean."

"You're very kind." Powerful emotions warred on his face as he stared at her. Then he opened the door. "Goodbye, Chelsea."

It was a strange thing to say when she was only going to her room, but Chelsea knew what he meant.

Chapter Eight

Mindy's bedroom door was closed when Chelsea passed it on the way to her own room. She thanked heaven for small favors, at least. After the traumatic scene with Roberto, she couldn't have faced her sister.

Chelsea's nerves were wound tightly as she changed clothes. Could she and Roberto possibly act normally toward each other from now on? Wouldn't the underlying tension between them be obvious? Even if Mindy failed to notice, Dolores was an intelligent, perceptive woman. Chelsea felt disaster hovering over her head. When a knock sounded on the door, she jumped visibly.

"A telephone call for you, *señorita*." Luis's words were muffled through the heavy door.

Her mother's voice greeted Chelsea, presaging a further ordeal. "Will you kindly tell me what's going on there?" Mrs. Claiborne demanded. "Why haven't I heard from you?"

"There really hasn't been anything to tell," Chelsea answered.

"What have you been doing all this time?"

"Oh, well, you know," Chelsea answered weakly.

"No, I *don't* know. That's what I'm trying to find out. What's happened to you, Chelsea? You don't even sound like the same person."

Chelsea gripped the phone. "We must have a bad connection."

"I can hear you perfectly," Doris declared. "You aren't telling me anything, though. Haven't you made any headway with Mindy?"

"It's a lost cause, believe me. You'll just have to resign yourself, Mother. *I* have." Chelsea closed her eyes briefly.

Doris sighed. "Well, tell me about the wedding. Will it at least be held in a church?"

"A very beautiful one. You'd be pleased."

"Don't overdo it," Doris said dryly. "How about Mindy's trousseau? You'll have to take her shopping. I don't want those people to think she comes from a family that doesn't know what's expected of them. And what about her wedding gown?"

"She's going to wear Roberto's grandmother's gown. I haven't seen it, but Mindy says it's lovely."

Doris started to sniffle. "My little girl is getting married, and I won't be there to see it."

"I'll take pictures," Chelsea promised. "Or at least, I'll get someone to do it. I'm going to be Mindy's maid of honor."

"Naturally." Doris's tears dried as she became interested in the arrangements. "Was Dawn disappointed that Mindy didn't choose her?"

"No, she, uh . . . no."

"That's good. A sister *should* take precedence, but sometimes these things cause such hard feelings. What color are your gowns?"

"Mine will be apricot. But that isn't important. I want to hear about Dad." Chelsea tried to head off the questions about Dawn.

"He's doing very well. He said to send you both his love." Doris returned to the previous subject like a homing pigeon. "I hope Dawn isn't planning to wear apricot, too. She's an attractive enough girl, but her skin *is* rather sallow. That color would make her look jaundiced."

"Don't worry about it, Mother."

Doris was reminded of her grievances. "I want my daughter's wedding to be perfect, even if I wasn't asked to take part. What color is Dawn wearing?"

Chelsea gave up hope of evading the issue. "She won't be in the wedding party."

"Why not? She's Mindy's best friend. Did they have an argument?"

Chelsea resisted the urge to take the easy way out. It was too risky, though, since she would have to tell her mother the truth if Carlos struck out. "I haven't been able to locate Dawn. She left the rooming house where she was staying, and the landlady doesn't have a forwarding address for her." Chelsea braced herself for the inquisition that she knew was coming.

"I told *you* that, days ago! What have you done to find her?"

"I spoke to one of her friends. She said Dawn had an argument with some of the other kids. That's why she left so abruptly."

"I don't care why she left, I'm only interested in where she is now."

"I am, too," Chelsea answered soberly.

Doris picked up on the tone of her voice. "Is there something you aren't telling me, Chelsea?" she asked sharply.

"Why would you think that?" Chelsea countered.

"I can't imagine, but you're being very evasive. Something is going on there, and I want to know what it is. Let me speak to Mindy."

"She can't tell you any more than I already have," Chelsea said quickly.

"We'll see. Call her to the phone. I want to talk to her anyway."

Chelsea knew it was useless to argue. She could almost see her mother's determined expression. "All right, I'll have to call you back."

"No, I'll stay on the line."

"That's foolish, Mother. Mindy sleeps late. I might have to get her out of bed."

"I'll wait. Stop wasting time and go get your sister."

Chelsea had to give in. She sped into the hall and knocked urgently on Mindy's door. She had only a few moments to warn her sister to be circumspect. When her knock wasn't answered, Chelsea went inside. Mindy wasn't in bed. She was in the bathroom being violently ill.

Chelsea rushed over to her. "Why didn't you call me when you felt sick?" she gasped.

Mindy merely groaned before retching again.

Chelsea hated to leave her, but Doris was waiting. She hurried back to the phone, wondering what excuse to give. Her mother was already suspicious.

"Mindy isn't in her room," Chelsea said breathlessly. "She must have gotten up early for once. I'll have to go look for her."

"This is very strange, Chelsea. I'm getting the feeling that you don't want me to talk to Mindy."

"That's ridiculous, Mother! I can't help it if she's not there. I don't keep track of her every minute." Chelsea's nerves were ready to snap. "I'll have her call you as soon as possible."

By the time she raced back to her sister, Mindy was in bed. Her face was very pale, and a fine sheen of perspiration dewed her forehead.

"This time you're not going to talk me out of it," Chelsea declared. "I'm calling a doctor."

"Don't bother," Mindy answered wearily. "I've already seen one."

"When?" Chelsea gave her a startled look. "You didn't tell me."

"I wouldn't have now, but I know you're not going to let up."

Chelsea's chest felt tight with dread. "Why did you go to a doctor? What's wrong with you?"

"I'm pregnant."

The words dropped like stones in a pond, distorting the calm surface. Chelsea stared at her sister, forced to face what she'd really known all along. Mindy's bouts of sickness, her excessive need for sleep, the wedding that had been arranged so hastily. All these things together were such obvious clues. But Chelsea hadn't wanted to believe it. She'd denied the possibility because she didn't want it to be true.

"Don't look at me like that," Mindy said peevishly. "It happens all the time."

"I'm sorry. I didn't mean to look disapproving."

"I guess it was kind of a shock, but at least you know now. It's sort of a relief."

"Why didn't you tell me right away?" Chelsea asked quietly.

"I figured you'd really have it in for Roberto. You were dead set against our marriage even before you knew about the baby."

"I still am. You don't have to get married. Come home with me. We'll all support you in every way."

"Can you give my baby a father?"

"That isn't important nowadays. A lot of children grow up happily in single-parent homes," Chelsea told her earnestly. "Your child will have plenty of love. That's what really counts."

"I want my baby to have his father's name."

"That shouldn't be a problem. Roberto has acknowledged paternity."

"Do you honestly think he'd give it up? Especially if it's a boy."

Chelsea's jaw tightened. "He doesn't have any choice."

"I wouldn't like to challenge him. Fortunately it won't come to that. We're getting married on schedule."

Chelsea gazed at her sister, wondering how to convince her that great sex wasn't enough to make a marriage work. Roberto was undoubtedly fantastic in bed, so it was understandable that Mindy would be dazzled by his expertise. Women a lot more sophisticated than she had fallen under his spell, Chelsea thought grimly. Mindy's infatuation was difficult enough to combat, without the added complication of her pregnancy. But Chelsea had to try.

"You've told me you want your baby to have a name," she said slowly. "Can you truthfully tell me you're not marrying Roberto for that reason alone? I'm waiting to hear you say you love him."

"Everybody makes such a big deal about love," Mindy answered impatiently. "It's just a word. Men say it all the time to get what they want."

"Okay, you learned the hard way. That doesn't mean you have to let one mistake ruin your life."

"Give it a rest, Chelsea. I feel rotten and I want to go back to sleep."

"Not till we get this settled. I can't let you go through with this marriage."

"You can't stop me." Mindy turned over and buried her head under the pillow.

Chelsea stood and gazed down at her, accepting defeat for the moment. Maybe she couldn't change Mindy's mind, but Roberto was another story. She had a few choice things to say to him, Chelsea thought darkly.

Luis told Chelsea that Roberto was in his office, a room she hadn't seen before. He directed her to the back of the house.

Unlike Dolores's plush sitting-room combination, Roberto's office was all business. Papers littered a large desk and file cabinets bulged with manila folders. He was talking on the telephone, issuing orders at a rapid clip.

Chelsea marched up to the desk and stood over him. He stopped in mid-sentence when he glanced up and saw her. Noting the expression on her face, he ended his conversation abruptly.

"I want to talk to you," she said in a clipped voice.

"Is it really necessary?" he asked quietly. "What more is there to say?"

"Quite a lot. Why don't you start by telling me how you seduced my sister?"

Roberto paled under his tan. "Did Mindy say that?"

"How long did you think you could keep it a secret?" Chelsea asked scornfully.

"Exactly what did she tell you?"

"She spared me the sordid details, if that's what you're asking. Not that I needed them. You gave me a few samples of the way you operate, remember?"

"I've apologized for that."

Chelsea waved that aside. "At least I was mature enough to think clearly. How could you seduce an impressionable young girl who didn't even have enough experience to take precautions?"

Deep lines were carved in Roberto's face. "I deeply regret that."

"Only because you feel you have to marry her."

"Doesn't that make me a little less reprehensible?"

"Not in the slightest. I might feel kindlier toward you if you'd fallen in love with Mindy, but we both know that wasn't the case. She simply happened to be there when you were feeling amorous and your regular playmates weren't around."

"That wasn't the way it happened," he said in a low voice.

"You expect me to belive you love her?"

He hesitated for a moment. "There are many ways to love someone."

"Oh, please! Don't insult my intelligence. Mindy even admitted she fell for a classic male line."

"Did she tell you I said I loved her?" Roberto asked intently.

"She discovered the hard way that men will say whatever it takes to get a woman into bed."

"Sometimes women have to share the blame." He walked restlessly to the window and stared out. "They're too willing to settle for instant gratification."

"Are you trying to say it was my sister's fault?" Chelsea asked indignantly.

"The time for placing blame is over," he answered in a tired voice. "It happened."

"No! I won't let you get away with weaseling out of the responsibility. You were the one who should have called a halt like you did—"

"With you?" He finished her sentence when she came to an abrupt halt.

Chelsea's color rose at the memory of that heated encounter in Roberto's bedroom, but she held her chin high. "I realize now that you were only playing games with me," she said bitterly.

He spread his hands in a gesture of helplessness. "How can I defend myself? I'm damned whether I agree or disagree."

"It doesn't matter. I wouldn't believe a word that came out of your mouth."

"That's not fair. I might have been guilty of evasion with you, but not of lying."

"Oh, really? How about telling me you'd never had sex with Mindy?"

Roberto stared back at her without expression. "Nothing I say would change your opinion of me, so it's futile to try."

"That's a cop-out. You have no excuse."

"Can we just leave it at that? You've made your feelings clear. I don't see what's to be gained by further recriminations."

"We have one more thing to settle, and then I'd be more than happy to end this conversation. I'm sure you realize the wedding is off."

"Is that Mindy's decision or yours?" he asked evenly.

Chelsea's only hope was to get Roberto to back out of the marriage. "She doesn't love you," she answered evasively.

"That doesn't answer my question."

"Being pregnant isn't enough reason to get married," Chelsea said stubbornly.

"The baby is a del Machado." Roberto's voice was austere. "It will bear that name."

"I don't regard it as highly as you do, but the child can still have your name."

"Not legally."

"What difference does that make? We don't want anything from you. You should be relieved. You won't even have to pay child support."

Roberto's eyes glittered with anger. "Whatever else you think of me, I don't deserve that."

Chelsea realized she was being unfair. "All right, you've been generous, but it's no longer necessary. We can take care of Mindy's baby. The child will be much better off growing up among our family and friends. All it would have here is a legal, but reluctant, father."

"You don't think my family has love to give?" he demanded.

"I suppose so, but *you* don't," she said bluntly.

He folded his arms and looked at her dispassionately. "I wish I had your omniscience. You're both judge and jury. You know exactly what happened and how it should be resolved."

"I'm not interested in being impartial. I want what's best for my sister."

"Regardless of her wishes in the matter?"

"You've dominated her so completely that she can't think straight."

"Mindy?" Roberto's laughter was his first light-hearted emotion.

"She isn't as secure as she appears," Chelsea said defensively. "The prospect of being an unwed mother must seem frightening to her."

"You think that's why she's marrying me?"

"I'm sure of it."

"You don't give your sister enough credit. On the surface she appears to be a typical teenager, interested only in having a good time. Mindy may have been guilty of errors in judgement, but she's a very caring human being. I respect her deeply and I suggest that you do, too."

Chelsea was impressed by Roberto's quiet words. Was his condemnation of her valid? Had she jumped to conclusions without knowing all the facts? Her experience with love had meant fireworks and roller-coaster emotions, but maybe she was the naive one. Perhaps there were other kinds of love that built slowly out of shared experiences—like a baby. Mindy and Roberto both wanted to get married. Did she have the right to interfere?

"If Mindy tells me she's changed her mind, I'll release her," Roberto said. "Otherwise, the marriage will proceed as planned."

His statement was measured, not exulting over her defeat, merely stating a fact. It was the sadness in the depths of his eyes that disturbed Chelsea. After an indecisive moment she went to the door without further argument.

Chelsea left the house, needing to be by herself. She'd made a terrible mess of things. What had happened to the competent, self-assured woman who'd come here a week ago?

Had it only been a week? How could her entire life have changed so drastically in such a short time? And what about Mindy? How would her life turn out?

Chelsea wandered blindly through the winding streets with no destination in mind. She was really trying to find her way back to normality, an impossible task.

After walking until her legs protested, she reached a pretty little square. A tinkling fountain gave an illusion of coolness, and a stone bench looked very inviting. Chelsea sank down on it to rest her weary body.

Her thoughts were so somber that she tried to banish them by taking an interest in her surroundings, although those were commonplace. A few people were talking together and a shopkeeper was sweeping the sidewalk in front of his store. A young mother did provoke a faint smile when she grabbed her toddler as he was preparing to climb into the fountain.

A welcome diversion was a young man with a backpack. He sat down on the bench next to Chelsea and brushed the hair off his forehead. It was very warm in the direct sun.

Slanting an appreciative look at her, he said, *"¿Como está, señorita?"*

She grinned at his atrocious accent. "Just so-so. How are you?"

"You're an American," he exclaimed. "Boy, am I glad to meet you! Everybody's been laughing at my fractured Spanish."

"You didn't have to struggle with it. Most of the people here speak English."

"They sure kept it a secret." He held out his hand. "I'm Eric Hansen from Cleveland, Ohio."

She shook his hand. "Chelsea Claiborne. New York City."

"Are you here by yourself?" he asked hopefully.

Her smile dimmed. "For the present."

"Maybe we can join up. At home that would sound like a pickup attempt, but it's different here," he said hastily.

"In what way?" Chelsea asked with amusement. He was a few years older than Mindy, and as ingenuous as a puppy.

"Well, you know. We're expatriates in a foreign country. We have to stick together." He gave her an appealing look. "Besides, it's no fun doing things by yourself."

"Are you traveling alone?"

"I started out with a buddy. Our parents gave us the trip as a graduation present from college. But Dwight broke his ankle water-skiing, and he had to go home."

"That's too bad."

"Yeah, it was a real bummer. I decided to stay on, but it isn't the same. That's why I hoped we could go see a few places together." He produced a guide book. "Have you been to the bullring yet? It's the oldest existing one in the world?"

"I've heard about it, but I haven't been there. Let's make that our first stop."

Chelsea decided this was just what she needed, a respite from her insurmountable problems. Sightseeing with a stranger would allow her to forget them for a while, and Eric was a perfect choice.

The bullring in Ronda was housed in a whitewashed building with an imposing entry. "The balcony was forged in Ronda, using motifs of a bull," Eric read from his guidebook. "Inside are 176 columns and nearly five thousand seats."

"I suggest you put away the book and look for yourself," Chelsea told him.

"I guess it's a holdover from college." He grinned. "I expect to be quizzed afterward."

They climbed down the stone tiers into the arena itself, gazing at the royal box and the gate where the bulls entered the ring. Although the stands were deserted now, Chelsea could almost hear shouts from imaginary crowds and the thunder of hoofs in the sand under her feet.

"The bulls average eleven hundred pounds, and have to be two to four years old." Eric was reading from his guidebook again. "'A *corrida* consists of six bulls and three bullfighters.' I guess each toreador takes on two bulls. One at a time, naturally. Those bulls are killers."

"I don't like to think about that part of it," Chelsea said. "Let's go through the museum."

A small attached building was filled with outfits worn by famed matadors from the past. The costumes were called suits of lights, and they were lavishly decorated with embroidery and braid. Eric was fascinated by the wicked-looking swords, but Chelsea was more interested in the photographs of handsome matadors who had performed there. All had an autocratic tilt to their heads, and bold, dark eyes that stared back at her challengingly. Like Roberto.

"Let's go to the next place," she said abruptly.

Eric's list included a former private home that could be visited for a fee. It was of more interest to him than Chelsea, who had experienced this way of life personally.

"Wow, get a load of those paintings and tapestries." Eric was gazing around the large living room. "Those old Spanish dons sure knew how to live."

"They still do," Chelsea answered briefly.

"So I've heard. I'll bet those people don't have a care in the world."

"You have a lot to learn," she answered somberly.

The day passed pleasantly, except for the inevitable reminders of Roberto. But Chelsea managed to keep them at bay until it was time to return to the house.

Eric left her reluctantly. "I told this guy I'd meet him by the Santo Domingo convent. He's my ride back to Marbella, so I'd better be there."

"It's been fun, Eric. I'm glad I ran into you."

"It was a real stroke of luck for me. Maybe we can do it again. Can I call you?"

"My plans are uncertain," she said gently. "I might be going home soon."

Chelsea's excuse was meant to soften her refusal, but the idea must have been in the back of her mind. As she walked reluctantly toward the del Machado house it became the only sensible solution. Her mission had been a complete failure. There was nothing more she could do here but add to the existing tension.

Mindy would be upset, but it was for her good, too. After all that had happened, Chelsea knew relations between herself and Roberto would be ghastly. It would be a miracle if they managed to keep up appearances. How could she possibly take part in the wedding under those circumstances? Chelsea's mind was made up by the time she reached the house.

She braced herself for a confrontation with Roberto. He always seemed to be lurking around waiting for her. But even bad luck had to take a rest once in a while. Dolores greeted her instead.

"Oh, there you are, my dear. Mindy wondered what happened to you."

"Is she feeling better?"

Dolores looked concerned. "Was she ill?"

Chelsea gazed at the older woman in speculation. Did she know Mindy was pregnant or didn't she? That would be a potent reason for approving of Roberto's choice. Otherwise, his mother would be likely to have the same objections that Chelsea did. Dolores wasn't easy to read, however.

"Mindy didn't mention feeling poorly," the older woman commented.

"Then I guess she's all right," Chelsea answered cautiously.

"I'm sure of it, since she went shopping. Come out to the courtyard and I'll have Luis bring us something cool to drink. It's been frightfully hot today, hasn't it?"

Chelsea trailed after her hostess, trying to decide how to explain why she was leaving. She waited for an opening while Luis brought tall glasses of lemonade and Dolores chatted about trivial matters.

"The dressmaker called this morning," Dolores remarked finally. "She'll have your gown ready for a fitting the day after tomorrow. That's cutting it rather close, but you musn't worry. Señora Melendez is very reliable."

Chelsea seized her opportunity. "Actually, I'm quite embarrassed to have put you to so much trouble. It seems I won't be able to stay for the wedding after all. Something has come up."

"Oh, I'm so sorry. I hope it's nothing serious."

"Well, yes, in a way. One of my biggest clients wants to—uh—review his portfolio. I have to go back and switch some of his securities around."

That sounded lame even to Chelsea, but it was all she'd been able to think of. She'd considered using her father's health as an excuse, but that would worry Mindy needlessly. She would also call home and discover the lie.

"Surely that can wait one more week," Dolores protested.

"No, he's a very demanding man. He expects immediate service."

"Couldn't someone in your office take over for you?"

"It's a very large account. I wouldn't want to lose it." Chelsea felt herself flushing under the other woman's steady gaze.

"Mindy is going to be terribly disappointed."

"I am, too, but it can't be helped."

"Are you sure?" Dolores asked quietly. "I've realized from the first that you aren't in favor of this marriage."

"Are *you?*" Chelsea asked bluntly. She wouldn't have brought it up, but she was unwilling to back down once the other woman did.

"I have no say in the matter. My son and your sister have made a commitment."

"Do you think they're right for each other?"

"How can anyone else decide that?"

"I'm asking your opinion," Chelsea persisted.

Dolores refused to be pressured. "I want what's best for both of them," she answered simply.

"I'm only concerned about my sister," Chelsea said heatedly. "I'm sorry to be rude, but you're right about my reservations. I can't bear to see her ruin her life."

"You think Roberto will do that?"

Even in the midst of her anger, Chelsea had no desire to hurt his mother. She framed her reply carefully. "I think they have too many strikes against them. The age gap, the difference in their backgrounds."

"Those obstacles have been overcome before."

Only when the people involved loved each other, Chelsea wanted to shout. Instead, she sat quietly.

"Are those your only objections?" Dolores looked at her shrewdly.

"Aren't they enough?"

"I can think of something else that might trouble you." Dolores hesitated. "Roberto is a very charismatic man."

"Exactly what are you implying?" Chelsea asked tautly. "That *I'm* attracted to him? That my objections are personal?"

"Not at all. I merely wondered if you questioned whether he would remain faithful to your sister."

"Oh." Chelsea regretted her outburst. "Well, I'm sorry to have to say it to you, but yes, that *is* one of my concerns."

"You're so wrong. I'm not depicting my son as a saint. He has had friendships with many young women."

"I know. I've met some of them," Chelsea said ironically.

"Whether you approve or not, they were consenting relationships."

"How does that qualify him to be a good husband?"

"I'm trying to tell you that Roberto isn't a callow youth who needs to be reassured of his manhood. He's an experienced, sophisticated man. Once he has made a commitment, he will honor it."

"If he made it willingly."

"Do you really think Roberto could be pressured into anything this important?"

Chelsea still wasn't sure if Dolores was aware of the facts. The clues had been there for her to see, also, but she was Roberto's mother, after all. Perhaps in her idealized vision he could do no wrong. Chelsea didn't want to be the one to shatter her illusions.

"I wasn't suggesting that he was being pressured. I merely meant he might feel a certain obligation for some reason or other," Chelsea said vaguely. "Perhaps there are things you don't know."

Dolores sighed. "Don't open up Pandora's box, my dear. Accept what cannot be changed."

She did know! Maybe it was her idea in the first place. "Are you forcing Roberto to marry my sister?" Chelsea demanded. "Did you tell him it was the honorable thing to do?"

"I can assure you I played no part in his decision."

Chelsea looked at her uncertainly. Although Dolores's answer was uninflected, something about her tone of voice indicated disapproval. Was her intention just the opposite? Had she tried to change his mind and failed?

If so, Dolores had bowed to the inevitable with her usual grace. "Mindy was Roberto's choice, and we will welcome her into our family with great pleasure. I wish you could share it with us. Won't you reconsider and stay for the wedding?"

Mindy joined them in the courtyard before Chelsea was forced to answer. Her arms were full of packages and she was in high spirits. Chelsea marveled at her sister's ability to act perfectly normal.

"Where were you all afternoon?" she asked Chelsea.

"I went out."

"I *know* that. I looked all over for you. Roberto wasn't here, either. Did he take you sightseeing again?"

"No, I just wandered around town," Chelsea answered without elaborating.

"That doesn't sound like much fun. You should have waited for me. I did some major shopping."

"So I see. I'll tell Mother she doesn't have to be concerned about your trousseau."

"I didn't buy clothes. I bought presents." Mindy handed Dolores a beautifully wrapped box. "This is for putting up with me all the times I misbehaved."

"Dear child, that wasn't necessary," Dolores said fondly.

"I notice you aren't denying it." Mindy grinned. She placed another beribboned box on the glass table. "This one's for Roberto. I got him a silk shirt. They had a really nifty striped number, but I figured he wouldn't wear it, so I stuck to the tried and true."

"I'm sure he'll be very pleased," Dolores said.

"I also got some things for Luis and Consuela."

Chelsea was touched by her sister's generosity. Mindy might seem heedless and self-centered, but underneath was a warm, considerate human being.

"And this is for you." Mindy handed Chelsea the last of the packages.

"You didn't have to buy *me* anything," Chelsea protested.

"You've put up with me more than anybody." Mindy's eyes held hers, the first acknowledgement of that morning's revelation. Then she smiled. "Besides, the bride has to buy her maid of honor a gift."

"I don't think it's written in stone," Chelsea said.

"Okay, I just wanted to. Open your present," Mindy urged. "I got you something you can wear to the wedding."

Chelsea couldn't bear to dim her sister's happiness, so she opened the small square box. Inside was a lovely little filigree bracelet. Her throat felt tight as she gazed at it.

"Do you like it?" Mindy asked eagerly. "It's handmade by a craftsman here in Ronda."

"I love it," Chelsea answered.

"I thought that bronzy color would be neat with your gown. When are you having a fitting?"

"Well, I . . . it won't be ready to try on for a couple of days."

"The wedding is in a week!" Mindy exclaimed. "Maybe we'd better buy you a backup dress, just in case."

"Don't you think you should tell her?" Dolores asked Chelsea gently.

"Tell me what?" Mindy looked slightly apprehensive.

Chelsea knew she couldn't let her sister down. The wedding would be the culmination of a week of torture, but she'd get through it somehow. Mindy didn't deserve to be hurt any more.

"The dressmaker couldn't get quite enough material for the style I picked out, so we're modifying the design."

"Is that all? You had me worried for a minute. I thought there was a *real* problem."

Chelsea mustered a smile. "Nothing I can't handle."

"Your mother must be very proud of you girls," Dolores said softly. "I would be, if you were my daughters."

As Mindy was about to answer, she noticed Roberto inside the house. "Hi," she called. "Come out here and join us. I have something for you."

"Later," he replied curtly, continuing on his way.

"What's the matter with *him?*" Mindy asked indignantly. "He was grouchy this morning, too. I'm almost sorry I bought him a present."

"It's the heat," Dolores said placatingly. "I've never known it to be this oppressive."

The weather continued to be unusually sultry for the next couple of days. The clear blue sky had turned leaden, and no breeze stirred to give even temporary relief. The still atmosphere felt threatening, making everyone jumpy. As if something ominous were about to happen.

Chelsea's nerves were already wound tightly. She and Roberto tried to avoid each other as much as possible, but they couldn't be too obvious about it. The strain began to take its toll on both of them, and the wedding was still five agonizing days away.

Chelsea would have been willing to swear things couldn't possibly get any worse. But that was before the telephone call she received on Wednesday morning.

Chapter Nine

Carlos's voice on the phone couldn't have been more welcome. He was like a breath of fresh air, giving temporary relief from the miasma surrounding the del Machado household.

"I'm so glad to hear from you," Chelsea told him.

"That really makes my day," he answered gallantly.

"Isn't this a scorcher? I suppose it's cooler near the water where you are." She hoped he'd take the hint and invite her to Marbella. It would be heavenly to get away from the house for a while.

Carlos didn't oblige, however. "I'm afraid it's hot everywhere, but they say relief is on the way."

"That's good. We can use it." She tried to mask her disappointment.

He hesitated for a moment. "I have something to tell you. I'm afraid it's bad news."

Concern drove Chelsea's own problems out of her mind. "Is it about Dawn? Has something happened to her?"

"She's all right, but she's in a great deal of trouble."

"What do you mean?"

"Your friend is in jail."

"What for? What did she do?"

"The police are holding her on a drug charge."

"Oh, Lord, this is what I was afraid of," Chelsea groaned.

"I wish I could have located her sooner," Carlos said regretfully.

"I'm grateful for what you've done. I wouldn't even have known where she was if it hadn't been for you. Did they pick up her boyfriend, too?"

"I didn't find out too many of the details. Only that the police raided a party she was attending. I got a tip that an American girl had been one of the people arrested. I checked with the authorities, and it was Dawn."

"How does she look? Are they treating her all right?"

"I haven't seen her. I called you as soon as I verified the information."

"Will you do another favor for me? Could you find out how much her bail is and call me back? I want to come prepared."

"I don't know if she'll be allowed out on bail."

"But that's outrageous! She's just a dumb kid. She isn't a hardened criminal."

"Drug use is a serious offense in Spain."

"I have to get her out! Where is she being held?"

After Carlos had given her the name of the jail, he said, "I'd come and get you, but it will be faster if Roberto drives you down."

Chelsea was so upset that she didn't even flinch from the prospect of the long ride down the mountain with Roberto.

He was in his office, working at his desk. His expression was hooded when he glanced up and saw her, until he noticed her distress. "What's wrong, Chelsea?"

"It's Dawn. Carlos found her. At least he told me where she is." The whole story tumbled out in a rush.

Roberto frowned. "This is very serious."

"I know. Carlos said they might not grant bail, but I can't leave her in a jail cell! Will you drive me down there? Maybe if I talk to the police and explain that Dawn had never been in any trouble before, they'll be reasonable."

He shook his head slightly. "It isn't that simple."

"Please help me, Roberto," Chelsea pleaded. "I don't have anyone else to ask."

He rounded the desk and took both of her hands in his. "Of course I'll help. Did you have any doubt?"

She gazed up at him, feeling his strength flowing into her, calming her panic. No, she never had any doubt. Roberto was two men. One might be a sensuous libertine, but the other was a compassionate man who cared about people.

"I'll back the car out," he said.

Chelsea started to follow him, then hesitated. "Do you think I should wake Mindy and tell her?"

"Why worry her needlessly? She couldn't go with us anyway. The Ferrari is only a two-seater, and it's faster than the Bentley."

"I guess you're right. I'll get my purse and meet you out front."

Roberto was exceptionally thoughtful on the ride down the mountain. He made small talk, asking Chelsea about the stock market to get her mind off Dawn. It didn't work, though. She had always found her job engrossing, but under the present circumstances, the world of high finance seemed inconsequential.

She remarked on that to Roberto. "I suppose you think I'm overreacting. Dawn isn't related to me. It isn't as if I'm responsible for her."

"That's not important. She's young and vulnerable. I'm concerned about her, too, and the girl is a stranger to me."

"Didn't Mindy ever introduce you to Dawn?"

"No."

"That's odd. Those two were inseparable at home."

Roberto smiled thinly. "They obviously changed when they came over here."

"It's incredible. I wasn't that close to Dawn, but I thought I knew my own sister, at least."

"No one can predict what young people will do."

Something told Chelsea that Roberto was referring to his brother. "I suppose you've had to pull Jorge out of scrapes like this."

"Not precisely. Jorge's escapades were merely pranks before."

"Is he in trouble, too? I'm sorry. You have your own problems, and here I'm dumping mine on you."

"It's all right. Jorge isn't in any trouble. He's one of those rare people who manages to walk away from any mishap unscathed," Roberto remarked sardonically.

"You should be happy about that."

"Not when he causes other people pain."

"I'm sure he doesn't mean to. Everything comes so easily to charming people that it makes them thought-less. Mindy is the same way."

Roberto's jaw tightened. "They'd make a good pair."

"Don't be too hard on Jorge. He'll grow up. They all do."

Roberto raised an eyebrow. "You can tell that without ever meeting him?"

"I wish I could have."

"You will next time."

"No. I'll never be back," she said quietly.

Silence pulsed between them. Then he said just as quietly, "I understand."

She wasn't leaving for five days, but Chelsea knew they were saying their goodbyes now. This was perhaps the last time they would be alone together, so it was fitting.

They were both lost in their own thoughts for the remainder of the drive. Neither spoke until Roberto stopped the car beside an official-looking building.

"Take it easy," he said gently as he took Chelsea's cold hand to help her out.

She clutched her purse nervously and followed him inside. The policeman sitting behind a high desk did nothing to reassure her. He was an intimidating man who stared at them suspiciously.

"You have an American girl here named Dawn Renzler," Chelsea began haltingly. "I'd like to see her."

"Are you her lawyer?" the man asked.

"No, I . . . no."

"A family member?"

"I'm representing her parents," Chelsea said.

"Nobody can see the prisoners but their attorneys or a relative."

The word prisoner jolted Chelsea. "I'm prepared to post her bail," she said hastily.

He thumbed through a stack of papers in a wire basket and pulled one out. After giving it a brief glance, the man looked up at Chelsea sternly. "The charge is possession of drugs. No bail."

"How can you do that? She isn't a hardened criminal," Chelsea exclaimed.

"Drug abuse is a crime in Spain," he told her.

"I understand that. I only meant that she isn't a threat to society. You don't have to keep her locked up."

The man shrugged. "You are more lenient in your country. Over here we see things differently."

"How long do you intend to hold her incommunicado?" she demanded.

"Until her trial."

Chelsea was appalled. If Spanish courts were anything like their American counterparts, that could take months! "You can't keep her in jail until then," she said with a sinking heart, realizing they could do just that if they chose.

"Let me handle this," Roberto murmured. "I understand your policy," he told the desk officer. "The girl is an American. She could leave the country to avoid prosecution."

"Exactly." The man gave Chelsea a reproving look, as though she were already guilty of aiding and abetting.

"Excellent reasoning," Roberto said approvingly. "But this *señorita* must answer to the girl's parents. I have a solution that should satisfy everyone. Release the girl in my custody and I will guarantee her appearance in court. I am a responsible Spanish citizen, a landowner. My family has lived here for generations. You may have heard of the del Machados of Ronda."

The policeman was impressed, both by Roberto's credentials and his authoritative bearing, but he was still forced to refuse. "I am sorry, *señor*, but I cannot go against the rules."

"Suppose Judge Caramoza were to vouch for me," Roberto persisted. "Would that make a difference?"

The man's face cleared. "*Sí, señor*. Then I could turn her over to you immediately."

"I will bring you such an assurance, but it might take a little time. Meanwhile, will you allow us to see the girl?"

By now, the officer's implacable attitude had softened. He gave his permission and called another policeman to take them to Dawn's jail cell.

As Chelsea and Roberto followed the man down a dreary corridor she whispered, "Do you really know that judge?"

Roberto nodded. "He is an old friend of my father's."

"Are you sure he'll go to bat for a stranger?" Chelsea shivered as she glanced at the metal cages they were passing. "I won't rest easy until I get Dawn out of this place."

"She will be soon," Roberto said soothingly.

The guard stopped at a cell. "This is it. I can't let her out, but you can talk to her from here."

Inside the little cubicle a young woman was sitting disconsolately on a narrow bunk. Her long blond hair was disheveled, and there were deep circles under her eyes. She glanced up when she heard the guard's voice. Apprehension changed to incredulous joy as she saw Chelsea.

"Oh, thank God!" Dawn rushed up to the bars. "I thought everybody had forgotten about me."

"Are you all right?" Chelsea asked.

"I will be as soon as I get out of here. You don't know how horrible it's been. They searched me and took away all my things, even my wristwatch. I was scared that nobody would ever come to get me out."

"We had no idea where you were. Wouldn't the police allow you to make a phone call?"

"I didn't know who to call. Mindy is my only real friend here, and I didn't know how to get in touch with her. I finally called one of the girls at the rooming house and asked her to phone my parents, but I guess she didn't want to get involved."

Chelsea made a small sound of disgust. "That's disgraceful."

"Well, you're here now. Tell that guy to hurry up and unlock the door. I feel like a hamster." Dawn's spirits were already rising.

"It isn't that easy. They don't grant bail for drug offenders. Roberto has to—"

Dawn interrupted before she could finish. "You mean you're going to leave me here?" Her eyes filled with tears. "I thought you came to help me."

"We did." Roberto took over. "Chelsea only meant it will take a little time."

"How much time?" Dawn asked suspiciously.

"It shouldn't be more than an hour," he assured her.

Actually, it took considerably more than that. Judge Caramoza was presiding over a trial and couldn't be contacted until the court took a recess. That period was taken up by the opposing attorneys seeking a judicial ruling, and then court reconvened. It wasn't until the next recess that Roberto was able to see his father's friend and arrange for Dawn's release.

After they returned to the jail with the authorization, a mountain of paperwork had to be completed. By the time Dawn was brought from her cell, she was on the edge of hysteria.

Flinging her arms around Chelsea's neck she sobbed, "I thought you weren't coming back!"

Chelsea patted her soothingly. "You knew better than that."

"No, I didn't. You said it would only take an hour, and I've been waiting all afternoon."

"We ran into a few complications, but everything is taken care of now. You'll be free to go in a couple of minutes."

Dawn's budding relief dimmed. "Where? I don't have any place to stay. I can't go back to that rooming house where Sancho and I were living. I never want to see him again!"

"You're coming home with us," Roberto said as she started to tremble.

Eventually the formalities were completed and they were able to leave. Dawn's spirits bounded back as soon as she was outside the building. But after Roberto had helped Chelsea into the front seat of the car and Dawn had squeezed in next to her, Chelsea wished she'd let Dawn get in first. Then Dawn would have been the one in the middle, close to Roberto. But since Chelsea was already seated, she could scarcely get out without making her objection obvious.

As they drove away, Dawn breathed a huge sigh of relief. "I don't ever want to be alone again. You can't imagine what it's like to be cooped up in a cell all by yourself."

"I don't want to preach—certainly not right now," Chelsea said. "But you did a very foolish thing."

"I know," Dawn answered soberly. "Everybody told me Sancho was no good. I had to find out the hard way."

"You knew he was using drugs. Didn't that give you a clue?"

"I'm not saying it was a smart thing to do, but Sancho didn't have the advantages the rest of us did," Dawn said defensively. "He was born in a slum in Madrid. While most of us were going to dancing class and taking tennis lessons, he had to drop out of school and go to work."

"Where are the violins when you need them?" Roberto asked derisively.

"Well, I believed him," Dawn said stubbornly. "The other kids were always putting him down, and I felt sorry for him."

"Even if he did have an unhappy childhood, there were other ways besides drugs to escape," Chelsea said.

"He said he'd quit if I helped him."

"Quit using, or quit selling?" Roberto asked cynically.

"Sancho isn't a pusher." Dawn's indignation didn't ring true.

"I'm afraid he is."

"People kept saying that, but it wasn't true."

"You said he comes from a poor family, yet he doesn't work. What does he live on?"

"Sancho told me he had a little money saved up. He was going to look for a job when that was gone," Dawn answered uneasily.

"You didn't really believe that," Roberto said.

"Of course I did. You don't think I'd have stayed with him if I thought he was dealing drugs."

"So Sancho was just a poor, underprivileged lad who needed a crutch to face life," Roberto's voice was rough with anger. "Does that excuse him for getting *you* to use drugs?"

Dawn gave him a shocked look. "I never went near the stuff."

"You had cocaine in your purse when you were picked up," Chelsea said. "Quite a lot of it. I saw the arrest report."

"But it wasn't mine! Somebody must have put it there when the police raided the party."

Roberto arched an eyebrow. "Somebody?"

"Okay—Sancho," Dawn said reluctantly. She heaved a huge sigh. "I was ashamed to admit how dumb I've been. He set me up, and then never even came to see me in jail."

"Why don't you tell us exactly what happened," Roberto suggested.

"Sancho did offer me drugs," Dawn admitted. "But I never took any. When he tried to pressure me, I threatened to walk out. After that he backed off."

"But you knew *he* was using drugs," Chelsea commented.

"He said he was trying to kick the habit. I've read about how hard it is, so I didn't bug him too much."

"You were remarkably understanding," Chelsea said grimly. "Did you also carry the stuff in your purse for him?"

"*No!* I told you how it got there. I didn't even want to go to that party, but Sancho insisted so I gave in. He said it would be a blast, but it wasn't my scene. I wanted to leave right after we got there. Sancho said he had to see somebody first, and then we'd go."

"Did he tell you what he wanted to see this somebody about?"

"No, and I wasn't interested. I just wanted to get out of that place. I didn't like the people. I was glad when the guy showed up."

"Was it somebody you knew?"

"No, he was an older man, maybe in his thirties." Dawn saw the smile Roberto and Chelsea exchanged. "You know what I mean—he was older than the rest of us. I didn't much like his looks. I wasn't too happy when Sancho left me alone and went outside with him.''

"How long were they gone?"

"Only a few minutes, and the guy didn't come back with Sancho."

Roberto nodded. "It all adds up—the arranged meeting, the large amount of coke. He was Sancho's supplier."

"I guess so, although I wasn't thinking about anything like that at the moment. I was just about to ask Sancho if we could go now when the cops started banging on the door. After that everything got crazy. People were yelling, and the police began searching everyone."

"It sounds as if they had a tip," Roberto mused. "I gather Sancho didn't have any drugs on him."

"How could he? He planted them all on me," Dawn said bitterly. "And then he split before I could accuse him of it."

"I'm just grateful that you're all right," Chelsea said. "A lot of people have been looking for you."

"You've both been so great. I really owe you."

"You have Roberto to thank." Chelsea turned her head to look at his strong face. "I couldn't have done anything without him."

He gazed into her eyes. "I'm not really all bad," he said softly.

Chelsea was achingly conscious of his long body so close to hers, his lips such a short distance away. Good or bad, she couldn't stop wanting him.

"Mindy is sure lucky to have you, Roberto," Dawn remarked.

Her innocent comment was like a pail of cold water over both of them. Roberto's jaw set and Chelsea moved away. The small space between them might as well have been a chasm.

"How is Mindy?" Dawn's question filled the silence. "I wanted to call her, but I didn't know where she'd gone."

"She'll be very happy to see you," Chelsea said. "Mindy was awfully disappointed that you wouldn't be at the wedding. Maybe you can still be a bridesmaid if we can get a dress for you in time."

Dawn shook her head. "I hate to miss it, but all I want to do right now is go home."

"I understand how you feel," Chelsea said sympathetically. "I'm afraid you can't, though. Roberto guaranteed that you'd show up for your trial. It was the only way they'd let you out."

"I was just an innocent bystander, but what if they don't believe me?" Dawn was in a panic again. "What if they send me to prison?"

Chelsea was worried about the same thing, but she tried not to show it. Dawn was free for the time being only. Roberto comforted both of them.

"You're borrowing trouble needlessly," he said. "The police are more interested in finding out who Sancho's supplier is. If you cooperate by giving them a detailed description of the man, I'm reasonably sure I can speak to a few people and get the charges against you dismissed."

"Oh, I will! I'll tell them every single detail. His name was Nick—I heard Sancho call him that—and he wore a gold medal on a chain around his neck, and—"

Roberto stopped her. "You can write it all down and I'll take it to the police."

"Then can I go home?" Dawn looked at him hopefully.

"Won't she have to stay until she's cleared?" Chelsea asked Roberto.

"I think we can safely assume that will happen. Why make her suffer any more? If it becomes absolutely necessary, she can return to Spain."

"Do you understand that?" Chelsea asked Dawn sternly. "Roberto has gone out on a limb for you. If you chop it off, I'll drag you back here myself." She was unaware of the tenderness in Roberto's eyes as he gazed at her.

"I'll do anything you say," Dawn promised fervently.

Roberto had called Mindy from Marbella, and she was waiting eagerly for them when they arrived at the del Machado house. The two girls threw their arms around each other in a joyous reunion.

"You have to tell me every single thing that happened," Mindy ordered.

Dawn proceeded to do so with great dramatic flair.

"You'd think she'd been held on Devil's Island," Chelsea murmured to Roberto.

He smiled. "I'm glad the experience didn't leave a mark on her."

"A small one might not be too bad."

"I believe she's learned her lesson." He looked at Chelsea critically. "You look done in. Why don't you go up and soak in a cool bath."

"I think I'll do that. The girls can't get into any trouble here."

Roberto grinned. "You want to bet?"

"No," she answered wearily.

"Relax. I'll take care of everything."

Chelsea didn't doubt that for a minute. She'd seen how good he was in a crisis. Roberto could solve any problem . . . well, almost any.

"I'll go tell Mother we're back with her new houseguest," he said.

Chelsea couldn't reveal her innermost emotions, but she could express one of them. "Roberto, wait." When he turned she said softly, "Thanks, again."

A nerve pulsed in his temple as he stared at her, reacting to her tone of voice rather than the conventional words. After a brief instant his expression changed to polite acceptance. "*De nada,*" he answered.

Chelsea repressed a sigh as she turned back to the girls. One task remained before she could relax. "You have to call your parents immediately, Dawn."

The girl's animation died. "Do I have to tell them everything?"

"That's up to you," Chelsea replied neutrally.

"I'll be grounded until I'm thirty," Dawn groaned.

"You mean middle-aged?" Chelsea couldn't resist the barb.

Mindy looked thoughtful. "I always feel I'm doing my parents a favor by not telling them things that will upset them."

"You're all heart," Chelsea remarked dryly. "This is strictly your decision, Dawn, but you have to call home right now. I'll wait here, in case your parents want to speak to me."

Dawn did as she was told, albeit reluctantly. She returned in a fairly short time, looking chastened.

Chelsea hazarded a guess. "I guess you told them."

"Most of the story," Dawn said cautiously. "I decided it would be better if they heard it now. That way they'll have a chance to cool off before I get there. They told me to be on the first plane home tomorrow.''

"You can't go!" Mindy exclaimed. "Didn't you tell them I'm getting married on Sunday?"

Dawn smiled wryly. "I think that was the deciding factor."

"Marriage isn't contagious," Mindy said indignantly.

"At this point, I suspect my parents are planning to send me to a convent."

Chelsea pushed her chair back. "I'll find out where Dolores is going to put you," she told Dawn.

"She can stay in my room," Mindy said. "We won't have much time together if Dawn has to go home tomorrow."

"Okay, but tell Dolores now, so she won't have a room made up."

Chelsea was lying on her bed reading, although her eyelids drooped now and then. The leisurely bath had relaxed her after the tension-filled day. It was also a relief to know that all her problems were behind her. At least the ones she could solve. She answered a knock on her door without enthusiasm.

Dawn looked apologetic when she saw Chelsea lying on the bed in a robe. After her bath Chelsea had put on only a cool chiffon peignoir.

"Oh, I'm sorry," Dawn apologized. "I didn't know you were napping."

"I wasn't. I was just reading." Chelsea looked at the young girl approvingly. "You look a lot better."

"I *feel* better. I washed my hair, and Mindy gave me some clean clothes."

"I forgot about that. We'll have to go by your rooming house tomorrow and pick up your things."

"They can burn them as far as I'm concerned. I'm never going back to that place again," Dawn said emphatically.

"You won't have to," Chelsea soothed. "I'm sure Roberto can arrange to have your belongings sent up here."

"I guess you think I'm overreacting."

"No. You've been through a rotten experience," Chelsea said sympathetically.

"The worst of it is, I don't have anybody to blame but myself."

"Facing the fact is a sign that you're growing up."

"What's so great about that?"

"Nothing much, but we all have to do it," Chelsea answered quietly.

She thought of Roberto, and the adult passion she felt for him. Not a teenage crush she'd get over, but an abiding love that would never leave her.

"I used to be in such a hurry to grow up, but it's not what I expected," Dawn said plaintively. "I didn't know everything would change."

"That's life," Chelsea answered without facetiousness.

"But it all happened so fast." Dawn gestured helplessly. "*I* goofed up. Mindy's getting married. Nothing is the same."

"You'll be getting married in a few years, too."

"I only hope I find someone like Roberto."

"Don't we all?" Chelsea replied in a muted voice.

"I can't believe there are men like him in the world," Dawn said in a tone of disbelief.

"He's one of a kind," Chelsea agreed. Part of her wished Dawn would get off the subject, but another part always welcomed a chance to talk about Roberto.

"You bet he is! How many men would marry a girl who was pregnant with his brother's child?"

Chelsea was sure she'd heard incorrectly. She sat up straighter. "What did you say?"

"I really liked Jorge. I never thought he'd turn out to be such a rat."

"You're joking, aren't you?"

"No, he came across as a real great guy. I thought he was in love with Mindy."

"Did Mindy love him?" Chelsea asked through stiff lips.

"She was out of her skull over him. Remember what a hard time she used to give all the guys who were crazy about her? Well, you should have seen her with Jorge. She was so starry-eyed you wouldn't believe it was the same Mindy. She didn't want to let him out of her sight." Dawn tilted her head reflectively. "Maybe that was the trouble. Do you think guys like it better when you play hard to get?"

"I don't know." Chelsea stared at her in shock.

"He seemed to like it, but look what happened."

"What did happen?" Chelsea whispered.

"It was a real whirlwind affair. Sparks went off the instant they met, just like in those romance novels. Jorge was staying in a friend's apartment, a really posh place in a fancy neighborhood. Not like that dump we lived in. Although it wasn't so bad," Dawn said pensively. "Except for the landlady, of course. She was a real witch, but the crowd there was great."

"How did Mindy meet Jorge?" Chelsea's nerves were wound to the breaking point as Dawn's reminiscences led her off on a tangent.

"At a disco in Puerto Banús. A bunch of us from the rooming house dropped in there one night. We used to hang out a lot together, not specially as couples, just in a group. It was fun. To think I gave all that up for a jerk like Sancho.''

Chelsea wanted to shake her till her teeth rattled, but she restrained herself. ''Jorge didn't have a date?''

''No, he was with a couple of pals. They started to talk to us, and Jorge asked Mindy to dance. They fell in love that night, and from then on they spent every minute together,'' Dawn said dreamily. ''I only saw her a couple of times after that.''

''Mindy moved in with him?'' Chelsea tried to keep her voice neutral, but some of her agitation came through.

''It's not as bad as it sounds,'' Dawn answered defensively. ''They were in love—at least Mindy was. She told me she wanted to marry him.''

''Evidently he had other ideas,'' Chelsea said tautly.

''It turned out that way. Go figure men! Jorge seemed as crazy about Mindy as she was about him. You should have seen the way he treated her, like a delicate piece of china. I guess it was the baby that did it. He must have freaked out at the idea.''

''You're sure Jorge knew Mindy was pregnant?'' Chelsea asked intently.

''Of course. She told him.'' Dawn looked at her curiously. ''Why are you asking *me* all these questions? Didn't Mindy tell you the whole story?''

''She left out a few details. I knew she was pregnant, but I just naturally assumed Roberto was the father.''

''Oh, wow. I've really done it this time! I'm sorry, Chelsea. I never would have said anything if I thought you didn't know.''

''Don't be sorry. I'm glad you told me.'' Chelsea stood up. ''Stay here, Dawn. I want to talk to my sister alone.''

Mindy was drying her hair at the dressing table when Chelsea entered her room without knocking. Walking over to the wall socket, Chelsea pulled out the plug.

"What did you do that for?" Mindy frowned.

"I want to talk to you."

"Can't it wait a couple of minutes? I'm almost finished."

"No, it can't wait. I need to talk to you *now*."

"Okay, okay. Don't get huffy. What's up?"

"I just had a talk with Dawn."

"I hope you didn't give her a bad time. It's all over."

"She told me about Jorge."

Mindy's mild annoyance turned to resignation. "I should have told her not to say anything."

"How could you keep something like this from me?"

Mindy shrugged. "Does it make you any happier now that you know?"

"I can't believe you'd marry one man while you're pregnant with another man's child."

"It's his brother's." Mindy's mouth curved sardonically. "At least I'm keeping it in the family."

Chelsea stared at her in a kind of horror. "I don't even know you anymore."

Mindy's pretense at brittleness cracked. "For Pete's sake, don't lecture me." Her voice had a catch in it.

"This isn't one of your little escapades, Mindy. You're doing a terrible thing. Can't you see that?"

"I'm not forcing Roberto to marry me. It was his idea."

"He's as crazy as you are!"

"Why?" Mindy asked calmly.

"You don't love each other!" Chelsea practically shouted back.

"I loved Jorge, and look where it got me."

"You made a mistake, but that's no reason to ruin your life."

"I expect to have a very good life here," Mindy answered stubbornly.

"Because Roberto is rich and moves in high society? How long do you think that will be enough? You need someone your own age, a man who shares your interests."

"Like Jorge?" Mindy's mouth twisted bitterly. "He fits the description perfectly. Unfortunately the commitment was one-sided."

"What happened, Mindy?" Chelsea asked less heatedly. "Dawn said Jorge was in love with you."

"That's what I thought. Those weeks we lived together were like a honeymoon. I was a virgin," Mindy said matter-of-factly. "Does that surprise you?"

That explained a lot. Chelsea hesitated for a moment. "From all I've heard about Jorge, he's very charming," she answered indirectly.

"Meaning, I'm making a big deal out of our affair because he was the first? I'm not that naive. Sex with Jorge was unbelievable, but I thought we had a lot more than that going for us." Mindy smiled briefly, a wistful little smile. "We didn't spend all our time in bed. We took long walks along the beach and talked about what we wanted to do with our lives."

"Was marriage included?"

"It was sort of taken for granted. Why else would he ask me to transfer to his university?"

Chelsea concealed the pity she felt for her trusting kid sister. "Dolores told me Jorge plans to be an architect. That means he had years of college ahead of him."

"I was willing to wait till he got his degree, if that was what he wanted. I intended to get mine, too. We just wanted to be together."

"But the baby changed all that," Chelsea said gently.

"Evidently." Mindy's eyes darkened. "That's what hurts the most. If he'd come right out and told me he wasn't ready to take on a wife and child I'd have been angry and disappointed, but that would have been the honest thing to do. He owed me that much. Leaving without telling me he wasn't coming back was really low."

"You didn't argue?"

"Just the opposite. When I told him about the baby he pretended to be ecstatic. He jumped out of bed and said he was going to buy me a present because I'd just given him the greatest gift in the world. That's a laugh! He was in such a hurry to get out of there that he even forgot his wallet. I found it on the dresser later."

"He didn't take any of his belongings?"

"Only the money he stuffed in the pocket of his tennis shorts. The last time I ever saw him was when he went out the door."

"Why did you go to Roberto?" Chelsea asked curiously. "I should think Jorge's brother was the last person you'd want to see."

"I couldn't believe Jorge had really walked out on me. I wanted to talk to him, to hear him tell me to my face that he didn't love me. I guess I kept hoping if I could just see him, everything would be all right again. But Roberto hadn't heard from him."

"So Roberto offered to marry you himself?" Chelsea asked incredulously.

"Not right away. He tried to find Jorge first. Roberto was furious with him. You know what a big deal the del Machados make about their honor—all of them except

Jorge," Mindy added sarcastically. "I told Roberto I wasn't interested in a shotgun wedding. I just wanted to talk to Jorge before I went home."

"Roberto couldn't find him?"

Mindy shook her head. "Jorge really went underground. I was staying up here at the house, and I finally faced reality. Jorge didn't want to be found. I told Roberto I was going home. That's when he asked me to marry *him*."

"But you knew it was only because you were pregnant."

"That's a pretty good reason for accepting," Mindy replied simply. "I want my baby to have a name."

"It *will* have," Chelsea said urgently. "Our name is as good as theirs any day."

"I want it have a father, too." Mindy's chin set stubbornly. "Don't tell me again about all the happy children who grow up in a single-parent homes. My child is going to have it all. Jorge might not want this baby, but I do."

"What kind of parent will Roberto make after being blackmailed—morally, anyway—into marrying you?"

"He'll be a very good father. Under that macho pose is a very gentle, caring man. I might not love Roberto, but I respect him a great deal."

"You think that's enough?"

"It will have to be. You still don't understand. What I felt for Jorge was the real thing. Nobody will ever take his place."

A flash of anger swept through Chelsea. "You keep talking about *your* feelings, *your* life. How about Roberto's? How can you condemn *him* to a loveless marriage?"

"I worried about that," Mindy admitted. "But he wasn't seeing anyone regularly. From what I hear, he's never been seriously involved, although he's dated some of the most beautiful women on the Continent. If he hasn't found someone by now, he probably doesn't want to.''

''You can't assume that. Suppose he meets someone and falls in love with her?''

''Then I'd give him his freedom.'' Mindy looked at her appealingly. ''I'm not taking advantage of Roberto. I know he's giving up a lot for me, but it was his choice.''

''He didn't feel he *had* a choice!''

Chelsea argued until she was practically hoarse, but Mindy stood firm. She was marrying Roberto on Sunday.

''Isn't there anything that will change your mind?'' Chelsea finally asked hopelessly.

''Only Jorge could do that, and we both know that's pie in the sky.'' Mindy's face was equally unhappy. ''So I guess you'd better get ready to watch me walk down the aisle.''

Chapter Ten

After leaving her sister, Chelsea marched down the hall to Roberto's room. Her state of mind was so chaotic that she forgot she was only wearing a robe.

She rapped sharply on Roberto's door, breathing rapidly. When he didn't answer, she knocked harder. He had to be inside getting ready for dinner at this hour.

As she was preparing to renew her efforts, he opened the door. Chelsea's surmise was correct. Roberto had been shaving. A white towel around his neck emphasized the deep tan of his bare chest. She paused, momentarily thrown off balance by his splendid physique.

Roberto was even more affected by the sight of her. After an instant's surprise, his eyes moved over her with a searching intensity. A flush of embarrassment warmed Chelsea as she realized her oversight. The floral chiffon robe merely camouflaged her body, making the small glimpses it revealed all the more erotic. Roberto's gaze was riveted on the small peaks her nipples formed, only thinly concealed by the pastel flowers that covered them. She quickly folded her arms over her breasts.

He shifted his eyes to her face. "Is anything wrong?"

"Just about everything!" Chelsea meant to tell him she'd be back as soon as she got dressed, but the urgency of her errand overrode modesty. "Why didn't you tell me the truth?"

"Your mood changes rapidly," he commented cynically. "A short time ago I was the man in the white hat. What have I done this time to incur your wrath?"

"You've been lying to me since I arrived—you and Mindy both."

"In what way?" he asked cautiously.

"Don't fence with me! You know perfectly well. You aren't the father of Mindy's baby."

Relief was one of the many emotions that crossed Roberto's face. He opened the door wider. "You'd better come inside."

"It's a little late for discretion. Everyone else in the house already knows," Chelsea stormed, but she followed him into his bedroom.

"How did you find out?" he asked after closing the door. "Did Mindy tell you?"

"No, Dawn did. She thought I knew." Chelsea uttered a short bark of laughter. "The entire world seems to have known, except me."

"Would the truth have made you any happier about the situation?" he asked gravely.

"No, but I would have understood better. You can't do it, Roberto. You can't go through with a marriage of convenience."

"Mindy is carrying my brother's child. What would you have me do? It's a matter of honor."

"Jorge's honor, not yours!"

"It's the same thing."

"No, it isn't. If anyone should be forced to marry Mindy, it's Jorge."

"Unfortunately he has walked away from his responsibility." Roberto removed the towel from around his neck and flung it forcefully on the bed. "I'm deeply disappointed in my brother. We've always made allowances for Jorge because he's young, and because we felt he could be trusted not to bring disgrace on the family. He's gotten into minor mischief, now and then, but he's always faced the consequences. I never thought he was a coward."

"What he did was reprehensible, but you're not making it any better."

"I'm offering Mindy my support and protection. Their baby will have its rightful name."

"I heard all of that from Mindy," Chelsea said impatiently. "There's one thing neither of you mentioned. What about love?"

Deep lines were carved in his face. "You ask a great deal, *señorita.*"

"You bet I do!"

"All of life is a compromise," he answered heavily.

"I don't buy that. Mindy can have her baby *and* a happy marriage. But not with you. She'll meet someone and forget all about Jorge."

Roberto's face was impassive. "You think it's that easy to forget someone you love?"

"It wasn't love with them, it was sex," she replied scornfully.

"You don't know your sister very well," he said quietly. "She wants this child because it's Jorge's."

Chelsea remembered the new maturity in Mindy's face when she talked about the things she wanted for her baby.

"All right, maybe it was love on her part, but you can't *make* someone love you in return."

"No, you can't do that." He stifled a sigh.

"She has to put all of this behind her and move on."

Roberto's smile had a mocking tinge. "How very practical you are. It's obvious that you've never been in love."

Is that what he thought? Chelsea's pulse rate accelerated as she became aware of Roberto, not as an adversary she had to convince, but the man she wanted so hopelessly. He had never looked more virile. She ached to run her hands over his broad shoulders, to rake her nails through the dark hair on his lean chest, to trace the tapering V down to his belt buckle.

Chelsea bit her lip and turned away. "My emotions aren't a consideration here."

"Tell me, just to satisfy my curiosity. Have you ever needed somebody so much that it was like a physical pain?" When she didn't answer, he turned her to face him, his hands burning through her thin chiffon robe. "Have you ever had a recurring dream that you were lying together in bed, joined into one person?"

"No, I—" She couldn't look at him, afraid he might see the lie.

"You're very fortunate." His hands were caressing now on her shoulders. "I have that dream every night."

"Then don't you see why you can't marry Mindy?" Chelsea pleaded.

A shadow passed over his face as he released her. "I can't break my word."

"You aren't being noble, you're being stubborn! You and Mindy are both in love with other people. Your marriage would be a disaster."

"Maybe we can console each other." He reached out and stroked Chelsea's cheek, trailing his fingers down to the corner of her mouth. "Since neither of us can have the one we want."

She caught her breath at the mind-spinning implication. Chelsea knew that Roberto desired her. The sexual tension between them was always just under the surface. But she'd never dreamed he felt any more than that. Was it possible?

"Am I the one, Roberto?" she whispered.

His hand dropped to his side. "You must have known."

"No! You said you wanted to make love to me, but I thought—"

"That's all it was?" He framed her face in his palms and gazed deeply into her eyes. "I do want to make love to you, *cara mia*. I want to touch your ivory skin and excite you so much that you'll beg for completion. I want to watch your face as I enter your beautiful body, and hear you call out my name when we share that final moment. I love you, my dearest."

Chelsea's body felt as if it were on fire. She trembled with need for this man. Nothing was more important at that moment than the two of them. Everybody else had ceased to exist.

Throwing her arms around his neck, she pulled his head down to hers. "Oh, Roberto, I feel the same way. I love you, too."

Incredulous joy blazed in his eyes, then his mouth covered hers urgently. Chelsea was sucked into a vortex of pleasure as Roberto loosed all his restrained passion. He parted her lips for probing kisses that made her smolder with desire. She returned them fervently, making tiny sounds of happiness.

Finally he dragged his mouth away and buried his face in her hair. "I've been so hungry for the touch and taste of you. I've never wanted any woman this much."

The contact with his hard body was still enflaming her senses, but now that Roberto had stopped kissing her, Chelsea was able to think more clearly. She unclasped her arms from around his neck and moved out of his embrace. This had only made matters worse.

"You've proved my point for me," she murmured.

"I don't understand."

"You certainly can't marry Mindy now." He was silent for so long that Chelsea looked up.

Roberto was staring at her with searing anger. "You're quite proud of yourself, aren't you? You think your plan worked."

"What plan?" she asked blankly.

"I was right about you the first time. You'd do anything to stop the wedding."

"I told you that from the beginning," she answered steadily.

"I didn't know you'd fight this dirty. Although I should have known when you came to me dressed like that. Or should I say undressed?" His eyes roamed over her lightly clad figure, but this time they held lust rather than love.

Chelsea folded her arms over her breasts. "I didn't mean to. I was so upset after talking to Mindy that I didn't realize I wasn't dressed."

"Isn't it time you were truthful with me? After all, I bared my soul for *you.*"

The taunting note in his voice and the dangerous glint in his eyes made her nervous. "That's what happened, Roberto."

"I really admire your strategy," he said, as though he hadn't heard her. "Did you choose that robe for the subtle effect? I can almost see your hidden charms, but not quite.'' His eyes continued their insolent scrutiny. ''That's very good. You can almost count on a man forgetting everything but his need for you. Then you can get him to promise anything you want.''

Chelsea was definitely alarmed now. Primitive passion blazed on Roberto's face, along with violent rage. She started to edge toward the door.

''There's no point in prolonging this discussion.'' She tried to sound calm.

He moved with cat-like swiftness to block the door. ''I agree. The time for talking is over.'' He gripped her wrists and opened her arms wide. ''Don't be modest with me, Chelsea. Let me see what you would have offered if I'd held out a little longer.''

She gasped as he tore her robe open. Every inch of skin heated as his eyes devoured her nude body. For a moment that seemed like an eternity, he simply stared at her. She was immobilized by the brilliance of his gaze, caught like a frightened doe in a headlight's glare.

Then Roberto reached for her and the spell was broken. She tried to run, but his arm snaked around her waist, and one hand curved around her breast.

''Let go of me!'' She pounded on his chest with her fists. ''Are you crazy?''

''If I am, you've driven me there,'' he snarled.

His fingers tangled in her long hair, jerking her head back so his mouth could crush hers. Chelsea attempted to resist, but he held her in a vise-like grip that was incendiary. Every struggle on her part caused their bodies to buck against each other erotically. Roberto was becoming even more aroused.

Suddenly he lifted her in his arms, carried her over to the bed and threw her down. When Chelsea rolled away he was on top of her in an instant, subduing her with his weight.

"You can't do this," she raged, striking out at him.

"I should have done it long ago."

He captured her flailing hands in one of his and pulled them over her head. While she squirmed helplessly he cupped one of her breasts and touched the sensitive nipple with his tongue. A bolt of pure sensation ripped through Chelsea and she arched her body reflexively.

Roberto looked down at her mockingly. "I can make you respond, can't I, my little Machiavelli? You like that, don't you? How about this?"

As his lips closed over her other nipple, he shifted his weight so his hand could glide down her thigh. Chelsea's muscles were strained to the breaking point as she tried to stiffen her body against his sensual assault. It didn't help. His hand trailed paths of fire, creating an almost unbearable need.

"Roberto, please," she begged.

"Please what, little devil? Is this what you want?"

Parting her legs, he stroked the soft skin of her inner thigh. Chelsea felt herself melting. Even in the midst of his contempt, Roberto couldn't help giving pleasure. The sensation heightened when he reached the juncture of her thighs and probed erotically.

There was no tenderness in his hard face as he stared down at her, only mounting excitement. She could feel the tension in his taut frame, the growing urgency.

"You're going to be mine, even if you didn't plan it that way."

Chelsea's willpower was almost at an end. Her awakened body was screaming for release, and this was the man she wanted to fulfill her. But she couldn't bear to be taken in anger.

"Is this the del Machado honor you're so proud of?" she asked quietly.

Roberto's long frame became rigid and his eyes lost their wildness. He levered himself off the bed and went to stand by the window, fighting for control.

When he finally answered her, his voice was low and tortured. "You're right. I'm no better than Jorge. We're both a disgrace to the family."

Chelsea retrieved her robe and wrapped it tightly around herself. Sorrow filled her, and frustration.

"If you thought less about your family and more about yourself, you'd be better off," she said curtly.

He continued to stare out the window. "Go away, Chelsea. You've gotten your revenge. Isn't that enough?"

"Is that what you think?" she asked bitterly. "I told you the truth, no matter what you choose to believe. I asked you not to marry Mindy because I don't want you to screw up her life the way you have yours and mine."

He turned then and stared at her. "You weren't simply trying to stop the wedding by saying you love me?"

"You don't have a monopoly on losing control," she answered wryly. "I never wanted you to know. What good does it do? We have no future together. Mindy would always think, as you do, that I was a conniving witch determined to run her life, no matter what it took. My feelings don't change anything, but just for the record I was being honest with you."

"What can I say? I thought I was doing the right thing," he said slowly.

"You aren't. Call off the wedding, Roberto."

"Do you want me to tell Mindy that a second del Machado man has run out on her?"

"She'd understand," Chelsea said uncertainly.

"She's made plans for herself and the child. Are you willing to tell her the reason they won't come about?"

Chelsea knew that was impossible. Mindy would feel a deep sense of betrayal, and she'd be right. How could they do that to her? She'd never trust anyone again, man *or* woman.

"I have to pay my brother's debt," Roberto said sadly.

Chelsea's shoulders slumped and she turned away. Maybe Roberto was right. She didn't know anymore.

Dinner that night was an agonizing ordeal. Everyone was tense and on edge, although they tried not to show it. Only Ramón and Rosa were oblivious to the charged atmosphere. They had dropped in for cocktails, and accepted an invitation to stay for dinner.

"This is an unexpected pleasure," Rosa remarked to her mother-in-law when they were seated in the dining room. "I just thought I'd have a short visit with you while Ramón talked business with Roberto. I didn't plan to stay."

"The pleasure is mine," Dolores answered, ever the gracious hostess. "I love having all of my family around me."

"Too bad Jorge couldn't be here to make the family circle complete," Rosa commented.

"Yes." Dolores rang the bell for Luis, who appeared immediately. "Perhaps someone would like more wine," she told him.

Rosa continued as if there had been no interruption. "Where is Jorge? I haven't seen him all summer."

"He's been keeping busy," Dolores answered vaguely.

"You must miss him terribly. It's thoughtless of him not to come home more often."

"I don't want my sons to consider me an obligation." Dolores's austere tone indicated she didn't wish to discuss Jorge.

But Rosa had never been very perceptive. "I should have known better than to criticize your baby." She chuckled and turned to the others. "Jorge is a wild one, but in Dolores's eyes he can do no wrong."

"I wouldn't call him wild," Ramón protested.

"You told me yourself that he has a different girlfriend every week."

"That's not my definition of wild. I'd call him lucky." Ramón laughed. "Right, Roberto?"

Dolores gazed down the table. Roberto's face was like a thundercloud, and Chelsea, Mindy and Dawn all had their heads bent over their plates. She changed the subject deftly, but not necessarily for the better.

"Did Rosa say you came to see Roberto on business, Ramón? Is there a problem?"

"Not at all," he assured his mother. "The crops have been excellent this summer. I had to come here to talk to Roberto because he rarely stops by the office anymore."

"You must realize that he has a lot on his mind with the wedding such a short time away."

Roberto frowned. "You don't have to make excuses for me, Mother."

Chelsea had never heard him speak sharply to Dolores before. It was an indication of his inner turmoil. They were all squeezed to the breaking point, and his brother and Rosa were turning the screws.

"I wasn't complaining," Ramón winked at Roberto. "I know what it's like to be engaged."

"Where are you going on your honeymoon?" Rosa asked Mindy.

"We haven't discussed it," Mindy answered absently.

"The wedding is in four days!" Rosa exclaimed.

"I meant we haven't decided yet. We thought we'd just . . . uh . . . drive until we saw someplace we liked."

"That's rather casual." Rosa looked at her disapprovingly. "What if you can't get a room on your wedding night?"

Mindy's eyes glittered as her scant patience came to an end. "Then I guess we'll just have to make out in the car. But don't worry. I'll tell Roberto to put the top up."

"Too bad you won't be here for the wedding, Dawn," Dolores said hastily. "Are you sure we can't persuade you to change your mind?"

"My parents made it up for me." Dawn smiled ruefully. "Although you might be stuck with me if I can't get on a plane. The end of August is murder to try and get a reservation."

"You're right," Roberto said. "I phoned the airline office when we came home. The best they could do was put you on a waiting list."

"So you might have to stay, after all," Mindy said happily.

"Don't count on it," Roberto advised. "The ticket agent told me they usually have a few cancellations. They'll call to let us know."

"Did you enjoy your stay here?" Rosa asked Dawn.

"It was very . . . educational," Dawn answered.

"I know I'm an overly protective mother, but I would never let my girls go so far from home," Rosa said. "So much could happen to them."

"Not bad things, necessarily," Ramón said. "Look at the evidence right in front of you. Dawn broadened her outlook, and Mindy found a husband."

"Only Chelsea is going home empty-handed," Roberto remarked sardonically.

''Not necessarily.'' Mindy's voice was equally derisive. ''She had a trip she'll never forget. Isn't that right, Chelsea?''

''It's been very eventful,'' Chelsea murmured. She couldn't match their brittle tone.

''We've been so busy with the wedding that we haven't had time to entertain for you properly,'' Rosa said. ''On your next visit we'll have to plan a series of parties in your honor.''

''That's very kind of you.'' Chelsea didn't bother to mention that she had no intention of returning. Ever.

''Rosa loves to give parties.'' Ramón glanced fondly at his wife. ''The only thing she likes better is matchmaking. I'm surprised she hasn't paired you up with someone by now.''

''I think Carlos took matters out of my hands,'' Rosa replied. ''He was quite taken with Chelsea at the rehearsal.''

''Who is Carlos?'' Dawn asked.

''A really nifty guy,'' Mindy answered. ''I hope Rosa is right. He'd be perfect for Chelsea.''

''Wouldn't it be nice if they fell in love? Roberto's best friend and Mindy's sister.'' Rosa sighed happily. ''You never can tell. Weddings are so romantic.''

After a glance at Roberto's rigid jawline, Dolores changed the subject again without bothering to be subtle. ''Tell us about your girls, Rosa. Carmen starts school this fall, doesn't she?''

Rosa was dependable in that respect. She launched into a detailed account of Carmen's emotions at the coming momentous event, her school wardrobe and probable accomplishments. Then Rosa recounted Milia's already documented triumphs.

Nobody listened, except perhaps Ramón. But at least the others were spared more of her bumbling remarks. They all retreated into their own troubled thoughts, although Rosa didn't notice. She droned on, delighted that for once, no one tried to head her off.

Dinner finally came to an end, and everyone dispersed rapidly. Now there were only three more days to get through, Chelsea told herself as she closed her bedroom door.

Dolores's dressmaker came to the house the next morning to fit Chelsea's gown.

"It looks all finished," Chelsea remarked as she turned around to be zipped up the back.

"The darts are only basted." The woman smoothed the dress over Chelsea's hips, inspecting her closely. "It's a little loose through the middle, isn't it? You have such a tiny waist."

"You did a wonderful job, Señora Melendez." Dolores gazed admiringly at Chelsea. "You look lovely, my dear. I knew that color would be becoming. Do you like it?"

"Yes, it's very nice," Chelsea answered tepidly.

The gown deserved more praise. It was princess-style, fitted through the midriff, then flaring out to a bouffant skirt. The shimmering fabric picked up highlights in Chelsea's auburn hair and lent a glow to her fair skin.

Roberto appeared in the doorway, scanning some papers in his hand. "Mother, did you get a receipt for—" He stopped abruptly as he glanced up and saw Chelsea.

Although he appeared unmoved, his hand clenched around the papers he was carrying. Chelsea held her breath as his gaze moved over the gentle curve of her breasts under the thin silk organza. The remembrance in his eyes warmed her cheeks. Roberto knew her body intimately now.

Dolores broke the small pool of silence. "Isn't Chelsea's dress beautiful? We were worried that it wouldn't be ready in time, but Señora Melendez is a miracle worker."

The dressmaker was gratified. "These darts won't take any time at all to finish." She placed a few pins in the seam at Chelsea's waist.

"Did you want something, Roberto?" Dolores asked.

"It can wait," he answered.

Mindy and Dawn arrived as Roberto was leaving. "Oh good, you're all together," Mindy said. "I'm going to show Dawn around Ronda. Who wants to come along?"

"I'm sorry. I have work to do." Roberto left abruptly.

Mindy shrugged and turned her attention to Chelsea. "Your gown is smashing! What do you think, Dawn?"

"I love it. That ballet neckline and little puff sleeves are darling. You look fantastic, Chelsea."

"Sure, rub it in." Mindy pretended to grumble. "Nobody's going to look at *me*."

"That will be the day," Chelsea told her fondly. "We're all just the opening act. You're the star of the show."

"Can I see your bridal gown?" Dawn asked.

"I thought you'd never ask." Mindy laughed. "Chelsea hasn't seen it, either."

While she was getting the dress from Dolores's closet, Chelsea changed back into her casual clothes. The dressmaker left with her gown, promising delivery the next day.

Mindy carefully unwrapped the sheet that shrouded a white satin gown with a small train. Tiny seed pearls were sewn in a floral design around the sweetheart neckline and at the wrists of the long sleeves. The same pattern was repeated at intervals over the full sweeping skirt.

They all marveled as they gazed at the exquisite dress. The heavy satin was like thick cream and the intricate workmanship was magnificent.

"It's to die over!" Dawn proclaimed.

"I couldn't have picked out one I liked better," Mindy agreed.

"I was so pleased that you wanted to wear it," Dolores said.

"Why wouldn't she?" Dawn asked wistfully. "Any bride would jump at the chance."

"Mindy will be carrying on the family tradition," Dolores said softly. "Her son's bride will wear this same dress some day."

"What happens if she doesn't have a boy?" Dawn asked.

"The del Machados always have sons," Dolores joked.

"It's obligatory. They don't allow anything to get in the way of family tradition." Chelsea's tone was brittle. She regretted her sarcasm when Dolores's expression turned to sadness and Mindy's mouth tightened.

"Well, I'm glad I got to see your gown, anyway," Dawn said after an awkward moment. "I guess we'd better get started now if I'm going to see anything of Ronda."

"Right. Are you coming, Chelsea?" Mindy asked.

"If you want me to," Chelsea answered tentatively.

"Of course I do." Mindy flashed her a smile, her momentary annoyance forgotten.

While she carefully covered her wedding gown and hung it back in the closet, Chelsea ran upstairs to get her purse. They were ready to leave when Roberto came out of his office.

"I just received a telephone call from the airline," he told Dawn. "They've had a cancellation. You're booked on the noon flight tomorrow."

"There must be dozens of people on the waiting list," Mindy complained. "Why did they have to give the seat to Dawn?"

"You'll have all day together," Chelsea consoled her sister. "Let's make the most of it."

In spite of the heat and Dawn's impending departure, the afternoon was a success. They walked around town, went into quaint little shops and drank iced coffee at a sidewalk café on a picturesque square. By unspoken agreement the wedding wasn't mentioned, or anything else that might spoil the mood. On the surface at least, they were three carefree companions enjoying the day.

As they lingered over coffee, the two younger girls debated what to wear to an engagement party that was being held that evening. Chelsea waited until they returned to the house to tell Mindy she wasn't going.

"Honestly, Chelsea, you pull this on me every time," Mindy said in exasperation. "What are you going to do at home?"

"Wash my hair and go to bed early."

"There's a scoop for the society columns."

After a protracted argument, Mindy finally accepted defeat. She and Dawn went to their room, and Chelsea went to hers. She would have taken a book to the courtyard where it was cooler, but she didn't want to risk a meeting with Roberto.

Later, after Mindy and Dawn had tapped on the door to say goodbye, Chelsea went reluctantly downstairs. She wasn't hungry and she didn't feel like making conversation, but she could scarcely hole up in her room all evening.

The courtyard was lit solely by candles flickering in little clay pots on the tile floor. One larger candle illuminated the glass table. Dolores was sitting nearby, her face pensive.

Chelsea joined her, forcing a smile. "No company tonight?"

"Only the two of us, I'm afraid. I was sorry to hear you weren't going to the party with the others. Are you feeling all right?" The older woman looked at her searchingly.

"Just a little tired, that's all." Chelsea glanced curiously at her. "You must be invited to these affairs. Why didn't *you* go?"

"I suppose you could call me antisocial." Dolores smiled. "I don't really care for large parties. I prefer small groups of close friends."

"That's understandable. I often think people try too hard to have a good time at those big bashes."

Dolores nodded as she rang the bell for Luis. "Will you have a glass of wine before dinner? I thought we'd dine out here. It's cooler than indoors."

"I do hope the weather cools off by Sunday," Chelsea remarked.

"It should. I've never known a heat wave to last this long."

They talked about nonthreatening subjects such as the weather, current fashions and places they'd both visited on the Continent. It was a surprisingly pleasant evening. Dolores's charm and sophistication almost made Chelsea forget that the woman was also ruthless. How could a mother sacrifice one son for another? Chelsea forced herself not to dwell on it. Since all the victims were willing, there was nothing she could do.

They were drinking coffee when Dolores made an unthinking remark that shattered the illusion of one big, happy family with no problems. They had been discussing the differences between American and Spanish customs.

"In my country we're always in a hurry," Chelsea commented. "I'm surprised at how fast I got used to your slower-paced way of life."

"You're welcome to return for a visit whenever the pressure builds up. Or even if it doesn't," Dolores added graciously.

"You're very hospitable, but I don't expect to have another vacation for a long time."

"I'm sure we'll be able to lure you back when Mindy has her—" Dolores stopped in chagrin.

"Her baby?" Chelsea finished the sentence for her.

"I'm so sorry," Dolores murmured. "I'm not usually that indiscreet."

"It's time we spoke plainly. We both know about it. What I only found out yesterday was who the father is."

Chelsea watched the other woman closely. A remote possibility existed that Dolores didn't know the whole truth. If not, someone had to tell her about the injustice to Roberto. Dolores's troubled face told Chelsea that that wasn't necessary.

"I deeply regret the pain my son has caused your family. Jorge's betrayal of your sister was inexcusable."

"I agree, but saddling Roberto with Jorge's responsibility is no solution. You knew the truth from the beginning. How could you allow this charade to go on?"

"I had no choice."

Chelsea's emotions got out of hand. "I don't believe you! I think you forced Roberto to do the right thing so your precious family honor wouldn't be tarnished. What kind of mother are you?" she demanded furiously.

"Not a very good one, obviously." Dolores sighed. "I thought I had instilled values in all my sons. But you're wrong about my pressuring Roberto. Quite the contrary. I discouraged this marriage for the same reasons you gave.''

''You were willing enough to go along with him.''

''What else could I do? I told Mindy the same things I told Roberto. I assured her that she and the baby would be welcome members of the family, no matter what her status was. We would cherish the child in any case. Unfortunately, neither she nor Roberto would listen to reason.''

''You would raise an illegitimate baby here in Ronda?''

''That's an ugly word,'' Dolores said reprovingly. ''It should never be applied to an innocent child.''

Chelsea couldn't help being skeptical. ''Suppose I'd convinced Mindy to return home with me. You're telling me you wouldn't have been relieved?''

''I would have been deeply saddened to be separated from my grandchild, but I'd have understood and respected her decision. Jorge has broken both our hearts.''

''I'm afraid I've misjudged you,'' Chelsea said slowly.

''It doesn't really matter. Our concerns are the same. Let's just hope that Mindy and Roberto will be able to build a life together. Some things are hard to accept, but time does blunt the pain, my dear.'' Dolores's voice was gentle.

So she knew that, too. Chelsea tried to smile. ''I hope Mindy appreciates what a terrific mother-in-law she's getting.''

''I wish it could have been…different.'' Dolores's true meaning hung in the air between them.

Everyone was up early the next morning in preparation for the long ride to the Málaga airport. Dawn was already packed, but she kept opening her suitcase to put in forgotten items, while Mindy gave her last-minute messages to deliver to friends.

"We have to leave here in fifteen minutes," Roberto called from the hall.

"Get in the car with him, Chelsea, or he'll give us five-minute warnings," Mindy said.

"I'm not going with you," Chelsea answered.

"You have to go." Mindy wasn't taking no for an answer this time. "We're going to stop for lunch at a fantastic place on the way back from the airport."

"That's right, make me feel worse," Dawn complained. "While I'm eating airline food, you'll be stuffing yourself with goodies. Tell me you're not going to Lucia's."

Mindy grinned. "I'll think of you while I'm eating one of those gorgeous pastries. Wait till you see them, Chelsea."

"I wish I could, but I promised Dolores I'd help her with some of the arrangements at the church," Chelsea lied.

"Can't you do it later?"

"You won't be back until afternoon, and by then she won't need me." Chelsea had no intention of spending the day anywhere near Roberto.

Under the circumstances, Mindy had to give in. "Okay," she said reluctantly. "I'll bring you back something chocolate."

"I appreciate the thought, but you'd better not. It would melt in this weather."

"You look cool." Dawn eyed Chelsea's white tennis shorts and thin T-shirt enviously. "I wish I could travel in shorts, but I'm in enough trouble at home already."

"You hardly ever wear shorts," Mindy remarked to her sister.

"I know, but since I'm not going anywhere I decided to be comfortable."

"I thought you were going to the church," Mindy said suspiciously.

"I'll change later. You'd better get moving before Roberto gets impatient," Chelsea urged.

"That's for sure," Mindy agreed. "Here, you take Dawn's tote bag, and we'll carry the luggage."

Chelsea hesitated. She hadn't intended to go out to the car, but avoiding Roberto completely would be noticeable. Her heart quickened as she followed the girls down the stairs.

Roberto was already impatient. He was pacing up and down the driveway like a thoroughbred racehorse charged with pent-up energy. In the moment before he turned and saw them, Chelsea drank in every detail of his chiseled profile and lean body. When he started toward them, Chelsea handed Dawn her tote bag.

"Have a good trip, and don't pick up any strange men," she teased.

"What if she meets somebody really foxy on the plane?" Mindy asked.

"I don't want to know about it." Chelsea laughed to cover her nervousness. She was aware of Roberto's silent scrutiny. Every nerve end was reacting.

"You're not coming with us?" he asked.

"No, I . . . no."

"I'm sorry it's so painful to be with me," he said in a low voice.

"Why can't you just let things be?" she pleaded in an equally low tone.

"We both know the answer to that." He left her abruptly and strode around to the driver's side.

Chapter Eleven

Chelsea wandered around the house like a lost soul after the others had left for the airport. Finally Dolores took pity on her. She sat Chelsea at a card table with a long list of names, and asked her to make out place cards for the numerous guests who would attend the bridal dinner. Chelsea didn't guess that another set of cards had already been written the week before.

After the place cards were finished, Dolores found other little chores for her to do. One was cataloguing the wedding gifts that had arrived, and writing the donors' names in a register.

"These things are magnificent," Chelsea exclaimed. "Mindy is the only nineteen-year-old I know of with an antique silver tea service and bone china service plates for twelve."

Dolores smiled. "People have been very generous."

"That's an understatement." Chelsea made a note of the final gift card. "Okay, that's the last of them. What else can I do for you?"

"You've been cooped up here all day. Why don't you take a walk and get some fresh air? I do believe it's finally gotten cooler."

Chelsea stood up and stretched. "Maybe I will. There's a heavenly breeze coming in, and I need some exercise. I think I'll poke around the outskirts of town where those lovely meadows are."

"That would be nice, dear," Dolores answered vaguely. She was entering figures in a large ledger.

The weather had changed drastically. The sun still shone, but the sky was blue now instead of a burnished pewter color, and a soft breeze kept the temperature down.

Chelsea felt her spirits lift as she ambled along aimlessly, gazing into shop windows. Beyond the stores was the medieval bridge. She paused in mid-span and leaned on the parapet, staring down into the awesome chasm.

A little farther on, the town gave way to country. Meadows stretched out on either side of the road, sweet-smelling pastures dotted with wildflowers. Chelsea would have picked a bouquet, but the tall fence along the verge was posted with No Trespassing signs. She inhaled the perfume instead, feeling her cares drain away momentarily in this tranquil setting.

Roberto and Mindy returned home about an hour after Chelsea had left.

"Where did she go?" Mindy asked Dolores.

"I sent her out for a walk," Dolores answered.

"More sightseeing?"

"No, she said something about a stroll in the countryside."

"That's not for me. I think I'll take a nap." Mindy was yawning as she left them.

"Did Chelsea say exactly where she was going?" Roberto asked his mother.

"Wouldn't it be better if you left her alone?" she asked gently.

He frowned. "All I want to know is where she went. Did you warn her to stay out of the meadows?"

"I don't believe so." Dolores's brow furrowed. "Surely it isn't important. They're all posted."

"What if she doesn't notice the warning signs?" After a moment's indecision, Roberto whirled around and left the room.

Dolores sighed as she heard the Ferrari screech down the driveway.

Chelsea moved over closer to the fence when she heard a car coming. There had been very little traffic on the narrow country road to disturb the peace and quiet. Her own peace of mind was disturbed when the car stopped and Roberto called to her.

"What are you doing here?" she asked in exasperation. Just the sight of him destroyed all her new-found serenity.

"Mother told me you were here and I—"

"You shouldn't have followed me. We have nothing further to say to each other." She resumed her walk, staring straight ahead.

The Ferrari crawled alongside her in low gear. "I didn't come here to talk. I know you don't want to see me."

"Then go away."

"First I have to tell you something."

"No!" Why did Roberto have to torture her?

"Just listen to me for a minute," he insisted.

She couldn't outrun him, so Chelsea did the next best thing. She began to climb the fence. He couldn't drive onto the field.

"Chelsea, *don't!*"

In his haste to get out of the car, Roberto hit the horn button with his elbow. A raucous blast of sound shattered the stillness, heightened by his urgent shouts.

Chelsea was almost to the top of the fence when Roberto grabbed her around the waist and pulled her down. She struggled wildly, needing to break his hold on her— both physically and mentally.

Suddenly in a rush of sound and fury, two bulls came charging out of a clump of trees. Their hooves sounded like thunder, and to Chelsea's dazzled eyes smoke seemed to be coming out of their flared nostrils. But she wasn't imagining the wicked curved horns that sprouted from the lowered heads of the dangerous beasts.

Chelsea went limp against Roberto. She was rooted to the spot while the thousand-pound animals came charging straight at them. Roberto transferred one arm to her shoulders and hustled her across the road. When she looked back, the bulls had stopped at the fence, but they were pawing the ground and snorting ferociously.

"Where did they come from?" Chelsea gasped when she could talk.

"That's what I was trying to warn you about. The bulls for the *corrida* are pastured out here."

"How was I supposed to know that?" she asked indignantly.

"There are signs on the fence, but I was afraid you might ignore them."

"I did consider climbing over to pick wildflowers," Chelsea admitted. She glanced over with horror on her face, even though the bulls had lumbered off.

"Don't think about it," he soothed. "You're all right."

"Except for my nervous system. Will you drive me back? My legs are still shaking."

When they were in the car and she had calmed down, Chelsea asked, "Did Dawn get off okay?"

"She's on her way. The airport was a madhouse, but I made sure they held her seat."

"This is the peak travel period. I'd better leave in plenty of time on Monday," Chelsea remarked. "Will you arrange for someone to take me?"

"I'll drive you."

"It's the day after your wedding," she murmured.

Chelsea had no idea if Roberto and Mindy were going on a honeymoon. Everyone would expect them to, as Rosa had. Would they go that far to keep up appearances? Chelsea didn't want to find out.

"I know what day it is," Roberto answered harshly. "You don't have to remind me."

"I just thought it would be easier if you got someone else to take me," she faltered.

"Nothing will make it easy to see you go." He drove into his his driveway and turned off the motor. Deep lines were etched in his face as he gazed at her. "It's torture to be with you, but it's going to be worse when you leave."

"We have to forget about each other."

"How? You haunt my dreams every night. I keep hoping the dreams are reality and this is just a nightmare."

"You're asking for a miracle, and they're in short supply." Chelsea opened the car door. "We'd better go in."

Mindy flew at them as soon as they entered the house. "Where have you been?" Without waiting for an answer she said, "We have to go to Málaga right away!"

"Don't tell me Dawn didn't get on the plane after all," Chelsea groaned.

"My patience has limits, Mindy," Roberto warned.

"You don't understand. This has nothing to do with Dawn. It's about Jorge!"

Roberto stiffened. "What are you saying?"

"He's in the hospital. At least they think maybe it's him. But I know it is. That would explain everything!"

Dolores joined them, looking uncharacteristically shaken. "Do you think it could be true, Roberto?"

"Will someone please tell me what you're both talking about?" he asked.

"Someone called from a hospital in Málaga. They have a young man there who has been unconscious for weeks." Dolores's knuckles whitened as she gripped her hands together. "He suffered a head injury while riding a motorbike."

"You see?" Mindy exclaimed. "That proves it's Jorge. He left on his motorbike that last day."

"Wait, Mindy, I have to hear the rest. Why didn't the hospital notify us sooner?" Roberto asked.

"The boy had no identification," Dolores answered.

"I told you he was only wearing shorts and he didn't take his wallet." Mindy was wild with impatience. "Why are we standing here talking? I want to see him."

Roberto put his hands on her shoulders. "Of course we'll go, and I pray to God it's Jorge. But you musn't get your hopes up."

Chelsea felt the same as Roberto. She was afraid to believe in something that would indeed be a miracle. "How did they know to call here after all this time?"

"He came out of the coma and said a few words," Dolores explained. "He's still disoriented, but he mentioned Ronda and the name del Machado."

"What more do you need?" Mindy tugged at Roberto's hand. "Let's *go.*"

She was supremely confident, but the others harbored secret fears. What if the boy was simply a friend of Jorge's, and was asking them to get in touch with him? Or suppose the young man *was* Jorge, and his injuries had left permanent damage? Chelsea could tell that Dolores and Roberto shared her apprehension.

The ride seemed interminable, but they eventually reached the hospital. Then they were shunted between the front desk and the admitting office.

"Can't I just see him while you're looking up his records?" Mindy pleaded.

"Dr. Muñoz will have to give his permission," the woman told her.

"Will you kindly get him out here? *Now,*" Roberto added.

After a glance at his grim face she picked up the phone.

Finally the doctor showed up, looking rather uncomfortable. Someone had evidently briefed him hastily about Jorge's case. Before they could ask any questions, he launched into a defense of the hospital's efficiency.

"I hope you understand our delay in contacting you."

Roberto nodded. "You can hardly be blamed for that. We were told the young man had no identification."

"Exactly." The doctor seemed relieved. "So when he did give us his name and a few other bits of information, we had to wait to be sure he was lucid."

"When did he do that?" Roberto asked sharply.

"Well, ah, a few days ago, actually."

"He told you who he was, and you didn't notify us?"

The doctor flinched slightly at the fury on Roberto's face. "You have to realize that we're terribly under-staffed, Señor del Machado, like most hospitals nowa-days. And of course we wanted to be very sure of the young man's identity before alarming you needlessly."

"I could have taken one look at him and told you," Roberto thundered.

Dolores put her hand on her son's arm. "What is his condition, Doctor?"

The man turned to her in relief. "I'm happy to say that he will make a complete recovery. We were concerned at first, but we've run tests and there is absolutely no brain damage."

"Thank the Lord," Dolores whispered. She had tears in her eyes.

"In addition to his head injuries the boy has a broken leg, but that will heal nicely."

"We'd like to see my brother now, Doctor," Roberto said.

"Certainly." He led them to an elevator. "I never saw the patient before the accident, but I can tell that he was in excellent physical condition. I'm afraid you might be a little shocked when you see him. He's lost a lot of weight."

"He'll look wonderful no matter what shape he's in," Mindy said happily.

The doctor led them into a large room with six beds, all but one occupied. The room was clean but austere. There were no flowers or magazines on the bedside tables, and venetian blinds on the windows screened out most of the light.

"Patients in the wards get the same care as the ones in our private rooms," the doctor said hastily when he noticed the look on Roberto's face. He left them precipitately.

Mindy didn't see anything but Jorge. Uttering a glad cry, she raced to his bed. Jorge acted as if he didn't believe his eyes, but when she threw her arms around him they hugged and kissed frantically.

"*Cara mia,* I thought I'd lost you forever." He closed his eyes and held her tightly.

"You can't get rid of me that easily." She was laughing and crying at the same time.

"When they told me how long I'd been here, I almost went crazy. I was sure you'd gone back to America."

"How could I do that? I have something of yours," she answered softly.

"My love," he whispered, gazing at her tenderly.

After giving the two young people their few moments together, Roberto and his mother approached the bed. Chelsea stood to one side, studying the youngest del Machado son. Jorge was as handsome as his portrait, although his face was gaunt now. But what pleased Chelsea the most was the adoration in his eyes as he gazed at Mindy.

"My dear boy." Dolores touched his cheek lightly, as if needing to be sure he was real.

Jorge took her hand and kissed the palm. "I'm sorry I worried you, *Madre.*"

"That's an understatement." Roberto tried to hide his emotion under a gruff tone that didn't fool any of them. "I trust you'll give up motorbikes from now on."

"Right. I was thinking of switching to a motorcycle," Jorge replied mischievously.

"You'd better be joking," Mindy declared. "I want you in one piece."

"What happened?" Roberto asked. "Do you remember?"

"Up to a point." Jorge's brow furrowed with the effort. "I was crossing an intersection when a car ran the red light and came straight at me. Somebody yelled. Maybe it was me. Then everything went black."

"I hope they caught the jerk," Mindy declared angrily.

"I don't know. I didn't think to ask."

"It doesn't matter," Dolores said. "You're going to be all right. That's the important thing."

"You'll get such tender, loving care that you'll be spoiled rotten," Mindy teased.

"My family thinks I am already." Jorge smiled.

"They don't know you like I do," she answered softly.

"You're two of a kind," Roberto joked. "No wonder you get along so well."

Jorge gave him a puzzled look as he suddenly realized that Mindy and Roberto were well acquainted. "How did you find out about Mindy?"

She was the one who answered. "I went to see Roberto after I waited and waited and you didn't come back. I thought he might know where you were."

Jorge groaned. "I can imagine what you thought."

"I tried not to, but when he scoured Marbella and couldn't find you anywhere I sort of figured you didn't want to be found."

"You didn't think of checking the hospitals?" Jorge asked his brother incredulously.

"I wasn't thinking about an accident. When Mindy told me about your relationship and how abruptly you left after... Well, I'm afraid I jumped to the same conclusion that she did."

"How much did you tell him?" Jorge asked Mindy.

"Everything."

"Even about the—" Jorge paused, glancing at his mother.

"It's all right." Mindy laughed. "Everybody knows about this baby except maybe a few people living in Outer Mongolia."

"And you thought I would walk out on Mindy and my child?" Jorge's face flushed with anger as he challenged his brother. "That's insulting!"

"You're right, and I apologize," Roberto answered quietly.

Jorge wasn't mollified. "We're in love and we're going to get married."

"I thought you'd never ask," Mindy remarked dryly.

"I *did* ask you."

"Not is so many words, but it's okay now. I accept." She smiled rapturously.

Jorge looked penitently at Dolores. "I'm sorry if you're disappointed in me, Mother. I didn't mean for it to happen this way. But you musn't blame Mindy. It was all my fault."

"I wouldn't say that." Mindy chuckled.

"Dear child, I love you both," Dolores said in a voice filled with emotion. "And I am very proud of you, Jorge. You have never disappointed me."

Mindy's face sobered. "Your mother is very special, Jorge."

"I've always known that." He reached out for Dolores's hand.

Roberto cleared his throat. "Well, that's settled. We're one big happy family again."

"Can we take him home now, Roberto?" Mindy asked.

"Home." Jorge heaved an ecstatic sigh. "I was beginning to think I'd never see it again, when nobody here would listen to me. I would have phoned you myself, but they wouldn't let me out of bed.''

"You won't have to lift a finger from now on. I intend to wait on you hand and foot. For a while, anyway." Mindy laughed. "When I get to be a little tub, you can return the favor."

"You'll always be beautiful to me," Jorge said deeply.

"I'll go speak to the doctor to see if he feels you're well enough to leave," Roberto said.

As he turned to leave, he noticed Chelsea for the first time. From the startled look on his face she knew he'd forgotten about her. Suddenly she felt like an intruder, although Roberto took her arm and led her over to the bed.

"Jorge, this is Mindy's sister. She's heard a lot about you."

"All bad, I'm sure." Jorge held out his hand. "I hope I can change your mind about me."

"You already have." Chelsea smiled. "Any man who loves my sister has to be a person with taste and intelligence."

"You should be flattered," Mindy told Jorge impishly. "Chelsea hasn't approved of all of my choices."

"I'll be right back," Roberto said.

"How long will you be staying?" Jorge asked Chelsea. "As soon as I'm up and around, even on crutches, I want to marry Mindy. I hope you'll be here for the wedding."

"Of course she will. Chelsea already promised to be my maid of honor." Mindy gave her sister an amused look.

"I'd like nothing better, but you don't know when the ceremony will take place," Chelsea said. "I can't stay away from my job indefinitely."

"Isn't my wedding a little more important?" Mindy asked with a pout.

"Of course it is, but I have to make a living. I don't have a husband to support me," Chelsea joked.

"That can be arranged. Jorge, we have to find a husband for Chelsea."

"How about Roberto? If she can throw a net over him, that is." Jorge chuckled. "Women have been trying for years without success."

"Oh, I don't know. He's rather partial to the Claiborne women," Mindy said complacently.

Until today, Chelsea would have included herself in Roberto's affections, but his present behavior left a chilling doubt. Naturally he'd forget about his own concerns in the first excitement over Jorge. But shouldn't Roberto have realized by now what this meant to his own future? Possibly he had. Perhaps this unexpected reprieve made him reluctant to rush into another commitment.

Roberto returned, followed by a nurse and an orderly. "The doctor says you can leave if you are very careful for the next few weeks. We've arranged for an ambulance to take you back to Ronda," he told his brother.

"I want to ride with him," Mindy said.

"I told them you probably would. I imagine Mother wants to go with you, also."

"Oh, no. I'm sure the young people want to be alone." Dolores's polite refusal didn't deceive them.

"Come along and keep us company," Mindy invited her generously. "Jorge's in no condition to make out, anyway."

He gave her a burning look that said, don't count on it, but Jorge joined in urging his mother. "The ride will seem a lot shorter with two beautiful women along."

Roberto took charge with his usual efficiency. He accompanied the gurney with Jorge on it to the ambulance, then saw to it that Mindy and his mother were comfortably seated inside. After they had driven off he went into the hospital office to settle Jorge's bill.

As Chelsea trailed along after Roberto, she reflected that most people had to pay their bill before they were released. But no one even suggested that to Roberto.

When everything had been taken care of and they were in the car, he said, "Now you've met Jorge. What did you think of him?"

"What everyone else does. He's a very personable young man."

Roberto nodded. "You don't know what a relief this is." As Chelsea's spirits started to rise, he continued, "It nearly killed me to think that Jorge would walk away from his responsibilities."

"Perhaps you shouldn't have rushed to judgment," she answered coolly.

"What else was I to think?"

"He's your brother. You've known him all his life. People don't suddenly do a complete turnaround."

Roberto stared at her remote profile. "Are you angry at me, Chelsea?"

"Where would you get that idea? I admire the way you handled everything. You're very efficient."

"There wasn't that much to do. The hard decisions will come later."

"Like what?"

"I'd like Jorge to finish college and become an architect, as he intended."

"That shouldn't be any problem."

"He might feel he has to go to work now that he's a family man. I think it would be a big mistake. I'd be happy to support them for however long it takes, but the del Machado men are fiercely independent."

"So I've noticed," Chelsea said dryly.

"You wouldn't admire a man who wasn't. Admit it."

"I suppose you're right."

Chelsea was becoming more and more desolate as Roberto continued to talk only about Jorge and Mindy. What about *us?* she wanted to shout. But if she had to ask, the answer was clear.

"It's too bad the wedding on Sunday will have to be called off," she remarked tonelessly.

"You don't really mean that." For the first time something flared in Roberto's eyes as he turned his head to gaze at her.

"I meant with a change of grooms, naturally."

"I certainly hope so!"

"You had a close call." Chelsea tried to keep her voice light. "I'll bet you've never gotten that close to the altar before."

"I've grown to love Mindy, but it wasn't an experience I'd like to repeat." His laughter held heartfelt relief.

Chelsea turned to look out the side window so he wouldn't see her expression. That's when she noticed they had reached Marbella. But they were driving toward the water, instead of away from it to Ronda.

"Where are you going?" she asked.

"To Carlos's. He'll want to know the good news."

"Dolores will be expecting us," Chelsea objected. She didn't want to spend any more time with Roberto than necessary.

"She'll be so busy fussing over Jorge that she wouldn't notice a brass band marching through the living room."

Chelsea had to resign herself. Roberto was filled with exuberance suddenly, as though the full realization of his preserved bachelor state had sunk in.

Carlos noticed his excitement as soon as he opened the door. "You look like the bearer of good tidings."

"The best!" Roberto told him all that had happened.

When he finished, Carlos glanced at Chelsea. "This explains a lot of things that have been puzzling me."

"I've been impossible to live with," Roberto admitted.

"You won't get an argument from us." Carlos chuckled. "Will he, Chelsea?"

"We've all been under a strain," she answered quietly. "I'm glad it's over with."

Carlos gave her a covert glance, but his joking comment was directed at Roberto. "You'll never find another woman that understanding. If I were you, I'd snap her up while you have a chance."

Chelsea spoke up quickly. "One Claiborne woman in the family is enough."

Roberto frowned. "You don't mean that."

Carlos looked from one to the other. "Why don't we all have a drink and unwind?"

"I want to talk to Chelsea," Roberto said. "Would you leave us alone?"

"That was going to be my next suggestion." Carlos smiled. "Make yourselves at home and stay as long as you like. I won't be back tonight," he added casually as he went out the door.

"We should go, too," Chelsea said. "We can talk on the way to Ronda."

Roberto brushed the suggestion aside. "We have something to settle first. What did you mean by that remark to Carlos?"

"Which one?"

"You know exactly what I'm referring to. You told me you loved me. I thought you wanted to marry me."

Chelsea's control snapped. "Don't worry, you made your feelings on *that* subject crystal clear."

"What are you talking about?"

"I got the message when you said you never wanted to get that close to the altar again."

"I meant with *Mindy!*" Roberto's rigid body relaxed and he gazed at her tenderly. "Or any other woman except you. Don't you know that by now?"

"You seemed to be having second thoughts," she said uncertainly.

"How could you think such a thing?"

"On the way here from the hospital all you talked about was Jorge. You never mentioned us or our future together."

"Because I didn't want to propose in the car, where I couldn't hold you and tell you how much I love you. And because if I even touched your hand I would have lost all control and made love to you on the spot." He took her in his arms and strung a line of tiny kisses across her throat. "I never have much control anyway when I'm around you."

Chelsea flung her arms around his neck. "Oh, Roberto, I was so miserable when I thought you'd changed your mind."

"You still don't realize how much you mean to me, do you?"

"Give me a little time. It still seems too good to be true."

He lifted her in his arms with a low male chuckle. "Maybe a demonstration will help."

He carried her into the bedroom and stood her on her feet. Chelsea clasped her arms around his neck again, not wanting to let go of him. As they stared into each other's eyes, the same incredulous joy was mirrored. Nothing stood between them anymore.

"This is the moment I was waiting for," Roberto said, framing her face between his palms. "But I couldn't have waited much longer."

Chelsea smiled tremulously. "You might have let me in on your plans."

"If I'd told you what I wanted to do to you, we'd never have reached here."

"Tell me now." She traced the shape of his mouth with her forefinger.

"I'd rather show you."

He kissed her finger and then her mouth, gently at first, then with more urgency. Chelsea parted her lips willingly, pressing against him and restlessly tracing the width of his broad shoulders.

Without removing his mouth from hers, Roberto began to undress her. Shivers of anticipation rippled down Chelsea's spine when he pulled her T-shirt free of her shorts and reached under it to unhook her bra. While his tongue continued to probe her mouth, Roberto pushed the loosened bra aside so he could caress her bare breasts. The sensation was indescribable. She drew in her breath sharply when his thumbs circled her hardened nipples.

"I need to see you again." He stripped off her T-shirt and bra, and feathered both breasts with his fingertips. "You're as beautiful as I remembered."

"I wanted you so much that other time," she murmured.

"It's a good thing I didn't guess." He put his arms around her waist and lowered his head to circle one rosy peak with his tongue.

Chelsea arched her back and closed her eyes. "I never knew I could feel like this."

Roberto's eyes blazed with triumph as he gazed at her passion-filled face. "Do you know how happy that makes me?"

He pushed her shorts over her hips, along with her panties. As they slid to the floor and she stepped out of them, he stroked her thighs tantalizingly.

"You're so smooth and warm," he said huskily. "I want to touch every inch of you."

"I feel the same way." She unbuttoned his shirt and ran her palms over his hard chest. "It's so heavenly to be able to touch you like this."

He guided her hand to his belt buckle. "Before this night is over, *cara mia,* we're going to know everything about each other."

Her fingers trembled in their haste to undress him. When Roberto kicked aside his clothes and stood before her completely nude, Chelsea was dazzled by his awesome masculinity. She reached out to caress the narrow strip of white skin between his tanned stomach and thighs, feeling a mounting sense of excitement.

Roberto gasped and reached for her convulsively. "Do you know what you're doing to me?" he asked hoarsely.

"I'm waiting to see you lose control," she teased, moving against him seductively.

"You've just achieved your goal."

He picked her up and carried her to the bed. Chelsea held out her arms to him and he covered her body with his. They stared into each other's eyes, prolonging the exquisite moment, their bodies on fire.

When the sweet agony became unbearable, Roberto parted her legs and completed their union. The initial thrust filled Chelsea with such joy that she surged against him, uttering broken terms of endearment. Roberto echoed her cries as he plunged deeper. They were welded into one person, experiencing the same throbbing ecstasy. The sensation increased in pitch until they reached the outer limits of endurance. Chelsea murmured his name over and over again as she achieved utter fulfillment.

They were silent in each other's arms afterward, awed by the intensity of their feelings. Chelsea had expected the culmination of their love to be beautiful, but she'd never imagined it could be this perfect.

Roberto finally stirred. "That was a dream come true."

"For me, too," she whispered.

"Will you marry me, my love?"

She laughed softly. "As long as you don't feel honor-bound."

He smoothed the tumbled hair away from her face. "I'm bound to you in every way there is."

She stroked his cheek tenderly. "The answer is yes. I'll marry you any time, any place, the sooner the better."

"How about Sunday? I happen to know of a church that's available."

Chelsea gave him a startled look. "I'd forgotten all about the wedding. It will have to be postponed."

"Not necessarily. Everyone is expecting to see the most beautiful bride in the world, so let's not disappoint them. Would you mind, angel?"

"It's the kind of wedding I've always fantasized about," she answered, misty-eyed. "I feel as if I'm living in a dream world."

Roberto's expression changed. "I hope not. Maybe I'm rushing you. Are you sure you'll be happy living here?" he asked soberly.

"How could you possibly doubt it?"

He hesitated. "You won't mind giving up your career?"

"It wouldn't mean anything without you," she replied simply.

"Sweet Chelsea. That's what I needed to hear." He hugged her close for a moment before drawing back to look seriously at her. "You won't regret it, I promise. Your new career will be even more rewarding, I hope."

"Taking care of you?" she teased.

"I'm hoping you'll consent to work with me in the family enterprises. I think you'd find it challenging."

"You're darling to offer me a job, but I don't know anything about farming or ranching."

"You know about investments and property. The rest you can learn. I really need someone to take part of the load off my shoulders."

"You'd honestly trust me to advise you?" she asked slowly.

"I'm turning my life over to you. Our marriage is going to be a partnership in every way." He kissed her tenderly.

"You're almost too good to be true." She sighed blissfully. As Chelsea was melting into his arms, a thought occurred to her and she sat up in bed. "We'd better phone your mother and tell her not to call off the wedding."

He pulled her down beside him once more. "She has other things on her mind right now, and so do I."

Chelsea relaxed, smiling enchantingly. "Could you share them with me?"

Roberto took her in his arms. "I plan to. Over and over again for the rest of our lives, my love."

* * * * *

Silhouette Special Edition

salutes

MOMENTS OF GLORY

from Lindsay McKenna

In a country torn with conflict, in a time of bitter passions, these brave men and women wage a war against all odds... and a timeless battle for honor, for fleeting moments of glory, for the promise of enduring love.

February: RIDE THE TIGER (#721) Survivor Dany Villard is wise to the love-'em-and-leave-'em ways of war, but wounded hero Gib Ramsey swears she's captured his heart...forever.

March: ONE MAN'S WAR (#727) The war raging inside brash and bold Captain Pete Mallory threatens to destroy him, until Tess Ramsey's tender love guides him toward peace.

April: OFF LIMITS (#733) Soft-spoken Marine Jim McKenzie saved Alexandra Vance's life in Vietnam; now he needs her love to save his honor....

From the popular author of the bestselling title
DUNCAN'S BRIDE (Intimate Moments #349)
comes the

LINDA HOWARD

COLLECTION

Two exquisite collector's editions that contain four of
Linda Howard's early passionate love stories. To add
these special volumes to your own library, be sure
to look for:

VOLUME ONE: *Midnight Rainbow*
Diamond Bay
(Available in March)

VOLUME TWO: *Heartbreaker*
White Lies
(Available in April)

 *Silhouette Books*®

SLH92

Silhouette Special Edition

is pleased to present

A GOOD MAN WALKS IN
by Ginna Gray

The story of one strong woman's comeback
and the man who was there for her, Travis McCall,
the renegade cousin to those Blaine siblings,
from Ginna Gray's bestselling trio

FOOLS RUSH IN (#416)
WHERE ANGELS FEAR (#468)
ONCE IN A LIFETIME (#661)

Rebecca Quinn sought shelter at the hideaway on Rincon
Island. Finding Travis McCall—the object of all her childhood
crushes—holed up in the same house threatened to ruin the
respite she so desperately needed. Until their first kiss . . .
Then Travis set out to prove to his lovely Rebecca that man
can be good and love, sublime.

You'll want to be there when Rebecca's disillusionment turns
to joy.

A GOOD MAN WALKS IN #722

Available at your favorite retail outlet this February.

NORA ROBERTS

Love has a language all its own, and for centuries, flowers have symbolized love's finest expression. Discover the language of flowers—and love—in this romantic collection of 48 favorite books by bestselling author Nora Roberts.

Starting in February 1992, two titles will be available each month at your favorite retail outlet.

In February, look for:

Irish Thoroughbred, Volume #1
The Law Is A Lady, Volume #2

Collect all 48 titles and become fluent in the Language of Love.

LOL192

THE LANGUAGE of LOVE